Earthbound

Earthbound

Chronicles of the Maca I

Mari Collier

Published 2015 by Creativia
Book design by Creativia (www.creativia.org)
Cover art by http://www.thecovercollection.com/

This book is dedicated to my children, Barbarie E. Collier-Bowling and to Lawrence D. Collier.

Contents

Chapter 1

Hunger

The crowd surged forward waving their clubs and staves. Screams of anger and desperation driven by hunger erupted from their throats. They needed food for themselves, for their families. If there was no food, vengeance would serve as their substitute for they would die either from hunger or the hated British troopers.

Three men stood in their path. One was a townsman serving as a guide to the other two. He promptly took to his heels. His pay as a guide was not adequate to cover this danger. One, a tall, red-haired gentleman clad in elegantly tailored clothes and fine boots, stepped forward, a serene look on his face as he pointed his index finger at the approaching mob. The other was his servant, a huge dark-haired youth dressed in dark clothing. He stared at the mob and began to edge backward, his fists curling and uncurling. This tis folly, thought the youth. They are too many. Even my great strength twill nay stop them.

The man pointing his finger at the mob realized too late that his mind could not penetrate any mind of the people in the foreground and a puzzled look came into his eyes. He sent his mind swooping among the crowd until he found one that he could control.

'You are to attack the person next to you,' his mind commanded. The mind command was too late.

The man given the mind instruction stopped, drew back his club, and began swinging it viciously at the man next to him. The crowd moved forward and knocked him down. With a roar the angry men attacked the red-haired, finely dressed interloper with the strange copper eyes.

Screams for food and yells to look for his purse came from some of the group. Others took after the youth fleeing down the road. They were too weak from hunger and the youth too strong and long of limb.

The youth stumbled into the pub where they had lodged and gasped out his tale of a master dying. A man was dispatched to inform the local priest. The priest then sent a message to his Lordship. By late afternoon a group of men on horseback arrived at the country lane and recovered the stripped and mangled body of the stranger.

The body was returned to the village and his Lordship sent a trusted man to speak with the youth named Llewellyn. To no one's surprise the youth was gone and the room vacated.

"Two strangers they were on a strange quest." The pub owner assured the Lord's servant. "They had questions about whether a different redheaded man with copper eyes and a golden ring around the pupils had been here. The man asked about the local cemeteries. Wanted to check out the tombstones, he did. His gold was good though. The gentleman's servant had a strong accent. He's probably from across the water." The owner cleared his throat before daring to put a question to such an important man.

"Do ye think we are in any danger from the prowling mobs?"

"His Lordship has sent an urgent message to the brigade stationed but a few miles from here. I'm sure they will heed his call for help."

“That won’t quiet all of the people. They can’t eat or sell their rotten potatoes.” The pub owner understood why the hungry mob prowled this part of Ireland. Still, it was worrisome.

“True, but 1842 has to be a better year for crops than the last two. We’ll have protection until then. Let us know if the young servant returns.” He turned and left the smoky establishment.

“He’s probably run all the way home or took a ship for the new world.” The last was muttered by the owner. Why in God’s name, he wondered, would anyone in his right mind stay in Ireland now?

Chapter 2

Freedom

Llewellyn sat under an outcropping of rock, a shield against the mist, and considered his options. That he was Maca of Don, hereditary administrator of one continent on the planet Thalia, meant nay more to these Earth beings than it did to the Justines who had beaten Thalia. Earth beings thought him to be about twenty-one, but he was nigh sixty-three according to the data aboard the *Golden One* when he checked about thirty days prior to landfall. Of all the places they had looked and scanned for signs of Toma's landing, Ricca, the Justine, had deemed this planet as the one that possessed areas where people were red haired and brown eyed. Ricca postulated that these beings might have the ability to evolve into a Justine like being. In time, these Earth beings could replenish the Justine gene pool. It was possible that Toma, the missing Justine, may have made the same assumptions. Of Toma's *Golden One* there had been no trace, but there was no other habitable planet that matched the encodings on the crystals Toma had left in the Justine knowledge banks. They had investigated two other countries and then went to the one called Ireland. Ricca had left this area as second to last as Ireland was an economic disaster. Another land, the United States, was a vast area of empty space and ill looking towns. Its scattered populace meant that any search there would take years.

Research in London had shown there might be small groups of people scattered over Europe and Asia, but those areas were unlikely places for Toma to dwell.

Llewellyn kenned that Ricca had planned to abandon him on this planet. Until then, Ricca had used him as a servant. It was also Ricca's way of avoiding mind contact with these primitive creatures as they caused him headaches. The realization that it wasn't the primitive ways of this planet that bothered Ricca, but the fact that many of these beings could close their minds to the Justine's mind probe gave Llewellyn immense satisfaction.

Llewellyn's Thalian-Justine mix of genes had endowed him with the Justine ability of mindspeak and entering another's mind. Ricca had taught him control while aboard the *Golden One* to keep him from killing any of the Krepyon crew. The one Krepyon's vomiting while he groveled before Llewellyn had been an accident. The Kreppie (as Thalians called them) had struck him and he had lashed out with his mind rather than his fists. He kenned that the use of fists would have caused Ricca to lock him away. Llewellyn did not know how he had managed to channel directly into the Kreppie's mind.

Ricca had taught him to mindspeak, to build walls in the mind when privacy or contemplation was necessary, and how to direct his mind into that of others. Like Ricca, Llewellyn was unable to enter the minds of all the Earth beings they had encountered. He had assumed it was because of his youth or the fact that his abilities were less than a full-blooded Justine's. He realized that Ricca could not enter their minds when an innkeeper in the last town cheated them, nor could Ricca's mind command make the man repay them. Ricca's headache had been ferocious that evening, and Llewellyn smiled in remembrance.

He was to be marooned to complete the sentence given when he was but one and twenty. The Justines denied the possibility of a mutant being born to parents from different planets, but he existed. They did not allow the beings on the planets they controlled to believe or teach that mutants could exist. To rid themselves of a perplexing problem and a refutation of their biological teachings, the Justines condemned him to isolation. The last forty odd years had been a darkness. Thalians needed to touch, to hug, to bed another, and he had had nay!

Ricca had detested that a servant be entrusted with funds. Customs in this land decreed that gentlemen did not soil their hands with money. More funds could be manufactured on the *Golden One* if one knew the proper procedures. The spaceship, manned by four Krepyons, was on the dark side of the Earth's moon where the Earth's primitive telescopes would miss it. The Scout from the *Golden One* was carefully hidden not far from here. It was guarded by two Krepyons in case a curious passerby chanced upon it.

Llewellyn could book passage on a ship to the new lands if he had more of the currency and gold from the *Golden One.* If he tried to hire on as a sailor on one of the ships sailing for the Americas, he feared he would kill one of these Earth beings before they arrived. He'd seen some of the brutality the sailors endured during their travels on this planet. If the Scout were in his possession, he could fly to the place called America and find somewhere to hide it, but he would still be without funds in a strange land. There was also the chance the Kreppies would scan for the Scout and locate him. Even if he avoided them, he would die here. Without Ricca, the Kreppies were apt to kill him anyway. If the *Golden One* were his, there was always the possibility that he would live long enough to acquire the needed information from the knowledge crystals aboard the ship to return to his planet and complete his Mither's revenge on the Justines. His Mither had destroyed the Justine planet. He would destroy the Justine Refuge and Thalia would be free. All were dreams until he procured the *Golden One.*

Night was beginning when he approached the cave. A light mist was falling as it seemed to do most of the time in Ireland. A three-quarter moon vied with a cloud as to which would dominate the space and the cloud was winning. Llewellyn dug out the hand com from the valise. It was hidden within the elaborate compass. He swung back the cover to access the audio.

"I have been sent to retrieve the rest of the funds. Ricca tis resting for the eve." It must have sounded plausible as the high sharp, quick speaking Kreppie named Aloyed answered.

"You are to wait outside. One of us will bring it to you." The com went silent.

Within two minutes the voice was back. "Why did not the golden Ricca appear?"

"I told ye, he tis resting. The primitive thoughts of the populace wear on his mind."

Again the com went dead. The bushes parted and the Kreppie appeared, glancing in all directions. He dared not let Earth beings see his greenish, brown facial skin with scales on his cheeks. He wore the usual tight fitting garb of a space being, but as a Krepyon, his uniform was light green.

"This is the last of the currency and gold we brought with us. Did the great one say if we should order more?"

"Aye, that he did as we have discovered nay trace of Toma." Llewellyn reached out as if to take the proffered valise and instead grasped the Kreppie by the head and neck and twisted. Aloyed died without a sound.

Llewellyn plucked the weapon from the Kreppie's holster, lifted the inert body, and carried it back to the Scout. Quaten appeared in the doorway. "What is wrong?"

"Catch." Llewellyn tossed the dead body to Quaten.

As Quaten staggered and fell, Llewellyn reached out and snatched the slight body towards him. A swift twist of the neck and the body of Quaten joined Aloyed's in the back of the Scout. Llewellyn retrieved the valise before he entered and sat in the navigator's seat.

He waited for an hour as darkness closed over the Earth before soaring upward. Most of the populace below slept at night and would not see the golden streak rising from Earth. Two of the Kreppies aboard the craft would also be sleeping for they worked in shifts. There was no way they would disappoint Ricca in caring for the *Golden One*. It was possible that three were sleeping as there was no danger from an Earth space vehicle.

Upon docking, he left the bodies inside the Scout and hurried to the lift. A faint bluish glow emanated from the curved walls and floor. He was surprised at the clacking noise the Earth shoes made on the metal flooring. Once in the lift he removed his shoes. Silence was essential as he had decided to take control of the Command Center first. The awake Kreppie or Kreppies would be there. If the Kreppies had been alert, they should know that someone had returned in the Scout, but no one had sent out a voice request.

It was as though the Gar his people named as Creator blessed his efforts. A surge of triumph went through Llewellyn as he entered the Command Center and saw the sleeping Kreppie hunched over the control panel. Revenge was sweet as he twisted another neck. That was for all the suffering the Kreppies had inflicted on Thalia and damage they had done to his Elder Lamar when they shrunk his right arm and took his seed. With a set face, Llewellyn marched down the hall towards the sleeping quarters. The bluish glow from the walls was dimmer here as though providing less light would simulate night. One of the Kreppies had boasted that his father died trying to prevent Llewellyn's Mither, LouElla, from escaping the asteroid. He had taken particular delight in making Llewellyn's existence miserable and bringing false allegations against him. Ricca had silenced him. A Justine knew when a Krepyon lied. None of the three rooms were locked. Llewellyn entered each room and performed the physical act of killing the others. He wrapped them in their blankets and grabbed three extra blankets before carrying them forward.

The body in the Command Center he wrapped in one of the blankets. He would need to clean in here, the rooms, and the Scout. He did nay care. He had time. Soon all six wrapped bodies floated outside to tumble downward and burn as they entered Earth's atmosphere.

Ricca had taught him to fly the *Golden One* within a gravitational orbit, but not the necessary math and system usage to chart starpaths. He was trapped until he acquired the knowledge to fly among the stars. He and the *Golden One* needed a haven where this violent planet would nay destroy it; a place that was quiet and away from prying eyes and curiosity seekers. He crisscrossed the planet letting the geological scanners probe underneath. Then he fled behind the moon while the data downloaded and he slept. When he awoke he would find the best areas and then begin the process of selecting one to bury the ship before beginning a new life. He realized it would take weeks, possibly longer to hide something as large as this craft. Creating a new life would take even longer.

Chapter 3

The Mountain Man

Zebediah L. MacDonald surveyed the wooden shack and pushed his hat back on his dark, straight hair. Like many of the buildings in frontier America, the ramshackle building was composed of logs, flat boards, and stone. The builders had used clay for mortar and then the clay, flat boards, and chimney had been whitewashed. Why one of the fierce storms of wind and rain had not demolished the place would remain a profound mystery. A weathered, carved sign proclaimed TAVERN, painted in faded black letters. The N was almost obliterated by a wide crack. Perhaps they twill have a brew, he thought. That thought was strictly optimism. Americans seemed to prefer whiskey or rum in these wild lands.

He heard shouts from within as he tied his reins to the hitching rail.

"Damned Dutchman! Yu all had that king palmed."

As he stepped through the door he blinked his eyes at the smoky darkness. Four men were sitting at a lopsided table playing whist and the blocky man with long blond hair was speaking.

"Like hell. I don't need to hide a card vhen playing mitt dumm kopfs like du!"

The sandy haired man jumped up, his hands throwing the table towards the last speaker. As if on cue, the other two had risen and moved to the side, extracting their bowie knives. They were tall, rangy frontiersmen dressed in homespun.

The man they were attacking was shorter, barrel-chested, and stocky. He was dressed in buckskin and moccasins. He proved nimble enough to avoid the table and pulled his own bowie knife. He crouched, his arms slightly extended, and his eyes turning hard.

For a moment the three men stopped, surprised by his swiftness. Then they separated to come at him from different sides.

MacDonald took one look, shrugged at the thought of missing the chance for a brew, and stepped behind one man. His knotted fist crashed into the man's head and the man crumbled to the floor.

The man at the bar was shouting while waving an old flintlock at them. "Get out, yu bastards, get out. Yu all cain't wreck my place."

The blonde man in buckskins was leaning forward to swipe at his opponents. One attacker moved in with his longer arm reach. The shorter man whirled out of the way, turned and drove his knife into the man's side, raking the knife outward and turning to meet the next man. He straightened and stared. The next man was kicking and turning red-faced while a giant of a man had him around the arms and was squeezing the air from his chest. The other man was stretched out on the floor. The owner of the place now had his flintlock aimed at the giant. His bowie knife went sailing through the air, straight into the owner's shoulder.

The flintlock jumped upward and the ball pinged against the ceiling beams. Then the ball and bark chips fell to the floor. The roar from the musket, however, caused the giant to turn and drop the man he had been squeezing.

"He appears to be in on the scheme to rob ye." Surprise mingled in the rumbling voice of the giant.

"Ja, sure, probably hired them. Du mitt them?"

"Oh, nay, I twas about to purchase a brew."

The blonde man shook his head. "Damn fool, du could have been killed." He walked over to the owner who was holding a dirty towel against his shoulder and trying to find another ball to ram into the flintlock.

The mountain man yanked the flintlock out of the man's hand and his knife from the man's shoulder. A scream ricocheted around the small room.

"I'll leave this outside. Du can vorry about your friends." He jerked his head at the three in various states of consciousness.

To MacDonald he said, "If du ain't mitt these fellows, du best come mitt me."

Something about the hard blue eyes, the competent warrior's stance, and the male self-assurance seemed to win the big man's respect. He nodded at the wounded owner and followed the man outside.

"Du know this country?"

"Nay, I have but arrived."

The man snorted. "Thought as much dressed like that. Du look like some city boy looking for adventure. Ve ride for awhile, then ve can introduce each other."

They pulled up under a grove of oak and ash trees near a large, rushing creek that was swollen from a summer rainfall. The blonde man rode a sturdy brown horse and led two mules packed with traps and camping paraphernalia. He dismounted and tied the reins to a tree trunk and MacDonald did the same.

For a moment they eyed each other and then a browned hand streaked out.

"I'm Herman Rolfe and danke, ah, thank du. One against three vas too many." A smile lit his face and eyes.

MacDonald's brown eyes filled with amusement and he returned the smile as he shook hands. "I am called Zebediah L.

MacDonald." How he wished he could have used Llewellyn, Maca of Don, but that must stay as hidden as the *Golden One.*

"Vant to say vhere du are going or du do vant to stay quiet about that?"

"I am nay certain. I had thought about going to Texas. They say it tis a good place for a man."

"Do du know how to cross Injun country?"

"I have a map I bought in St. Louis."

For a moment the blue eye regarded him. "Du are going to get yourself killed, boy. Let's jaw a bit." He sank down on his haunches and MacDonald followed suit.

Rolfe grabbed a twig from the ground and used it to draw a crude map. "Ve are about here. To get to Texas, du have to go through Missouri and Indian Territory or Arkansas. Then, depending on vhere du go, du go through parts of Texas that ain't settled yet. There's Kiowa, Osage, Platte, Choctaw, Cherokee, Comanche tribes, and Apache. All of them raid for horses or any other damn reason. Most of the Cherokee are more like us, but there's always a vild bunch. If they stop du, they'll vant something to let du pass or they'll take your scalp und your horse. They could do that anyway if du don't know how to avoid them. Then there are men who run from the law. Some are dangerous, some just vant to be left alone."

MacDonald swallowed. He did nay have the Thalian Warrior training for being among primitives. Nay did he ken this land, but the *Golden One* was buried deep in the earth of Texas. He had spent months searching for a safe place and then more months enlarging a tunnel and cave to house his spaceship. All of the excavating was done at night away from the prying eyes of anyone that might ride through the area. He had seen no one. It seemed to be a vacant land, but this man was telling him there were inhabitants.

He had taken one of the Scouts and hidden it near a small city. There he had purchased clothing that did nay fit. Llewellyn changed his name and rented a room before he hired a woman to sew him trousers and shirts. She also knitted socks and a cobbler made the boots he was wearing. Only then did he buy a horse, saddle, and equipment that the store owner said he would need if traveling alone across the plains. Somehow he had to possess the land where the *Golden One* rested below the earth.

Rolfe looked at him. "Me, I'm a fur trapper. I'm heading back up towards Ft. Laramie. Once it's cold enough, I'll start laying my traps. Dat's vhy the two pack mules. My partner von't go again as he got married. I'll teach du how to trap and survive. Du get ten percent of der profits."

"I'm grateful for the offer, but I have nay kenning of how much that tis or how long this twould take."

"It depends on the market for furs. This year not so good, but I made enough to put avay about a thousand dollars. Dot's after ve split the take. Dot means du vould haf about one hundred dollars or more."

"How long does this take?" He remembered how rapidly his funds had dwindled.

"About six months."

"That twould be but sixteen dollars per month."

The blue eyes hardened. "Ja, but that's a damn good vage, and I supply the equipment. Du might stay alive and learn how to survive. I teach du how. The only vons better than me are the Injuns. And I provide grub."

He saw the frown on MacDonald's face. "Dot's food, boy. Don't du understand American?"

"It seems I dinna ken what ye said. Nay do I ken what wages are here."

Rolfe sighed. "If ve make a good profit and du learn fast, I'll up it to fifteen percent. But du buy the coat and blanket du vill need. Once ve're out on the prairie, I can kill a buffalo. If there's time we'll tan it enough for making a varm tent."

His words left MacDonald's mind reeling. This man was one who would not let MacDonald's mind into his. It was obvious if he were to get back to the spaceship, he needed money to survive and he needed to learn the ways of men in this land.

"That tis much fairer. I shall earn that fifteen percent." He grinned and they both stood.

"Ve shake on it now."

Neither man tried to show their strength in the grip of shaking. Rolfe because he knew the big man/boy was stronger. MacDonald did not because he did not need to prove what was obvious.

"I'll teach du Deutsche too. Dot's German in English." He grinned. "Now ve ride to the next town vhere du can buy the things du need. I'll make sure that they don't cheat du."

He hesitated a moment. "How about I call du Mac? It sounds better than boy if du vorking mitt me."

"Aye, it does sound better. Someone is apt to laugh if ye call me boy and I'm towering over ye."

Rolfe broke off a chew and plopped it into his mouth. "Und du buy your own tobacco"

Chapter 4

The Maca

The sound of terror in the horses' whinnies and mules' braying brought the sleeping men to their feet. MacDonald and Rolfe had camped with another group of free traders heading into St. Louis. It had been a disastrous year for trapping. The danger of a larger group from the fur brigade stealing what few furs they had was real. They intended to sell their furs directly to the American Fur Company in St. Louis. They had found an abandoned squatter's cabin on the edge of western Kansas. It took minimal work to make the fence sturdy enough to hold their animals.

The fear of losing their horses and mules added swiftness to their movements. Men were grabbing their clothes and at their loaded rifles when Rolfe noticed a Kentuckian reaching for the door.

"Don't open that door. It could be anything from Injuns to bears. Vait till ve are ready."

He bent to pull on his moccasins when the blast of cold morning air hit him.

"It's Mac," someone yelled. "He's gone loco. It's a damn grizzly out there and he ain't got nothing but a bowie knife."

Rolfe pushed the others out of his way to get to the door. There were no windows in this cabin. One look and Rolfe stopped.

MacDonald was almost to the grizzly, his long legs cutting the distance in that peculiar rolling bear-like gait. He had on nothing but his under clothes and moccasins. The grizzly had its back to him as it tore at the fence rails, pulling one board loose and then another to get at the stock. It stood a bit shorter than MacDonald's six foot nine inches. He leaped the remaining distance to land on the grizzly's back.

MacDonald grasped under the open mouth and ran the knife across the middle of the right side of the throat towards the back of the neck. The grizzly roared and tried to claw at his right side, then at the left. MacDonald had released his grasp, but the claws still raked at his arm. Blood gushed from the grizzly's jugular vein. The wind and turning grizzly spewed blood in all directions. As his feet hit the ground, MacDonald reached upward and thrust the knife into the grizzly's left eye. He tried to retreat keeping behind the grizzly, but the beast stood, roared, turned, and charged.

"Get down du damn fool." Rolfe was shouting.

The men watched as MacDonald managed the impossible. He had gotten to the side of the charging animal and was back up on the beast's back. He had transferred the bowie knife to his left hand and was ripping at the jugular vein on that side. This time the blood oozed out and the bear dropped to his four feet, shaking his head as to clear his sight and charge at his antagonist.

MacDonald stepped back dragging the cold air into his lungs and creating clouds of iced vapor as he expelled the air. He could not explain to these men that for one moment he was back in the Sky Maist Mountains that bisected his continent of Don and that he, the Maca, was proving his worth by killing the wild elbenor with a knife. That he should have been wearing only a thong was irrelevant. The grizzly was close enough in size and the bowie knife sufficient in killing efficiency.

The grizzly shook its head and more blood spewed. Then the bear turned to peer at the livestock with its remaining eye, turned again toward the men at the cabin, and reared before toppling to the ground.

MacDonald threw his head back and his yell rolled out into the prairie sky. "I am Mac," and he hesitated just a moment, "Donald." I am Maca screamed in his mind. He bowed to the beast on the ground and walked back towards the cabin and the wide-eyed men staring at him in awed disbelief.

"Du crazy, Mac. Vhy didn't du let me shoot him?"

"Because, Friend Rolfe, I needed to do that. Now the frustrations of this year's hunt are somewhat alleviated." MacDonald smiled at him and his brown eyes filled with amusement.

Rolfe shook his head. "Vell, at least ve can sell the fur. Too damn bad du ruined der face."

"Why sell it? We can keep it, or ye can. Mayhap it twill keep us warm one of these nights." He realized the cold was biting into him and he stepped inside the cabin.

The others hurried out to check the animals and to keep them contained. Rolfe started skinning the bear. There was still plenty of salt left to start the curing, and the bear meat could be eaten that night.

Chapter 5

An Era Closes

MacDonald and Rolfe walked out of the American Fur Company, their backs straight and their shoulders swaying. MacDonald walked with his rolling gait and Rolfe was not much different with his legs bowed from the time spent in the saddle. Not until they were outside and mounted did they speak. When Rolfe did speak, it was in German.

"I still have to go home and tell Mrs. Rolfe what happened to the prices. You wait a couple hours and then come by. Don't do anything stupid, Friend Mac, and drink up what little you do have."

MacDonald looked at him. "It twas a good two years." It was their normal conversation pattern. Rolfe spoke German, MacDonald his own brand of English.

"No, there was one good year, one halfway decent year, and this year we barely made a profit. We've got to plan for next year. I have an idea, but don't want to bray it all over the streets. Now that I think about it, you have enough to rent a place. Come by in the morning and we'll make our plans."

MacDonald decided to save his pittance from this year. He was up to thirty percent after three years of working with Rolfe, but it looked like 1845 was the last of the good times for fur trappers. The men in the camps the last two years had been different, rougher, and meaner. Rolfe claimed they were far less educated than the earliest trappers and most of them were Frenchmen out of Canada. They were a dissipated lot and drank their furs away before they even made it to St. Louis or left the Rendezvous. The Indians were prone to drinking and trading their women. The tribal women and men appeared slovenly compared to the first year MacDonald had seen them. Rolfe was different from the other trappers. He had a wife and an established home here in St. Louis. MacDonald still puzzled over the rapidity in which the female of the Earth species bore their young. Rolfe had married Miss Clara Reiker in 1842 and their daughter, Maria Gretchen, was born that same year. Maria died before her second birthday, Olga had been born last year, and now another was expected or already born. Rolfe had even been prudent with his funds, either leaving them with his wife or securing letters of credit.

Banks were risky. They were given to collapsing and their script became worthless. MacDonald had either carried gold coins in a belt around his waist or left his funds in the care of Mrs. Rolfe. He was afraid to speculate in land in Missouri or anywhere else. Right now he planned to visit a bathhouse, find an eating establishment, and then spend the night outside of town hidden away for a needed rest. The hotels would be bedbug infested or filled with people ready to take what funds someone dressed as a trapper might be carrying. Sharing a bed with a snoring, farting, probably unwashed stranger did not appeal to his Thalian sensibilities.

The sun was well over the eastern horizon when MacDonald knocked on the Rolfe's door. Rolfe opened the door with a wide grin.

"Welcome, Friend Mac. Frau Rolfe is in bed with our son, and the midwife is still with her. As soon as they wake, I'll introduce you to Martin Luther Rolfe. Maybe he will be a pastor or a rich merchant."

"I rejoice with ye." MacDonald used the formal words of Thalia.

"Twould ye rather I come back tomorrow?"

"No, with another mouth to feed, I need to make our plans. I think with all that has happened this will work." He continued speaking as he closed the door and led MacDonald into the small kitchen. "We will become traders out of here and Santa Fe with a route clear into Texas."

"But Texas might go to Spain. Last night at the restaurant, I heard men discussing that it would be a protectorate under Britain."

"The South won't let that happen. They want Texas for a slave state. Once it becomes a state, we won't have to pay the country of Texas anything for trading there. There are German communities in the state and they would welcome us.

"Are you ready for a cup of coffee, Mac? There's some damn good coffee cake a neighbor brought over. Then we can look at figures. We'll need one, maybe two wagons. If we have two, we'll need to hire one or two men."

"Aye, to the coffee and the treat. I dinna ken about selling merchandise till I see yere costs and what we twill be selling. It sounds risky. Mayhap we should do more trapping or join the army. If the Union takes in Texas, there may be war with Mexico. They twill nay like it."

"The army doesn't pay enough to live on, Mac, but they need supplies. That's where an established firm would make more money."

"Are there nay traders there?"

"Ja, but they can't fight off marauders like we can. Some might know the country, but it's always an iffy business. If we get lucky, we can become rich. Then I'll move Mrs. Rolfe and the family to Santa Fe or Texas. That way we'll see each other more often."

"What kind of merchandise do we sell? Do ye ken about keeping accounts?"

"We sell doodads for the ladies, blankets, fabric, some whiskey, some guns and ammo, some beads for the tribes we run into, and maybe some metal pots and pans. First we go see what other traders are buying. That will tell us how we need to plan. Don't want food goods. Too heavy and might spoil. Ships take that in faster anyway."

"Don't they take the same goods ye are planning on?"

"Yes, but they don't make it to the little towns and smaller settlements. Even if the goods get that far, they cost double, triple, or more. A trader coming in from the north would be welcomed."

Chapter 6

Hard Times

Millard Hurley fought to unhitch the mules from the last wagon and get them hobbled. His shoulders were strained and hurting from the effort and one of the damn mules had stepped on his foot. It had been a fight with the mule teams everyday. His employers were not shy about telling him they were replacing him in the next civilized town.

Millard was in his middle forties with a sun lined face and graying hair, his exact age uncertain. Who bothered with such things anyway? He wouldn't have been hired out of Lawrence, Kansas except the other man had the bad luck to keel over dead. Millard was convinced the mules must have brought on a fit of apoplexy.

Rolfe appeared with an antelope. God knew how the bastard could find game when no one else could. Not in this dry, rocky place. MacDonald had hobbled and fed his horse and now was starting a fire behind one of the wagons. Dust stirred with every movement. This was a hellish part of Texas, all sand and rock unlike the prairie they just came through. MacDonald and Rolfe were delivering supplies to one of the new Army forts that had sprung up since the Mexican War. Millard was seriously wondering why he had agreed to work for them. These two drove men like animals and treated the animals better than men. He would have preferred a wagonload of whores instead of sundries for the dragoons.

Rolfe threw the antelope down and started to dismount when his horse began lifting its nose to the wind.

"Mac, something ain't right. Saddle your horse and bring your rifle. Hurley, du best grab your gun and be ready to ride a mule." He swung his horse around to gaze at the horizon.

MacDonald never questioned Rolfe's instincts. He tossed dirt over the fire, grabbed his rifle and saddle before running towards his horse. On the horizon appeared a line of warriors that broke into a gallop, whooping and shaking something in their hands that looked like a stick with feathers on it.

Millard tried to mount the mule and was promptly dumped on his backside, cursing mules and the men who had brought him to this godforsaken country.

Rolfe aimed a shot at the oncoming men.

"Vhat du think, Mac?"

"There's too damn many of them." MacDonald voice roared out over the mesquite and scrub brush savanna.

Millard was fighting the mule, trying to get it to stand still. The roar of Rolfe's Henry had startled the mules and they began running, some towards the oncoming men, others back the way they had come. There was a sinking feeling in his stomach and he raised his fist to hit the mule when he was grabbed from behind and lifted bodily off the ground.

MacDonald had one arm around his chest and was carrying him as his feet made running motions.

"Hold still till we get off a ways. Then ye can mount behind me," came the roar in his ears and mind.

How the hell was the man holding on to him? Millard didn't care. A couple of the yelling bastards were riding after them, but the other yells seemed to grow dimmer.

Rolfe and MacDonald raced around a boulder and drew up.

"Get on behind me." Millard found himself dumped on the ground and MacDonald's hand extended downward.

Rolfe had slid off his horse and took a quick shot around the rock. Then he jumped back in the saddle and pointed to the north before riding off. With a nod, MacDonald followed.

Two hours later they pulled up and dismounted. Rolfe took a swig out of his canteen and looked at MacDonald.

"Vhere's yours?"

"Back in the saddlebag that tis on the ground."

"Damn careless."

"Aye, it twas."

Millard was shaking. "Be they gone?"

"Mayhap." The big man shrugged. "What do ye think, friend Rolfe?

"I think they chased down the mules and now they're having a party mitt our goods and tonight's dinner. Vhat the hell do du think they're doing, Mac?"

The big man let out his breath. "Any chance we can make our own attack and recover our merchandise?"

"Vhen ve stopped at that boulder, I saw smoke. Vhat they ain't took, they've burned along mitt der vagons." Rolfe fought to keep the German out of his speech. "Damn Kiowa. Du think the Comanche vould keep them too busy to bother mitt us. Ve need to move on, Mac. Ve valk the horses now and find wasser, then a good place to camp."

"What about food?" Millard was regaining his courage.

"Ve go hungry tonight. No fire, and don't complain. Du damn lucky to be alive." Rolfe glared at him and Millard swallowed. Rolfe probably would have left him back at the wagons.

Chapter 7

Friendship and Gold

MacDonald and Rolfe sat near a small campfire. Their one meal of the day, a small, skinned deer, was in a pit that was lined and covered with hot rocks. A small fire burned over the heated rocks. It was an improvised a cooking chamber constructed by Rolfe. Their money was gone and the people in this part of Texas did not know them.

Their conversation was low and grim. They had dropped Millard Hurley off at the nearest pueblo, a town more Mexican than the towns the Americans and immigrants had built or were building near their farms and plantations. They had left the hot, dry lands of Texas to the Comanche and the 2nd Dragoons. Here the land was green prairie grass with juniper and scrub oak. High bluffs and red rock mountain-like hills covered with trees jutted upward from the plains.

"We're busted, Mac. Do you have any ideas that will get us home alive?"

MacDonald was on his haunches and he rocked back and forth. He kenned where he was. The *Golden One* was hidden to the north, mayhap three or four days ride. There was still gold there. He had taken enough to buy a horse, equipment, clothes, and food when he left.

The year was 1850 and Texas and California were now part of the United States. It meant this land was being sold to white men like him and Rolfe. He had learned that land records were kept at the county seat and would have the legal description of the land covering his secret. Then he could find out if anyone owned the land, purchase the land from the owners, or from the state of Texas. He would probably need a lawyer, but he could use his mind to determine if people were honest or trying to cheat him.

Still, he had to consider Herman; his friend had taught him to survive in this wild land, lent him money to start in the trading business, and then made him full partner. Rolfe had given him the cover he needed to learn the ways of this world. How could he convince Herman that he had left the gold hidden all these years? Earth beings' short life spans meant they reckoned time differently than Thalians. Would his reaction be indignation or would he agree to go partners and become a rancher? MacDonald relished the idea. In Thalia, Don had supplied the kine to all of the Houses. It did nay matter that kine were called cattle here. It twas the same brown-eyed beastie.

"I have been thinking, Friend Rolfe. I like this land. Most of it tis open grassland and cattle do well here. They are running around free since the turmoil of the Mexican War and Texas claiming the Spanish land grants here and the United States in California. How would ye like to become a rancher?"

"Have you gone stark, raving mad? What the hell would we use for money?"

MacDonald glanced up. "Before I met ye, I stumbled on a cache of uh, well, it tis gold. I twas new in this land and did nay ken how to use it or where. It remains hidden, and the location tis near here; about four days ride at the most. Without yere teachings, I twould have died in this land or been reduced to starvation. Tis more than willing I am to share it with ye."

"And this isn't a way to keep me silent if it's been stolen?"

MacDonald stood. "Friend Rolfe, ye canna believe that!"

"Well, was it stolen?"

"Nay by me. The owner twas nay there."

"How much gold?"

"I am nay sure. It seemed a great amount, but then I did nay ken the currency of this land."

Rolfe looked at him and weighed his choices. "Coins or bars?"

"They are bars, ingots I believe ye call them."

"What did the marks on it look like?"

"There twere nay marks that I recall."

"Mac, I've not been in church out here, but that don't mean I don't believe God's Word. You show me this gold, and then I'll decide."

"I ask only that ye nay divulge its location. I have kept it secret all these years."

"If it's stolen from some bank or company, I can't keep it a secret."

"How can ye determine that from looking at it?"

"The marks on it, dammit, they tell where they are from."

MacDonald gave a tight smile. "I told ye, there are nay marks."

* * *

They had ridden for three days through gently swelling prairie, the grass high, green, and sweet smelling. On the fourth day they were into the foothills of an almost mountainous area covered with pines and scrub oak that rose above the prairie. They had ridden past a small spring in a flatter area surrounded by trees.

Damn, thought Rolfe, a perfect place for a camp. He had noted the abundance of game, wild cattle, and signs of wild horses. This was verging on perfect land for ranching. Water flowed here and there were trees for felling, trees that could be used for building or for heat. They continued winding their way upward until they rounded a large rock and entered a small flat area between the piles of beige and rose-beige boulders. This side was hidden from view by the tumbled rocks and hilly terrain. One small tree tried to battle its way heavenward from the rocky soil. The stunted vegetation growing out of the cracks in the rocky face looked as though they were trying to overcome some type of contamination.

"This tis where the gold tis hidden." MacDonald dismounted and tied his horse to the tree.

Rolfe eyed the area and looked at him. He spewed out his chaw. "Mac, this place doesn't look natural. Everything is too stunted. Why did you even stop here? And how the hell do you intend to get into any cave?" He pointed at the large, almost round boulder.

MacDonald gave a half-grin and walked to the boulder. He put his back to it, set his legs and began to push. The boulder moved slowly scattering the small stones that had gathered or fallen in the ensuing years until an opening wide enough for a man became visible. MacDonald straightened and took several deep breaths. His face had reddened during the exertion and sweat poured down from his forehead and temples.

"If ye prefer to wait, I twill go in and bring it back. It twill take a few minutes as tis deeper than the front of the cave. Someone did nay wish it found." This wasn't a lie. He hadn't wanted anything found and had hidden the *Golden One* deep in the earth after finding this earthquake-free region. He had discovered the extra gold in Ricca's quarters when he searched for anything that would aid him in surviving in this alien world.

Rolfe frowned and swung down from his horse. "Why do I get the feeling you are hiding something from me, Mac?"

"Because, I am."

He turned to face Rolfe. "If ye see what I have hidden below, ye twill have the knowledge to destroy me and my time here."

"Who did you kill to steal the gold? Are there bones hidden by the gold?"

“Nay! Ye ken me better than that.” His voice was emphatic.

“Friend Rolfe, if the world sees what tis below, certain people twill wish to claim it. Without me, they canna enter it. They twill nay understand it, they twill try to possess it or destroy it. The weapons available in this world canna do that. Then they twill fear it and me.”

Rolfe’s face was devoid of understanding. “You are not making sense. You said ‘world.’ Do you mean the U.S. or Texas?”

“I meant this world. Come with me, and then ye decide if ye twill keep my secret.”

He turned and moved sideways through the open space.

Rolfe tied his horse to the tree, not really sure it was sturdy enough to hold both horses if something should frighten them. Like MacDonald, he had to turn his wide frame sideways to enter. For a moment he stood, blinking, waiting for his eyes to adjust to the semi-darkness. When he could discern the features of the cave he looked up and around. The place was wrong; the walls too smooth, the ceiling looked as smooth as the floor. He turned to face MacDonald and his mouth fell open.

The huge form was standing at the mouth of a tunnel waiting for him and in his hand was something giving out a beam of light stronger than any lamp Rolfe had ever seen. Questions, curse words, all ran through his mind in a jumble, but he was unable to utter a word for a few seconds. He fought the urge to run and stepped closer.

“What the hell, Mac? Can you explain that?” The light was so strong he could even see the half-smile on MacDonald’s face.

“I could, but ye twould nay believe me until ye see what tis below. Shall we walk?”

Rolfe reached out and grabbed him by the bicep. “How far do we walk, Mac?” His voice sounded strangled to his own ears. “Will you let me walk back up if I don’t like what I see?”

“Twould ye kill me, Friend Rolfe?”

"Ja, if you tried to kill me." His mouth was in a stubborn line and his blue eyes hard. He saw the white teeth of MacDonald flash and heard the laughter in his voice.

"That tis what I like about ye, Herman. Ye are the most honest man I ken. I could nay kill the man who taught me so much. If ye come with me, the decision tis yeres as to what we do next." He turned and began the descent.

Rolfe's emotions fought with his reasoning, but something was down there—something that his friend had discovered. That MacDonald could have possibly fashioned the tunnel never occurred to him as the height and width of it rivaled that of a three story mansion. The light began to recede and Rolfe hurried after MacDonald rather than be left to wonder the rest of his life.

As they descended, Rolfe could see a faint glow becoming brighter, sending the darkness back into the walls. As they neared the bottom, MacDonald shut down the light in his hand and Rolfe realized that the golden dome he had spotted was a huge ovoid-F-shaped machine built by men. But when? How?

MacDonald kept striding toward that monstrosity. Rolfe found he could not move. He had faced blizzards, floods, Indians, madmen, thieves, and grizzlies, but whatever squatted in front of him was beyond his comprehension. If the tunnel had not been dark, he would have turned and fled upward. The world began to dim and he remembered to breathe.

MacDonald stopped at the machine and turned. "This, Friend Rolfe, tis the vessel that brought me to this world. . . " He realized that Rolfe had not followed him into the chamber and he hurried back to him.

"The gold tis inside. Do ye wish to go in with me or do ye prefer to remain here?"

Rolfe could not take his eyes off the golden machine, but MacDonald was in front of him, blocking his view.

"Mein Gott! It's… it's… inside? How the hell do you go inside, Mac? There isn't a door. Are you going to tell me that you walk through metal or whatever that thing is made of?"

"I canna walk through metal, and, yes, tis made from metal. The metal twas manufactured on another world perhaps three hundred years or more ago by another race of beings called the Justines."

"Your people didn't make that? What did you do? Take it from them?"

"Nay exactly, Herman. My people do not have the ability to build this *Golden One.* I twas aboard this ship when it came here looking for another Justine. A mob in Ireland killed the navigator. He twas a relative of the missing Justine named Toma. I twas left with the ship. I canna fly it back to their land or mine. I dinna have the training or kenning to pilot through the stars."

Rolfe closed his eyes and shook his head as though trying to clear it. "You know what, Mac, I think I'll wait right here."

MacDonald started to ask him if he would be all right, but decided against it. That would be an insult and right now his friend did not need an insult to his bravery.

"It twill take a few minutes."

He returned to the *Golden One* and laid his hand on the correct panel. It slid back into the frame and a ramp extended downward. MacDonald left the panel open, although in normal circumstances he would have closed it. He hurried to the lift and ascended to the third level to access Ricca's quarters.

The bluish glow from the walls and floors were a familiar, comforting emanation. His biggest regret was the fact that he would need to hurry and there would nay be time to take a shower. How he longed to enter the cleansing room and feel the flow of warm, soapy water. It was impossible to take proper cleansings in this land, but Herman twas too upset for him to linger. He entered Ricca's room and pulled the gold from the storage unit beneath the bed. Ricca had placed the gold in a box purchased in Denmark while they were there. The key remained in the lock. No Kreppie would have dared remove the gold while Ricca lived.

In Denmark, it had been fascinating to hear how rapidly Ricca could assimilate an alien language. A few words and he would grasp it. Llewellyn found it took him several days to master an alien tongue and he could nay erase his Thalian speech. His German was still heavily accented.

The box was heavy and he hoisted it to his shoulder as he began the trip back. Once outside the *Golden One*, he paused to close the panel before striding back to Rolfe. The box was beginning to bite into his shoulder and he hefted it to the other side.

Rolfe was leaning against the tunnel opening looking at the *Golden One* and him as he approached.

"Isn't there anybody in there?"

"All are dead."

"All? You said a mob in Ireland killed the man who navigated this thing and he owned the gold. Who else was there?"

MacDonald swallowed. He had made a verbal slip. The years with Rolfe had eroded the caution he used when speaking to most beings on this world.

"There twas a crew—six in all."

"And what happened to them?"

"I twisted their heads off and buried them in space."

Rolfe looked at him, his eyes still hard, but puzzled.

"Mac, I never knew you to be a violent man. You protect yourself and others, but you don't kill for the fun of it. Why did you kill them?"

"We twere enemies. There had been a war between our worlds and there tis much bitterness. They would have killed me rather than take me back to their world. They twere a bit hampered as they could nay navigate the *Golden One*. I did nay want them loose on this world. They twould have tried to take over and rule it."

"Six men take over this world? That's crazy."

"They twould have had the *Golden One.* Ye have nay idea of the fire power that exists in its weapons. They could have destroyed every civilization on this planet."

"Can you still do that?"

"Why? I dinna wish to rule this world. I want to return home, but I canna do that. So since I must stay, I wish to stay here and own this land to keep the *Golden One* safe till I learn to navigate through the stars."

He looked at Rolfe. "Did ye wish to see the gold here or above?"

The desire to flee showed in Rolfe's face, but the desire to look, to touch real gold overcame his fears. He took a deep breath. "Here, Mac, if it looks all right, I'll examine it more thoroughly in the sunlight."

MacDonald set the box down, sat cross-legged, and unlocked it. Then he threw open the lid.

Rolfe sank down to his knees, his mouth open. "Gold," he whispered. "Mein Gott, gold." Somewhere in the back of his mind, he had rejected the idea that there would be any gold. People, no matter how advanced, could not produce gold. Alchemists had tried it and all had failed. He drew in his breath and ran his fingers across the top and picked up an ingot to examine it, turning it over and over. He did the same with another piece.

"There aren't any marks." He looked over at his friend.

MacDonald gave one of his half smiles. "I told ye, nay marks."

Rolfe's eyes were wide, an avid expression on his face at the sight of all that gold. It was as exciting as a fight.

"You can buy this land, Friend Mac."

"Aye, that we can. Are ye satisfied?"

Rolfe took a deep breath to relieve the tightness in his chest. "Do we go partners or each of us own a ranch?"

"What do ye wish?"

"It's better we each have our own land, and have our own brand for the cattle."

"Brand? Oh, aye, the mark to tell the world they are our beasties. Does that need to be settled now?

"Yes, we will need to file that when we file the deeds. If we have it settled now, we won't have to think about it." Rolfe had forgotten he was deep within the earth. He had always prepared for any contingency. The only things you couldn't control were weather, men bent on murder, or death.

"Do ye have a preference? I can think of nay right now."

"It must be something that tells the world the cattle and horses belong to you."

MacDonald grinned, a soft chortle coming from his mouth. "And what, Friend Rolfe, reminds ye of me?"

"A rearing grizzly."

MacDonald rocked slightly backward and then forward. "Then what do ye think of the Rearing Bear Ranch?"

Rolfe grinned. "Good name, Mac. Now it's your turn. What do you think of when you see me?"

"I think of a bowie knife."

"I can't name a ranch after a knife. Somebody might think Jim Bowie came back from the dead."

"How about a knife slash?"

"A brand is static. It doesn't go anywhere except where the cow goes. I can't show a slash. It would be too easy to change."

MacDonald slapped the lid back down and locked the box.

"All right, how about Crossing Blades?"

"That'll work." Rolfe grinned at MacDonald. "You know what, Friend Mac? We're both crazy."

Chapter 8

Austin

MacDonald and Rolfe strode out of the filing office with Matthew Rutledge, an attorney who had been representing them. MacDonald towered over the six-foot tall Rutledge and the other men on the street. MacDonald and Rutledge were dressed in the suits of the 1840's: heavy dark woolen suits with wide lapels, a double-layered vest over a white shirt with stand-up collar and the properly tied string bowtie. MacDonald wasn't certain whether he would choke or not. It was a wonderment how Earth beings wore undergarments, summer and winter. They put on layers of clothes without showing signs of extreme stress. In the West, men wore boots or the brogan type shoes and they did all manner of exertion in the hot, muggy weather without dropping from heat exhaustion.

Rolfe was still dressed in his buckskins and moccasins. He had adopted a gray, wide brimmed hat during his trader years rather than the fur caps he had worn as a trapper. They had just filed the deed to the Ortega Spanish land grant and their respective brands. The grant had been purchased from the state as Texas had insisted on retaining all public lands before being annexed into the United States. The deed and filing documents were in MacDonald's valise. At the corner of Congress and Pecan Streets they shook hands.

"Thank ye, Mr. Rutledge."

"My pleasure, Mr. MacDonald. Remember, should you ever need an attorney, we are able to handle all manner of contracts."

Rolfe cut a chaw of tobacco and nodded at the man. He had let MacDonald carry the bulk of the conversation. People respected Mac, accent or not, but they took his accent for stupidity or labeled him as Dutch. The latter had ended in fights at times. He had no reason to antagonize this man, and so he let any misconception continue.

"Now we need to take those legal papers to a safe place," he said once they were alone on a street crowded with wagons, surreys, and men in business suits hurrying from one location to another. "Then we need to celebrate, but damn if I can think of a safe place where we both can celebrate at the same time."

"Neither can I." Both spoke in German on the theory that fewer people would understand them. "I suggest we eat and then ride out of town before we decide how to do this. We need to go to Arles next and hire a surveyor. Perhaps we can toss a coin to determine who celebrates this evening. We can dine quite well before we decide."

"I have a better idea. We celebrate when we get back to St. Louis. Then I can set Frau Rolfe's mind at ease and explain that we will be moving in a year or two. She has enough money until we get there. We aren't expected back until spring."

"There is one thing I wish to do before starting back."

Rolfe looked at his friend. MacDonald's face was set and he was staring straight ahead.

"And what would that be, Mac?"

"I need to visit a whorehouse, a respectable one. If you wish to celebrate this evening, I'll guard our deeds and the remaining funds. I will wait until tomorrow evening."

Rolfe considered. Living with a native woman a few months while trapping, never bothered his religious beliefs. The tribe didn't consider the arrangement immoral if he left enough trade goods and meat for the family, but he had avoided whorehouses. He was married and whores usually harbored a disease. He did not wish to take that back to Clara. MacDonald had visited houses when flush, but for some reason never seemed to contact one of the diseases, not even clap.

"Why don't we both go to the whorehouse? I'll have a drink while you finish your business and then we can ride out and take turns guarding each other."

"You might be drunk by the time I finish. I intend to visit every whore in the establishment, perhaps more than once."

"That's a pipe dream, Mac. No man can do that."

They entered their hotel and collected their belongings for the trail. The stables were a few blocks away, set among a wainwright, a blacksmith, tanners, and lard merchants. The stench was everywhere, but no one seemed to notice anymore than they noticed the grey air drifting over the city from people cooking with wood or coal.

A few blocks away from the stable, they stopped at a large restaurant where men wearing suits were seen entering and leaving. They ordered steaks and hash browns with gravy. Both ordered beer.

"I have heard they have seafood and much fancier houses down in San Antonio or Galveston." MacDonald's voice had a longing in it.

"We don't have time to go that far. What's the matter with you Mac? You're acting like you want to fling away everything we just gained."

MacDonald attacked the steak trying to find words to explain to his friend that frontier food was not Thalian food. How could he explain the Thalian need for the caress of another being or how emotions transferred physically and mentally between Thalians? Every bedding with a prostitute had left that need unfulfilled and a steady fire had grown inside of him. He had never had his First Bedding rite, although Leta, an older female from Donnick's Enforcers had taken pity on him and instructed him in certain matters while granting him a bedding. When he returned he would reward that lassie if she still lived.

When no good words emerged, he changed the subject. "I'll camp tonight, but tomorrow I am going to the whorehouse Rutledge recommended."

"All right, Mac. We go there together tonight. I'll have a drink and wait for you."

"It will take me awhile."

Rolfe snorted and downed his beer. "You're crazy, Mac."

Chapter 9

A Refined Place

Madame Collette smoothed her brown hair and slid her hand down her maroon faille dress. She slipped a heavy pearl necklace over her head and smiled at the round face in the mirror before entering the lobby of her domain. She nodded at Doris arranging the glassware and whiskey bottles. Twilight had begun and her girls were in place awaiting her inspection, each deliberately posed in their most alluring position. She studied Suzette as she checked them. This would be Suzette's last season here. She was getting too old. Worse, it looked like the woman was pregnant again. She shook her head. Too damn stupid to use the correct douche. She nodded at the maid to unlock the front door. She could see two looming shapes outside. This might be a good evening for midweek if someone were here this early.

Doris opened the door with a beaming smile and two men crossed the threshold. The huge form of one made some of the smaller girls suck in their breath. There were times when such men could rip the insides of a petite woman. At least he was well dressed. The other man was dressed in buckskins. Not a good sign for someone with money to drop.

Madame Collette tried to gauge whether to ask that they leave or accommodate them. The large man solved the problem by removing his hat, bowing, and speaking in French.

"Good evening, Madame Collette. Mr. Rutledge recommended this as a refined place to visit before leaving your fair city. It seems you have those that will please a man and your drinks received almost as much praise."

Madame forced a smile to her lips. The girls be damned, she thought. Rutledge was her link to the law. This man was entitled to anyone in the place.

"If we both could have a drink, I'll make my selections."

"Selections, monsieur?"

The dark eyes smiled down at her. "Aye, I'll select two now and more as the evening progresses." He had reverted to English.

Madame Collette stared for a moment and gave a low chuckle.

"I like a man who knows what he wants. The fee is twenty-five dollars per room." In her establishment, it was the room that was rented not the female. "Since you are selecting two, it would be two rooms. It is a bit difficult to be two places at once. Do you intend to spend the evening? Then it becomes one hundred dollars."

MacDonald's smile was becoming a bit fixed. "Tis there a time limit on the two rooms?"

"Only if you spend the evening, then, as I said, the fee is one hundred dollars for each room. One room could be empty, of course, if that is what you prefer. We do make our gentlemen feel quite at home here."

Relief flooded MacDonald's face. "Of course, the fee changes with each selection. Tis that nay correct?"

The girls were twittering in the background. Madame could see someone else's shape at the door and the knocker clanged.

"Doris, admit the gentleman."

She turned to MacDonald. "That is correct."

"Then for now I twill take the two tallest. I should be back down in about two hours."

"Wouldn't you prefer a drink first, or one to take with you?" She thought this a most curious way to choose.

"Nay for myself, but friend Rolfe twould like one." He pulled out his bills and added a nickel for Rolfe's beer. He then looked at the young women for none were over twenty-four.

He nodded at two of them and they rose and went to him. Somehow he knew this would not fulfill the desire raging in him, but the physical could no longer be denied. At least his Elder Lamar had instructed him and Leta had more than taught him. They ascended the stairs.

True to his word, MacDonald returned in about two hours. By now the room was filled with cigar smoke, men talking loudly, the smell of alcohol floating about the room, and fewer women. Most of the men were waiting for a certain woman to return. Several men had started a poker game. The Madame did not mind. They bought drinks more frequently and added to her profit. MacDonald selected two more and sighed at their short stature. He bought Rolfe another beer. Rolfe raised his eyebrows. It was now after nine o'clock.

Two hours later he returned. That had been time enough for the first two females to spread the tale of an incredible lover who was capable of more than once without assistance. Both were hoping to be chosen again. Rolfe was trying to guard their valise and not fall into a slumber when MacDonald went back up the stairs with two more.

It was enough to make Rolfe sit upright. He decided to join in the poker game. The men looked tired and they had definitely downed more booze than he had. Rolfe laid down his gold piece and was accepted. They knew they were sharp business men. What could a buckskin-clad frontiersman know?

At one fourteen in the morning MacDonald walked down the stairs again. By this time the lobby was almost deserted except for a very drowsy Rolfe. Madame Collette was pacing back and forth.

"Will you be choosing another? I have but two left who are not engaged for the evening."

MacDonald looked at the two. They were but mere slips of womanhood, barely standing an even four feet. He shook his head.

"Nay, they are far too wee. I might injure them. If I may have my hat, please?"

"Of course, Mr. MacDonald, and may I say this has been one of the more interesting evenings of my life." She motioned to Doris to bring his hat. "You have given us something to dwell on for many an evening. Please come back at any time." She did not address her remarks to Rolfe. He had managed to upset two of her better customers by winning their evening funds.

Doris handed him his broad brimmed hat and he handed her a nickel, bowed to the Madame, and walked out the door with Rolfe. Once the door was closed, they untied their horses and mounted.

"I heard dem vimen say du fucked two times for each visit. Dat true?"

"Aye, I did that."

"Do du know vhat, Mac. Du ain't human." He swung his horse out into the empty street.

The darkness hid MacDonald's smile, but inside he still hungered. He had made up for the physical fire raging within, but the mental and emotional transfer had been missing. It was something the beings on this planet lacked.

Chapter 10

Arles

MacDonald and Rolfe rode back to the town of Arles, the county seat and the nearest town to their ranches. While in Austin, they had divided the land grant into two separate ranches and the purchase was recorded as such.

They hoped the drawings of the rivers and springs in the old Spanish land grant were correct as well as the measurements. MacDonald believed the *Golden One* was on his portion recorded in his Earth name. They also knew the river on one side of Rolfe's ranch was his boundary no matter if the course had changed. No one could really be certain of any boundary after that. They pulled up at the sheriff's office, dismounted, and entered. An official could tell them where the surveyor, if there was one, was located in town.

Sheriff Franklin looked up at the two dust-covered men; one a giant, the other a hunter in buckskin with a sheathed bowie knife slung on his right hip. Neither looked like the type that would bother with a law officer if something was wrong. He felt his shoulders tightening, ready for trouble.

"Good day, sir, I am Zebediah MacDonald and this tis my friend, Herman Rolfe." The voice had a rumbling quality to it and the r sound was rolled. Probably from Scotland, thought Franklin.

"We are in need of a surveyor as we have purchased the Ortega Land Grant. Could ye tell us if one tis in this town and if so, where he tis located?"

Franklin took a moment to study them a bit more closely. Where did two men come up with money for that? Why here? There were a couple of spreads up north a bit, but the Tillman brothers did as much farming as they did ranching. Still an honest question deserved an honest answer.

"Welcome to our community, gentlemen. I'm Sheriff Franklin." He stood and extended his hand. A handshake could tell you a lot about a man. He blessed Providence when his hand wasn't crushed by either.

"You all will find the surveyor, Mr. Smeaton, behind the Blue Diamond freight station. If you all run into any problems, let me know." No need to antagonize potential voters. He realized both men were probably in their thirties and ready to settle down. "We're a fine growing community. There's everything here you all might need in the way of sundries."

"Thank ye, Sheriff Franklin. We twill keep that in mind." Both nodded at him and left.

Outside they mounted and rode to the surveyor's office. It was a small wooden building tucked away behind the freight depot.

"Things look slow, not like in Saint Louis." Rolfe spat on the rutted street. It wasn't the heat of the day and no one was loading wagons or acting like freight needed to be delivered. Blue Diamond's freight buildings were normally a hive of activity.

"Perhaps they have down days here.

"Did ye wish me to speak again?"

"You might as well. He might try to cheat us else."

"If he rides out with us, ye canna remain silent."

Rolfe grinned. "Then he would think me a real blockhead."

They entered the building and found a small man dressed in a chambray shirt and canvas trousers laboring over a plat for future lot sales in Arles. His brown hair was rapidly receding from his forehead. He looked up as they entered.

Once again MacDonald performed the introductions and Smeaton rose to shake hands.

"We have purchased the Ortega Land Grant. Tis split twixt the two of us, but we need to ken where the boundaries are on all sides. What tis the cost for a survey like that and how long twould it take?"

"That would cost at least one hundred dollars and it would take at least two weeks. The river probably serves as a natural boundary for the land bordering it. The lands to the east that run into hilly country pretty well end at the highest rock, but no one knows for certain. The Spanish didn't have time for precise measurements here. They just sent whoever was rich enough and daring enough to settle." He waited for the men to object outright to the price. At least their interruption gave him an excuse to stand. The town council was becoming downright demanding about the plat.

"That seems a bit high," rumbled out of MacDonald's throat. "Ninety dollars sounds fairer to me."

Smeaton swallowed. Either the man was a skilled negotiator or he was reading his mind.

"All right ninety it is, but I can't get out there until next week."

The two men looked at each other and nodded.

"Very well, Mr. Smeaton, we twill expect ye then. Now if ye twould draw up a contract, we twill sign it."

It meant, thought Smeaton, that one of them was capable of reading. He sat and pulled a sheet of paper from his desk.

It took but a few minutes for the contract to be written. As he laid it out to sign, MacDonald smiled at him.

"Why do we nay walk over to the sheriff's office or Blue Diamond? Someone there should be willing to sign as a witness.

"It's legal the way it is. People know me here." His face flushed.

"Aye, but we are new."

"All right, we'll go over to the Justice of the Peace. Mallory's the Notary Public too." His voice was sharp. "But first I'd like to see the color of your money."

MacDonald removed a gold coin from his money belt, but held onto it. "Payment twill be after the job tis completed."

Smeaton recognized the coin as a twenty dollar gold piece and realized the bulge around the man's waist was not extra flesh, but a money belt. Greed overcame dislike. He nodded, grabbed up his papers, and led the way out the door.

It took less than one half hour to complete the signing, dating, and stamping. MacDonald relented and paid out two five-dollar gold coins for expenses before heading to the dry goods store.

Stanley, the owner, nodded at them as they entered. He was busy totaling up an order for a matron. The two looked around and decided dried beans, salt, sugar, flour, hard tack, some cheese, chicory coffee, and canned peaches would sustain them while camping. Before leaving, Rolfe selected another plug of tobacco for his chewing habit.

The salesman in Stanley came to the fore and he looked at Rolfe when handing him the tobacco. "We just had a shipment of ready made shirts and boots. They are in your size. They would be more comfortable than those Injun duds."

"Du crazy? Aint nothing more comfortable than these. Vhite men's boots don't fit any von." He turned and left the store with MacDonald while Stanley scowled at their backs. It was the beginning of animosity between the townsmen of Arles and the Yankee interlopers that would worsen over the years.

Outside the two men mounted and rode out of town towards their holdings. They had already arranged to meet Smeaton by the river where the high bluffs were on Rolfe's portion of the grant. They discussed their plans while sitting by the campfire that evening. Dinner had been a couple rabbits washed down with the peaches.

"After we find out our boundaries, I think we should trail up to Indian Territory and see Chisholm on our way to St. Louis."

"Why tis that, Friend Rolfe?"

"Because we've got to earn a living and he might want some cattle next year. We can trail cattle to New Orleans, maybe, but Chisholm knows me and he can always use beef on that reservation. Hides and tallow aren't going to bring in much. Not when California and Mexico keep shipping as much as they do."

"What about Mrs. Rolfe and your children?"

"I'll build a home here. See those bluffs? A man could dig out a sizeable house and be nice and cozy."

MacDonald eyed the bluffs that had once stood at the river. He cleared his throat.

"Herman, Mrs. Rolfe doesn't strike me as someone who wishes to live in a dirt house."

Rolfe considered. "Ja, but the funds we have won't keep us forever in St. Louis, and she wants all of us to be together. Martin is three now and he needs to be here and learn to be a rancher, not a townsman. He isn't going to be a Pastor.

"If we can't sell cattle, I'll be hunting wolves. It pays well when they've been killing livestock." That this scheme would leave Mrs. Rolfe and the children out on the prairie while he traveled did not upset him. This looked like a peaceful land. It was western Texas that was ruled by the Comanche.

"I have been thinking of signing up as a scout with the Dragoons or the Army if ranching does nay provide an income. They dinna pay that much, but I have heard it tis a way to get one's citizenship. It twould also allow me to keep the funds until I am ready to build a house. The money twould be safe in the *Golden One* and we twould nay need to worry about a bank failure."

Rolfe's face cleared. "I hadn't thought of that, but what if I need the money and you aren't here. How would I get it?"

"If ye went with me into the ship when we store the extra funds, I could instruct the system to allow ye to enter. It twould just need yere palm print and eye readings."

"What the hell are you talking about? What does that machine do, take off my hand and extract one of my eyes?"

MacDonald grinned widely. "Nay, it takes an electronic picture of yere eyes and the pattern on yere palm and implants them in the memory banks. Then I instruct it to recognize ye. Ye twould need to memorize where to stand when opening the access panel, but that tis easy for someone like ye to do."

Rolfe considered. He did not want to go into that machine. It was a terrifying concept, but the thought of a bank failure, losing his money while drunk, or entrusting the whole amount to a woman was equally terrifying. MacDonald was sure to see how frightened he was if he went near it. There was also the possibility that when the moment of actually stepping over the threshold came, he would be unable to do so. Trains had been hard enough to accept when he was younger. This thing, whatever it was, Mac claimed could fly between stars.

"Mac, you know I'm not a coward, but that, that machine, it scares me. It's like it could swallow me alive and not let me out. I don't know if I could go into it or what I would do once I'm in there. Why don't we just store the gold in the tunnel? No one is going in there. They won't bother that stone if they go up there. It's too out of the way for anyone to find. I'll use my horse to roll the rock away."

MacDonald eyed the fire for awhile and then looked up. "We could do that while we're waiting for Smeaton. I'm going inside though. I want a real cleansing and I twill sleep in a real bed and not worry about bedbugs."

Rolfe shook his head. "Mac, I was right. You aren't human."

Chapter 11

The Lay of the Land

Smeaton spread the paperwork out for MacDonald and Rolfe. It had taken a month to get all his readings and another two weeks to prepare both drawings. His face was tanner and if anything, the clothes a bit baggier as though the time on the prairie had squeezed the moisture out of him

"You all might want to refile your claims right here in Arles. They can record it and send everything to Austin. The state's lines were drawn up on old records.

"Mr. Rolfe, your land is pretty much the way it's drawn and abuts the Tillman ranches." His finger pointed to the plat he had drawn out on one set of papers. "The only thing different is that the river has moved about one-half of a mile to the east.

"Mr. MacDonald, I'm sorry to say that your land ends here." His finger touched a point on the map. That's only about a mile and a half up into the timber. It doesn't go to the top. Somebody had purchased a chunk of that land to look for silver and gold way back before Texas was a state." Smeaton cleared his throat. He had already warned Franklin that there could be trouble to-day.

MacDonald stared at the paper with the black ink lines in disbelief. He did nay own the land where the *Golden One* rested. Somehow he had to get control of it.

"Who does own it? Tis it someone here in town?" His mind was racing. "Twould they be willing to sell?"

"Right now, someone with the first name of Buster and the last name of Miller or his descendants, if he or they exist own it. The state of Texas isn't interested in rocks and neither is anybody that wants to ranch or farm. That's damn poor land up there. Why would you want it?"

"Dot's vhere the mustangs like to hide in the summer. Und there's a good spring up there und lots of timber." Rolfe realized that his friend had taken this like a blow to the temple. Disappointment can mess up a man's mind. "Ve planned to build a shack up there for vhen ve go after vood or horses." Not that the former was true, but both saw Smeaton nod his head.

"Well, I don't think anyone will stop you. Like I said, no one knows who really owns it and no one wants it."

He cleared his throat again. "Is everything else satisfactory?" He waited.

Rolfe felt like kicking MacDonald, but that wouldn't do much good. The man had already been kicked by fate twice. Rolfe dug into his money belt and took out two twenty and one ten dollar gold pieces. "Dot's for my side. Mac, pay the man and I'll buy du a drink."

MacDonald gave his head a slight shake. He checked Smeaton's mind. The man hadn't lied. Reluctantly, he put his own two twenty dollar gold pieces into Smeaton's hand.

"Thank ye, for a job well done. Tis there really any need to file these papers again?"

"Not really. A problem could develop if someone starts to claim land next to yours or on it. Like I said, Mr. Rolfe's boundaries are so similar, it would take another survey to prove they aren't correct, and no one wants the land y'all thought was yours. My signature and date are written there and the notary has stamped it." Smeaton figured the two were close to broke.

It was just like a frontiersman to blow all his remaining funds on booze.

"Good day then, Mr. Smeaton." Rolfe and MacDonald rolled up their papers and stepped outside. A light breeze was blowing from the South and grey clouds scudded high in the sky.

"Well, it's not going to rain for a while. You want that drink, Mac? You look like you could use it."

"Nay, I dinna. I wish to go out and get rid of this anger or I may hurt someone." He stalked to his horse and mounted.

"I twill meet ye up at that spring. Then we can deposit the survey with the gold." He turned the huge stallion and rode north, anger surging and waning. Strange, 1850 had started out so promising.

Chapter 12

Anna

Anna Louise Lawrence nee Schmidt's grey eyes were focused on the knapsack she was hurriedly packing. Time was short. Her black curls refused to stay in the braided bun and five-month-old Augustuv, called Auggie was protesting his filled wet diaper. Her stomach and lower regions were warning her that the danger was almost here. Twelve-year-old Margareatha stepped into the doorway carrying the other canvas bag from the barn when the screech of four-year-old Lorenz racked through her system.

She turned to see both boys on the floor. Eight-year-old Daniel was on the bottom, his eyelids blinking up and down, his arms at his side as though unable to move them. Lorenz was landing blow after blow on his brother, screaming, "It's mine."

Anna stepped forward and heaved Lorenz upward. Then she found herself screaming, red rage boiling through her at the thought of being delayed and that her handsome grey-eyed son had the same abilities as her husband. Lorenz might hurt his brother and was too young to realize what he had done.

"Du cannot do such things. Du cannot ever, ever get so angry again. Do du hear me?" She shook him. Hurt, fear, anger from the knowledge that her beloved son could do to his brother what their two-hearted father was capable of doing to other people shook her to her core. Margareatha had not shown any such abilities although she also had two hearts. How could she or Margareatha control Lorenz?

Lorenz's grey eyes were looking at her with hurt and surprise.

"Margareatha, take Lorenz and go to the corn patch and some early ears pick." Anna was frustrated, but both her husband and twin brother insisted she must speak English not German to the children. Auggie was wailing louder. Daniel had pushed up on his elbows and then scrambled to his feet. She had to get them out of the house; them, Auggie, and herself.

"Daniel, your father go help in the fields." Surely Mr. Lawrence would protect his own son. That cold, somber man with the two hearts and golden circles around his eyes couldn't be that unnatural.

Auggie continued his lusty crying while Anna piled bread and rolls into the other canvas sack. She added a sack of sugar and salt. She would put the ears of corn that Margareatha picked in there. She added a flint box and turned to Auggie. Poor baby, his diaper was full.

She grabbed the basin, rag, and cloths to change him. She dug the cornstarch sack out, wiped and washed him, and quickly sprinkled his pink little bottom. At least this baby didn't have the two hearts and there were no gold circles around his eyes. He was a normal baby like Daniel and they would grow into normal men. What was she going to do about Lorenz? He was so smart, so quick, and he could use his mind on people just like her husband. She did not let Mr. Lawrence into her mind. She could stop him. He had tried it when she first told him she was pregnant. She became so angry that the force of it threw him out. She learned to set her mind and he was blocked.

Outside a whoop cut through her thoughts and she snapped the last diaper pin into place and put Auggie back into the crib. Auggie promptly resumed his screams.

His screams were covered by the whooping going on outside and the whinny of a horse. Anna ran for the front door ready to face whatever was out there and yet she knew.

She looked upwards over the door to two empty gun racks and knew it was futile. Mr. Lawrence had taken both the rifle and the shotgun. She grabbed the broom set by the door and rushed out. Three Comanche warriors sat there looking at the small ranch house and buildings. It was as if they knew there was no one inside but a woman. Comanche women didn't fight. They were trained to grab their children and then run and hide.

As Anna ran out the door one of the men slid down from his horse and started up the one step onto the porch. She was holding the bottom end of the broom and swung the hard hickory shaft against his knees. They had not expected her to fight; nor had they expected a woman taller than they were. The man's knees buckled and he went down. Anna swung the broom again with all her strength and smashed it into his head. Her next blow was straight down into the ribs and she heard one crack. She whirled to face the next man coming towards her.

The first man's horse had reared and fled towards the cornfield. It wanted no part of the flailing broom. The horse next to it began to rear and back away, but his rider had it back under control. He was grinning as though this were some sort of fluke; a woman downing a Comanche warrior. The other man was up on the porch. He was watching her, waiting for her to swing the broom again. Anna realized he was waiting to catch it, sure that his masculine strength was more than hers.

She edged to the side. Perhaps she could draw them away from the house. Her teeth were set, the lips drawn tight. She would stop them somehow and she started to swing and then hurriedly pulled the broom handle back. The Comanche grabbed air and she swung the broom into his arm, side-stepped, and slammed the hickory handle into the man's head. He went down to his knees.

The other Comanche stepped out of the house carrying the squalling Auggie by one heel, swinging him back and forth. Anna's mouth dropped and her eyes widened. The man looked ready to bash Auggie's head into the doorframe. All the while he was looking at her, his head cocked to one side.

Anna dropped the broom and held out her arms for her baby. The Comanche stepped up to her and started to let Auggie drop. She grabbed him and held him tight. The other one had risen and approached with a knife, but the man that had held Auggie shook his head and said something in their language. He directed the man to go inside. He motioned Anna to walk over to the other one. He nudged him with one foot. To Anna his words had no meaning.

The one with the broken rib pulled himself up and looked for his horse. It was gone. His voice rose in anger. The one in charge said something to him. Anna was able to understand the contempt in his voice. There was no pity for a warrior bested by a woman.

She saw movement coming from the field. Was Mr. Lawrence coming to rescue them? And her heart sank. It was two more Comanche warriors and Daniel was riding in front of one.

Chapter 13

The Mad Woman

"Schwein Hunds!" Anna screamed at the women around her as they ripped and cut her clothes away from her body.

The Comanche women did not understand the vile insult of pig dogs and words of damnation she was spewing at them. They wanted her in clothes like theirs. There wasn't much left of her clothes after that hellish two week journey to the Comanche camp. Anna wanted to strike them, bruise them, destroy them, but her arms weren't free. She was holding Auggie, and striking at them meant she would need to put him down. They would trample him or take him from her, and he still needed her milk.

They had already taken Daniel. The man he was riding with kept going once they were in camp. A chanting Comanche woman had trotted beside his horse. Auggie was fussing for she was holding him tight against her body and he was hungry. She hadn't been given much in the way of water or food on the journey here and her milk output had shrunk. These women were fiends, laughing at her, at her clothes, and then it was over and she was naked.

One knife pricked too deeply at her ribs and red rage engulfed her. She grasped Auggie tightly in her left arm and smashed her right elbow down into the woman's face. She towered over them as no Indian woman matched her five feet ten inches in height.

Her worst fear was realized when someone grabbed Auggie. She was taken down to the ground by a group of screaming witches, and suddenly the attack stopped. The women were looking at her wide eyed for her menstrual period had started and blood was running down her leg.

They dragged her into the segregated tent for women and several Comanche women entered. One was pushed forward while an older woman spoke in Comanche.

"Stop fighting them," the pushed forward one hissed in English. She was dark-haired, brown-eyed, tanned from the Texas sun, but white. "We will make you a human. One of our brave warriors has chosen you as a mate for your courage and strong boys."

"They are mine." Anna was screaming. "Gott gave to me them. Vhy are du helping them? Du are vhite."

The woman glared at her. "I am Comanche." She threw the buckskin dress at Anna. "Cover your body."

Then the woman pointed at the pile of cattails. "Open them and use them for the flow. When it stops, you'll be allowed out. If you don't calm down there won't be any food and very little water."

"My baby needs my milk." Anna was speaking slowly to get the English words out correctly.

"You have no more children. They are with their new families. You must never go near them again. The baby is going with his family to a different group."

Anna threw herself at the speaker intent on destroying her tormentor. She used fists, elbows, and kicks as though she were still fighting her twin when they were growing up. Her blows were hard and the attack furious.

"Mein sohns," she kept shouting. "Mein sohns!"

The two white women in the group thought she was screaming, "mine sons," which was exactly what Anna was saying.

They explained to the older woman why Anna was so upset. At first her face softened, then hardened.

"Hold her down," she commanded.

It took six of the women to accomplish this while Anna continued to struggle and scream damnation at them. The older woman held a knife in her hand.

"Explain to her we understand her grieving for those children are dead to her. When Comanche women grieve for their sons they show their loss by giving part of themselves."

This was duly translated.

"Now hold one hand down." The old woman bent and with one expert stroke sliced off the end of Anna's right little finger.

The pain was so unexpected it stilled Anna for a moment, but only a moment. She almost heaved herself free.

"The next hand," commanded the woman. Just as quickly she cut the end of the left little finger off at the knuckle.

"Hold up her hair." Anna's long, curly dark tresses had come unbound. It was so thick the woman had to grasp first one side and then the next. Instead of hair that hung to her hips, Anna's hair now hung to her shoulders.

"Tell her to use the inside of the cattails as a bandage for her fingers. If she starts acting like a human being, she will be allowed to become a Comanche once the other stops. If she tries to come out of here before it stops she will die. Someone will push in food and water. It will be enough to keep her alive. She will be cleansed once this is over. When one of the other women enters, she is to stay away from them or she will die." After the translation, the group filed out.

There was no fire in the fire pit as it was summer. The upper tepee flap stayed open in summer, but now it was laced shut. Since Anna had no pelt or blanket to bring with her, there was nothing to sleep on but the ground. Anna came up on her knees. Gall was in her mouth and frantic thoughts of her children in her mind. Should she rush out and end it all? But her children, where were they? Where were her sons, her beautiful Margareatha? If she died, she would never find them again, and she closed her eyes. A low moan escaped from her lips and she began praying. She found she could not. Her body ached from the blows and her hands were wracked with pain. The bleeding from her fingers had slowed. If she let it continue, she could still die and what of her milk? It had diminished because of that strenuous trek and insufficient water, but there was still milk. If it hardened inside her breasts, she would have mastitis.

"Oh, my God, my Lord, help me to understand. What am I to do?" The wail became a primeval scream. She beat her fists on the ground, unmindful of the pain and the blood. She stood and stalked the width of the teepee and back. She wanted to kill, but she was naked and had no weapon. The dress they had given her lay crumpled where it had fallen during the fight.

Exhaustion finally stilled her wild movements and occasional scream. She collapsed onto the hardened dirt floor and slept.

In the morning, someone pushed in a water bag and a bowl of cooked squash. Anna looked at it with distaste. What sort of disease lurked there? Since no one had left anything like a commode here, she had used a spot on the far side of the tepee. The smell had dissipated, but Anna dreaded what the odors would be like if she ate the squash. Her hands had swollen, but she used them to milk her breasts into the bowl. Her own milk she would drink. By afternoon she had drank some of the water and her mouth was still dry. She barely touched the squash but what little she ate was with her fingers. She needed to wash them, but there was no basin, no soap. Dear God, she would die here. She hid her face in her hands, but no tears came. Nothing emerged from her mouth but that wild scream.

* * *

The next morning another bowl of food and bag of water were pushed in. The woman peeked in to see if the other bowl was close and saw Anna. She began running, screaming for the old woman.

"Her hair, her hair, it has turned white."

They found Anna glaring at them as they entered. The group stared. Anna had donned the buckskin dress, but it was ill fitting and far too short for her tall frame. The bodice was pulled tight. It was stained from the leaking milk. No one had arrived to escort her to a place of privacy and nature's leavings were in a pile in one corner; the odor permeated the entire area.

Whispering broke out. What could cause this? They had taken everything she brought with her. There was nothing in here that could have changed her hair color. Finally the oldest woman pointed at Anna and commanded.

"She is to clean that mess. Nothing has changed, but someone will escort her to the woman's area. Others will need to use this soon."

The white woman who translated had light brownish hair and blue-green eyes.

"Clean it yourself." Anna was still seething, anger overriding good sense.

The younger women looked at each other, and to Anna's ears, they began jabbering. One middle-aged woman stepped out of the tent. She returned within minutes carrying a flat piece of wood and a large stick.

"If she doesn't clean it, we will use this on her."

They left Anna bruised and stunned on the dirt floor. Most were certain there was a trickster involved or she had gone mad.

That afternoon, one of the younger women moved into the tepee. Two others accompanied her for her protection.

Chapter 14

The Woman Who Would Not Listen

"Why have you not listened to us?"

Anna's woman's cycle had ended. Her clothes smelled. The tent reeked, her body was a mass of bruises, her hands were swollen, but healing, and still she glared at them.

"Do you promise to act like a human being?" It was the dark-eyed white woman.

"Vhat does dot mean?"

"You will be given to one of our warriors and never speak to the one that came with you."

"He ist mein sohn." There was no mistaking her words. "I vill not such a promise make. God vould punish me. I vill not go mitt von of your men. Du are all savages."

This time they left Anna lying on the ground with both her ears cut off. Blood streamed down both sides of her face. They had not killed her as they were not sure she was sane. Her hair had turned white overnight. Women did not fight as she had when the warriors raided the ranch. Women were to run and hide. Women accepted what men decided for them.

"If she lives, the Great Spirit wills it. She will become a slave. Let her be. She will remain on starvation rations. Sane people soon eat." The old woman led the others out.

Anna crawled over to the cattails and split two down the middle and then held them against the sides of her head. The white woman had stayed just long enough to translate.

She stopped at the tent flap before leaving.

"Stop being so stubborn. You can have a good life here. My man doesn't beat me like the one in my other life. All of the men here ain't like him, but most are." Pride was in her voice. "They got a really good way to live. It's just different. Just remember, you caint ever talk to that boy you called son. He has another name and he likes it here." She stepped out into the sunshine.

Anna had tried not to hear her words. How could Daniel like it here? Didn't he remember any of her lessons, her hugs, her blessings, her prayers, the joy of sitting in church, and at the holiday family dinners?

She felt dizzy, her stomach ready to heave, and her chest was hurting. It was the heartache of losing all of her God-given children. She would not give in to their pagan ways. She was Christian. She prayed she would be brave enough to hold onto her faith in Christ. Anna collapsed on the fur pallet one of the other women had left.

The next morning another woman entered the tent. Anna was still asleep, her face flushed with fever. The woman set the water jug and bowl of food down and backed out of the teepee. There was no need to wake this mad woman. Maybe she could be the slave of her family. Her warrior was a brave hunter with many coups.

Chapter 15

Schmidt's Corner

A discouraged Kasper Schmidt returned to the Rolfe ranch house where his wife, Gerde, and son, Hans, were waiting for him. Dirty, rough workmen's clothes and boots comprised his outfit. His features, his carriage, his speech all seemed ill-suited to any hard toil. While he had been in Arles, the town's women had looked at him with approval; rough clothes and boots made no difference to their lingering eyes. He was a handsome man, standing five feet and ten inches when most men were at least three inches shorter. His shoulders were broad, his features straight, the mouth firm, and a small cleft split his chin. The dark mustache was luxurious and glossy.

When the word of the Comanche attack on a small ranch in Texas reached the Schmidt's in St. Louis, he had not been surprised. Anna was his twin. He had known she was in mortal danger that summer of 1854 when he doubled over in pain at the parochial school where he taught. His frantic search for information from Texas was futile. Who should he write to beside an unknown lawman in a town called Wooden, Texas? No one knew. His father was too busy with his new family and farm to pursue a lost daughter and her children. Their father felt that all had been murdered by the wild men of the West. Kasper had decided then that he must go to Texas to look for Anna and her children. He knew it was not Christian, but he had always disliked that cold, arrogant man she had wed. He felt honor bound not to read the letter she had given him when she left until he was certain she was no longer living.

The pastor in St. Louis had mentioned that a former parishioner had been a hunter and a trapper who had moved his family to a ranch in Texas. The man still did hunting and tracking on the side. Rolfe's partner was serving as a scout for the 2nd Dragoons. Perhaps both men could help in locating his sister. Kasper had eagerly written down the name, Herman Rolfe and his address. He had written to Rolfe with the offer to hire him as a guide to the town of Wooden. Perhaps they would discover or detect something at his sister's burned homestead. Gerde insisted that she and Hans travel with him.

"What if you never return from that wild place? We are your family."

She was very efficient in packing what they needed. Kasper had spoken wildly of a new beginning, perhaps even farming his sister's farm. Gerde set her lips in a straight line. Her brown eyes smiled only at Hans and Kasper. She was quite aware of the wild schemes Kasper could propose when he was really a teacher or a pastor by nature. The latter was too late for he had married her before finishing school, but he was more than qualified for any teaching post. She would make sure he stayed on the right path.

Rolfe had met them in Arles. Gerde had been horrified at the primitive buildings, the rough men, the streets of ruts, mud, dust, and a whorehouse but one block off the main street. She refused to stay in that sinkhole of iniquity with their three-year-old son. Worse, there was no Lutheran church and no one who spoke Deutsche. Rolfe had solved the problem by suggesting they stay with Mrs. Rolfe and their two children. Mrs. Rolfe was in the family way and needed someone there. She, like Gerde, did not like the town of Arles. Gerde would act as midwife and defray part of the cost of searching for Anna and her children.

Wooden had been a terrible disappointment for Kasper. A plantation owner by the name of O'Neal with the lilt of Ireland in his speech had shown them the Lawrence's farm and two graves.

"We buried two of the children there. Tis said the Methodist preacher came out to say their prayers for the dead"

"Which two did you bury?" Kasper found it difficult to get the words out.

"There was but one girl in the family that wild, redhead of a daughter, and she's buried there." He pointed at one of the graves. "I can't say which one of the older boys it was. The baby they took."

"Comanche don't kill redheads. They avoid them. Young girls they take." Rolfe had objected.

"Sure, and someone forgot to tell them that. Maybe it had something to do with Lawrence." O'Neal had sneered on the surname. "One of my hands saw him talking with the Comanche before the attack. He probably set it up. No good Yankee bastard. Why else would they kill a young lass and not the man? We didn't find a trace of him. I've heard he headed south towards Galveston."

"Who told du dot?" Rolfe could see that Kasper was looking sick.

O'Neal stared at him. "You talk like she did. I thought he was the relative." He jerked a thumb at Kasper.

"Gentlemen, please, what happened to my sister, Mrs. Lawrence?"

Both men looked at him puzzled. Who would ask such a fool question?

"They took her and the other boys. Do ye want a description of why?"

Kasper had turned white. "No."

"Did anyvon trail them?" Rolfe was insistent.

"No, we had better things to do than go riding after them without any soldiers. Good day, gentlemen. My Christian duty here is done." O'Neal mounted his horse and rode off leaving Kasper and Rolfe standing beside two graves set along a crumbling stone fence.

Kasper's voice was bitter when he spoke. "That man did not like my family. Do you have any idea why?"

Rolfe shrugged and spoke in German. "It could be because he considered them white trash. Southerners are that way. If you can't afford a plantation and a couple of slaves, you are white trash. If your brother-in-law had an education, that probably upset him too. He's what they call a 'Mick on the make.' He's not going to admit that his people had nothing when they arrived here."

"Will it do any good to pursue this in Wooden?"

"No, they directed us to O'Neal. You must have noticed the man that owned the general store had the same surname, and the sheriff directed us to him. I think they pretty well own this corner of Texas."

"But why is there animosity for Germans? O'Neal has a brogue."

"Who knows why? Maybe he wanted this land. Maybe your brother-in-law made him feel inferior."

Kasper had not understood then and he never understood their thinking or the prejudices in all the towns they went through. Men seemed to respect Rolfe, but were not particularly friendly when they heard Kasper was from St. Louis. Too many Yankees lived there. It was good to be back at the ranch where a certain amount of sanity ruled.

Gerde appeared in the barn doorway. "Welcome home. Mr. Rolfe, you should go in immediately. Your wife has given you another son."

"Is anything wrong with either one?"

"Why, no, there isn't. Young James is a handsome young boy that looks very much like Mrs. Rolfe." Gerde was staring at him as he turned back to the horses. He was as rough as the rest of the male populace. She addressed her next question to Kasper.

"Were you successful?" She knew they were not as Kasper looked dejected.

"No, mein Frau, we weren't. There was nothing but two graves and no information on the rest of the family other than Mr. Lawrence might have instigated the attack and had traveled south."

Kasper dumped some hay into the manger, walked to his wife, and gently hugged her. Society forbade a more vigorous reunion in public.

"Where is Hans?"

"He is outside somewhere with Martin and Olga. I let them have a bit of play between now and chore time."

All three walked into the house. Kasper paused to wash his hands at the basin set outside, but Rolfe hurried into the house.

Gerde looked after him with distaste. "I hope he is going in to see Clara. She and I have become good friends."

Kasper smiled at her. "That is good news as I have decided to settle here."

"What?"

"Yes, I used my inheritance from my Grandfather Zeller to buy five acres from Mr. Rolfe. The deed is filed at Arles. We will be to the north by two lots. I'm going to build a general store and livery stable for people traveling through here. A man in Arles has already bought two acres from me. If I sell the next lot, we will come out even on the land. The man bought the two acres that are next to Rolfe's home. He told me that he was moving his horseshoeing and ironworks business here as Arles already has two smiths.

"We stopped at the lumberyard and they are shipping the lumber and work crew here through Blue Diamond. They'll start building as soon as they arrive. I've drawn a rough sketch of our new store and home."

"But, Herr Schmidt, there is no school here for Hans."

Kasper smiled. "I intend to start one for extra income. I'll be teaching Olga and Martin for now, and Hans when he is old enough. Herman tells me that the older Tillman brother has a boy that is of school age and Ben Tillman, the younger brother, and his wife have two girls. Both are younger than Martin."

Gerde was unable to say anything for a moment. She took several quick breaths while her mind tried to find a way to leave here.

"There is no Lutheran pastor or church." Surely, that would convince Kasper.

"That is true, Gerde, but now we will be two families. We can apply to the Synod for a circuit rider to come through here. Some of the Lutheran churches in Texas are affiliated with the Lutheran Synod of Missouri." Satisfied that he had met all her objections, hunger reasserted its demands.

"Is there something to eat now, or shall I just wait for supper?"

Gerde almost ground her teeth. How could the man be so considerate on one matter and so dense and inconsiderate on another? Still, she was the good Frau and she responded.

"Ach, ja, mein Herr, you must be starving. You can't have eaten decently during your travels. Come in, come in. I have some stew and biscuits left for you and Mr. Rolfe to share."

Herman appeared in the doorway from the bedroom and saw that Gerde was setting out the bowls. "We could wait until supper. There's work to do. The ropes, extra saddle, and branding irons all need to be ready plus we need to clean out the saddlebags. If Mac can't make it, I'll be hiring a man to help with a cattle drive up to Chisholm in Indian Territory."

Gerde looked with horror at Kasper and her voice lowered to a whisper. "Are you going with him?"

Kasper raised his eyebrows. "No, Frau Schmidt, I must remain here to see about our store, stable, and home. Mr. Rolfe needs someone far more accustomed to cattle than I am."

He smiled at them. "However, if I can be of any assistance now, I gladly offer my services."

Chapter 16

The Saloon Keeper

Jesse Owens reined in his mule when he topped a small rise and looked around. He had seen smoke billowing several miles back and wondered who was out in this empty stretch of the Texas plains besides wild animals, wild cattle, wild horses, wild men, wild Indians, and occasional foothills of stone trying to be mountains. This was prairie grass with stands of juniper and scrub oak. Cottonwood and oak trees grew where water ran or percolated up in a spring, but it was too dry for good farming land. He'd seen what looked like maybe two ranches a couple of miles back, but this smoke was more than what came from a couple of stoves. It couldn't be a prairie fire as the smoke was fairly constant and remained in one place. To the east were several high bluffs, more prairie, and rolling hills. The hills became higher and carpeted with trees and continued upward into stone mounds that some might call mountains. They were too low to be like the mountains back in the South where his folks came from. When he looked southward he saw a settlement of three houses, a stable, and two other buildings. One had a steady stream of smoke and now he could hear the clanging of metal against an anvil.

"Well, now, maybe they have something liquid to offer a man." His brown eyes lighted at the thought and he tapped the mule lightly and rode on down.

He dismounted in front of the building that had a sign proclaiming, "Schmidt's Corner." The building had been whitewashed and the black lettering over the door announced this to be a General Store. It wouldn't hurt to see what they had. Jesse tied the mule to the hitching rail and entered.

A slender, dark haired man was emerging from what looked like a hall running back to a storage area. "Welcome, you are my first customer of the day." Kasper smiled as both men took stock of each other.

To Jesse, Kasper looked more like a city person than someone out in the middle of Texas. Kasper's shirt was white and starched, he wore a grey vest, and dark trousers with shined, laced up shoes.

Kasper saw a medium-sized man, tending to the stocky side, dark hair and eyes, dusty, trail-worn clothes and boots. When Jesse removed his hat, it was obvious his hair was beginning to thin although he didn't look more than about thirty.

Kasper moved behind the counter. "Is there anything I can help you with?"

"I was hoping to find a drink, some beer. It's been a dry trip."

"I do have beer, but it is by the bottle. Mrs. Schmidt prefers that you drink it outside."

Kasper bent and brought up a bottle. "You're in luck. I still have a few left before the next freight load comes through." He became a business man. "That'll be a dime since it would fill two mugs."

Jesse considered. "I don't suppose there is a tavern here?"

"No, there isn't. I stock the beer because my customers want it. The other business is the Jackson's ironworks and blacksmith shop."

Jesse fished in his pocket for a dime and came up with two half dimes. "I don't suppose you offer any food with that."

"No, we don't as we aren't a tavern."

"Do you get much traffic through here?"

"Not a whole lot." Kasper hated to admit it, but he depended on travelers passing through, the two Tillman ranches, a few scattered small spreads, thc Rolfe's, and MacDonald whenever the man chose to be in the area. He was thankful that Gerde had never upbraided him for settling here. The search for his sister had yielded no information. Rolfe wouldn't be back for another month and who knew when MacDonald would ride in?

"While our neighbors appreciate the fact that I stock the beer, my wife really doesn't like the idea. It brings in the rowdies." He smiled. "They're not bad men, just young. Our home is in this building and we have a small son."

"Do tell." Jesse laid his change on the counter as Kasper opened the bottle. "Since you ain't overrun with customers why don't you step outside with me and tell me more about this area."

"Gladly, I don't have any children for lessons today." Kasper removed his apron and walked outside with Owens.

"If you wish to water your mule, the river is behind us. It's not too far and the water is free." He smiled again. The elder Jackson was a taciturn man and Kasper enjoyed talking with people.

"I'll do that in a bit. I was wondering how much you do in the way of business." He saw the quick flash of concern in Kasper's eyes.

"This looks like a good place. There's plenty of grass and water. The way you talked, you get enough business with the booze to upset your missus."

"She'd like for me to give it up, but it is rather profitable and it keeps people coming into the store to buy their sundries here. We get the ranchers, any hands they might have, travelers going between here and the farm settlements further north. While travelers aren't many, there's enough to make a profit on the stable, plus the freighters stop here if it is towards evening when they arrive."

"So you wouldn't object if somebody came in and put up a saloon." Jesse winced as soon as he said the word, but why not? Taverns were considered old-fashioned places. He just hoped this Yankee wouldn't take offense.

"My name is Jesse Owens." He shifted the bottle to his left hand and extended his right.

"Kasper Schmidt." The two men shook.

Jesse took a pull from the bottle. "Who owns the land between here and the blacksmith and ironworks place?"

"I own the land back to the river on this side of the block up to the blacksmith shop. Herman Rolfe owns most of the land on the other side of the road. His ranch starts on the other side of the blacksmith's house and lot. Across the street a wainwright is planning to open a business and build a house. I was hoping to purchase the land across the road someday, but Mr. Rolfe has already seen the wisdom of dividing it up into lots. We intend to build a church on the other side, but a little farther north."

Jesse stuck the information in the back of his mind that he had landed among a bunch of Dutchman.

"Mr. Rolfe has taken a small herd of steers up to Chisholm in the Indian Territory. It seems they knew each other while they were trappers. His wife, Mrs. Rolfe, is in the larger house at the end."

"Y'all interested in selling that land?"

"What sort of saloon do you intend to open?"

Jesse scratched at this scalp under his hat and took another swig while he considered.

"Well, it'd be a small-sized one. Just a regular place where a man could come in, buy a beer, and play a game of cards. Y'all know, like the corner tavern in a big city; a place to get away from the missus and kids for awhile and relax." He assumed

Kasper would find the opportunity a plus since he'd mentioned having a son.

Kasper considered. "As long as it isn't a rowdy place with women, I think it would be an excellent addition to Schmidt's Corner."

Jesse eyed the man. This one was definitely different. He had a strange sounding name and he was talking like a scholar, plus he seemed to have a bunch of highfalutin morals. It wouldn't matter. Jesse couldn't afford to bring in women. He'd be lucky to afford putting up the building and a smaller place in back to live.

"Suppose we came to an agreement, where can we make it legal like?"

"We could go to the courthouse in Arles. It's the county seat. There's a Justice of the Peace and a Notary there. It takes about four and one-half days to get there. They also have a lumber-yard."

"Well, now, suppose we talk about price?"

Kasper smiled. "The lot is yours for fifty-five dollars."

"Can y'all make it fifty? Of course, that's after I look at this river to see if there'll be water enough."

"I believe Mrs. Schmidt and I will accept that. Right this way."

They walked around and behind the store. He doesn't want to bother his missus, thought Jesse. The walk led to an open space of about forty feet from the river.

"Why is everything set so far back?"

"In case the river floods, we do not have to worry about the damage it could do."

"Who owns that shack across the river?"

"That belongs to a Mexican family. They were there before I arrived. They have a cow and the woman raises some vegetables. They have a little girl named Olivia."

"They ever cause any trouble?"

"Why would they?" Kasper was puzzled.

Jesse shrugged. "Y'all never know with a Mex. Does he do any work?"

"Once in a while Mr. Rolfe or Mr. MacDonald will hire him."

"No complaints from them about his work?"

"I've not heard any. They wouldn't hire him again if it wasn't what they wanted."

Jesse nodded. He figured he could hire the woman to do some cooking for the saloon. He'd been on the road long enough. It was time to settle down and plant some roots.

"Will this Rolfe have any objections to a saloon?" Jesse realized that a man with a wife or kids could object if the man let his wife browbeat him into doing something to protect the morals of their children.

"Why, no, I don't believe he would. He would probably be one of your steady customers when he is here."

Jesse smiled widely. "Mr. Schmidt, you've just made a sale."

Chapter 17

Rescue

The men and horses were moving as silently as possible through the night's fading moonlight and starlight. They were following their Captain and a huge form on an oversized black horse. Grey light had begun to peak over the far away hills when the signal came to halt. The sergeants rode forward, received their orders, and rode back to deliver the command to spread out. No smoking, talking, spitting, or hacking until after the attack.

They formed a huge arc. Those that were looking forward saw the scout point out the direction to the Captain and then he moved to the far side of the attackers. The scout was allowed to join in the attack, but he was not part of the 2nd Dragoons. His risks were his own and he was to note if any large segment of the Comanche men or horses escaped, the direction they went, and report to the Captain immediately.

The arc surged forward. MacDonald, the scout, was kicking his heels into his horse to chase a man fleeing back to the village. The Captain waved and the bugler raised his horn. As one the men unloosened their revolvers and they surged forward at the sound of the bugle. Dust rose in the air and men began crawling out of the teepees as the horsemen poured into the village firing their dragoons. They fired six shots per man, holstered their revolvers, and pulled out their swords. By now the dust was rising from the ground, dogs were barking and yelping, teepees were being pulled over, and women and children were screaming, crying, and running as they looked for a place to hide from the Dragoons circling the area.

One tall, white-haired woman clad in a mended deerskin dress was shoving other women and children out of her way as she tried to head for the hills to the north. MacDonald rushed his horse into the trooper riding towards her.

"Nay, she tis too tall." He yelled at the Dragoon chasing her. "She must be white." He pushed his animal closer and his long arm shot out to pull the woman up.

"Ye twill be killed if ye run with yere back to the soldiers. They canna tell that ye are white." He was yelling to be heard over the noise and confusion.

Fists beat at the air and the woman tried to turn and fight him. Her feet were kicking at his horse. MacDonald galloped back to the wagon and swung down, the woman still held tight against his side. As soon as he dismounted, he released her and her angry, ice-cold grey eyes were glaring at him. Tiny white curls surrounded her face and fought to be loose from the braids. Her lips were white with fury.

"Mein Daniel, mein sohn." Her teeth clenched together and she balled her hands into fists, and she turned to run back.

He grabbed her arm and spun her around. "Dear Gar, are ye Anna Lawrence?" He began speaking in German. "Are you Kasper Schmidt's sibling? Do you mean one of your sons is alive and up there?"

For a moment she drew in her breath, swallowed, closed her eyes, and snapped them open. "Ja, I must go to him." Desperation and hardness filled her eyes, and she started to kick.

He picked her up by the waist while her arms and legs flailed the air. He lowered the back gate of the wagon and smacked her down on the hard wood. "You will stay here. I shall go see if there is anyone up there, but I doubt it. They are not shooting arrows at the troopers. How many are in his group and how tall is he now?"

She swallowed and shook her head. "Two, three others I, I, am not sure." The two years of not speaking German or English were dragging at her tongue and Anna felt a rising frustration. She wanted to speak clearly, but in her panic the words jumbled in her mind. The tribe had given her youngest, Auggie, to another group and Daniel to a family in this one. She could not lose her one remaining child.

"He's ten, but tall. Go, go. Do not let them take him." She continued to use German even if this man's speech was badly accented.

"Will you stay here? If you go out there someone is apt to think you are Comanche and kill you. Promise me you will stay."

Anna tightened her lips. How to fight this man? She knew she had lost weight and strength, and he was so strong; so rock hard.

MacDonald looked up at the driver. "This tis Mrs. Lawrence. She has relatives at Schmidt's Corner. Dinna let her go."

He swung back up on his horse and rode off. Anna was left blinking in the soft morning sunlight. Relatives? That word she understood. Here? Where? In Texas? Was she still in Texas? Where was Schmidt's Corner?

Confusion and dust filled her senses and mind. Auggie she felt was dead, but Daniel she knew was alive just a few minutes ago. In her innermost being, she knew that somewhere Margareatha and Lorenz were alive. Was God giving her this chance to get them back?

The yells grew dimmer, but women and children were still screaming. A contingent of troopers was herding another woman and two children back towards the wagon. Anna recognized the woman as the wife of one of the main hunters. That one had been with the group for seven years and had gone completely primitive in Anna's mind. Anna had starved and endured torture rather than succumb to the Comanche or bear children that might die tomorrow. They had let her live because they were not certain of her sanity. She was as strong as a man when it came to certain chores and they set her at them while withholding food. No sane person willingly refused food when starving.

The dust cleared enough that Anna realized the few Comanche women left were being stripped and raped before being killed. Their screams were muted and hoarse. She turned away, sick at heart. These men were no better than the savages that had captured her.

Anna hated the savagery of the world that had taken her children. She had prayed for God to help her to forgive, to take the hate out of her heart, but every child's cry made her see an image of her children and her heart wept for them and the red rage inside would begin again.

Chapter 18

A Way Home

Captain Lewis was trying to interrogate the women found in the Comanche camp. It was late morning, and most of his men were preparing for their ride back to the fort. The younger woman (he assumed she must be younger as her hair was not white or grey streaked) sat cross-legged on the ground, holding her youngest of three children, rocking back and forth, and refusing to look at him. Her lips were compressed and almost white. The white-haired woman was looking at him with a strange glowing light in her grey eyes. The younger woman's buckskin dress was clean and intact. The older woman's was dirty, a bit ragged, and too short.

"We can return you to your family if you will tell us your name and when and where you were captured."

Anna was standing and she looked first at the other woman and then at him when finally the English words came back. "I am Mrs. Anna Lawrence. She has so primitive become she vill not tell anyvon her real name. The babies have savage names." Anna continued, slipping back into German.

"I was taken in August of 1854 from a small farm in central Texas. We were about five miles out of Wooden." She saw the puzzled look on his face and bit her tongue. English, she thought, speak English like Kasper. She repeated her words end-ing with, "Ve vere about five miles out of Vooden. I had four children then. My daughter has red hair. Has the army found a girl named Margareatha Lawrence and a dark-haired boy named Lorenz?" Her grey eyes were intent on his face.

"No, I'm sorry to say we have not found any children like that, but thank you, Mrs. Lawrence. Would you be able to get her to speak?"

Anna's face stiffened to hide the bitter disappointment. She then turned to the woman and in halting, garbled Comanche words tried to ask the same questions. The woman looked first at Anna and then at the Captain before turning to Anna and spewing out a string of hate-filled words.

"She says du her home have destroyed." Anna did not add the part about the woman wishing all of them emasculated, dead, and rotting.

Captain Lewis turned to Anna. "Do you know her name or where she is from?"

"Nein, no, she vas going to von of the forts up north. Her father vas a trader. She said her Comanche (Comanche came out like a dirty word) name is her name."

He leaned back in his chair. "I'll be sending you both to Fort Davis under escort. From there you will be transferred to Fort Lawrence. You will be able to contact your relatives and return home. Be ready to leave in the morning." He stood.

"Has MacDonald returned from his scouting?" he asked one of his Sergeants.

"Yes, sir, he said he would like a word with you concerning one of the captive women. It seems her brother is in Texas and has been looking for her."

Captain Lewis almost heaved a sigh of relief and caught himself. "Good, I was planning on him guiding the rescued women to Fort Davis while we finish here. He can return her to her family from there and it won't cost the command anything.

"Return these captives to the cooking wagon and post a guard for them." He waved a hand toward the women and children. I don't want them running off when the men are in such high spirits. Then, have MacDonald report to me."

The Sergeant motioned the corporal and private closer. "Nobody comes near them. Understand?"

The two men hid smirks and answered, "Yes, sir." They both looked at the women like they were somewhere between dirt and maybe a good roll. White women who lived with Indians weren't no better than Indians in their minds. Their families weren't likely to want them back and if they did, they'd probably lock them away.

"Anyone that so much as disturbs them is court-martialed. Tell MacDonald that Captain Lewis wants to see him."

Chapter 19

Fort Davis

"Whoa up." The trooper pulled back on the reins and brought the mule team to a halt. The dust rose around their hoofs and half-way up the wheel spokes. It was nearing autumn and this was the dry part of Texas. Rain would come, but maybe not for another month. The buildings were primitive. The lumber rough, the windows small or nonexistent, and all were coated with dust waiting for the rains to wash everything clean. The so-called streets would become running streams to be cut into a maze of ruts.

Some of the washer women and their kids gawked at the two women and children. They had never seen a white woman in Indian clothes. Some of them pointed and moved closer before their mothers grabbed their arms as if they went too close to those creatures they might be contaminated.

MacDonald dismounted and tied his mount to a rail and looked at Anna seated in the wagon.

"Mrs. Lawrence, there tis the sutler's store but a few steps away. Twould ye like to purchase anything?"

Anna looked at him puzzled, and then straightened her shoulders, the look in her grey eyes becoming cold. "I haf no money."

"I am sure yere brither, Kasper, twill be happy to pay the small cost of what ye should want. Mayhap some clothes, although they have nay for lassies." The puzzlement on her face returned and he switched to German.

"Why don't we speak Deutsche until you regain your English skills?"

Anna was still puzzled. Who would call using English a skill? She knew the words, but they would not go right and she closed her eyes and nodded.

"Your brother, Kasper, will want you properly clothed and will not begrudge the amount it takes to do so. You need something else to wear and shoes. I suggest you buy men's clothing until you are home."

"You keep saying Kasper is here? Where is here?"

"Kasper, his wife, and little boy came to Texas to look for you. When they couldn't find you, they decided to stay. He has a general store and a livery stable at Schmidt's Corner. It is north of Arles and south of the German settlements further north."

For a moment hope surged in Anna and then she remembered. Would white people accept her again? Would they turn their backs on her like some foul, fallen woman, something to be hidden away? And she closed her eyes trying to keep the sobs out of her voice and the tears out of her eyes. A look of pain spread over her face.

She snapped her eyes opened and held her head higher. "You are right. I cannot disgrace him and Gerde by looking like this. There is one more problem. I cannot go about the countryside with a strange man. So I thank you for your offer, but the Army may send me back with the others."

MacDonald was looking at her in amazement. How could she change so rapidly? There was no crying from this woman; simply a steely determination to continue living after having her whole life ripped away. The same had been done to him at a young age. How old had she been at the time of the attack? Kasper was but thirty-three. Dear Gar, as his twin this lassie twas nay older, but thirty twas considered old for a woman on the frontier. Still she had courage. Had she nay fought him? He smiled at her.

"They will send you to Fort Lawrence in Kansas. That could take months. Then you would wait until they contacted your family. It will take another month for them to come for you. The whole procedure would take almost one year. I can return you to your family within three weeks.

"I promise you, Mrs. Lawrence, as Kasper's friend I will guard you and your honor with my life."

Anna calculated the time in her head. It would mean another year of being separated from her children. Margareatha, she knew would not forget her, but Lorenz had only been four years old. How could he survive? But he had. She knew it. She could hear him crying for her. She looked at MacDonald.

"Do you know Kasper that well?"

"Yes, Mrs. Lawrence, I do." His face was solemn and his voice emphatic. The driver broke into their conversation.

"Mrs. Lawrence, if you are getting out here, you'd best climb down. I've got to deliver the rest of the cargo."

His words angered her. The man wasn't thinking of them as women and children.

"Very well, Mr. MacDonald, but when we are at Mr. and Mrs. Schmidt's place, perhaps I can sew your clothes and do your laundry to repay you."

MacDonald gave a slight smile and amusement was back in his brown eyes. She had assumed correctly that there were no readymade clothes for him either.

"Maybe they will have a pair of boots to fit your feet or do you prefer the moccasins? There are some that do."

"I want to be rid of everything that stinks of that camp." Her voice was as harsh as her words.

"Then you had best step down. The other woman will be locked away to await transportation."

Two troopers had swung the gate down and looked like they were ready to pull her off.

Anna stood. "I can down get by myself, thank du." Thank Gott the words came out right that time. On the ground, she too towered over the two male troopers. MacDonald offered his arm and they walked towards the Sutler's store. Those in the vicinity stared at the two.

Upon entering, they both blinked at the darkened space. It was small and cramped, every conceivable item needed by man and beast was stacked on the floor, the shelves, and the counter except for the space the man used to set merchandise, make change, or run up a tab. One small window above the counter area provided the only light in the room, effectively hiding any grime or dust covering the wares.

"Good day, Hawkins, tis something in more conventional apparel Mrs. Lawrence tis needing."

Hawkins, short, lean, blue eyed, large bulbous nose, and brown, stringy hair regarded Anna. "Aint got no wimmin's clothes. There's a bolt of white muslin, iffen she can sew." It was a skill he was certain Indian women could not master.

Anna looked ready to attack the man and MacDonald straightened his shoulders. "As I said, Mrs. Lawrence tis needing more conventional apparel. I ken ye have blue bolts of cloth too. She twill look at both."

Hawkins looked at the scout and decided a paying customer was better than none. Her skin might be white, but she was a squaw. Not that it mattered in this hellhole. Any kind of woman was better than none.

Anna looked at the two bolts of poor quality cotton and swallowed. She would need enough material for a skirt and underskirt. There should be more underskirts, but there wouldn't be time. Her sewing would be confined to the evening hours. She looked at MacDonald.

"Are there men's shirts here?" She still spoke in German.

"Yes, and men's boots and socks."

"I don't need two bolts. Is it possible he could cut some off?"

"He will for me. How much do you need from them?"

Anna face flushed. "I will need seven yards from each. She dare not say she needed the muslin for the undergarment. "I will also need a needle and some thread. If you have a sharp knife, I should be able to do without the scissors." Anna wanted the scissors. The man might prove untrustworthy and scissors could be a formidable weapon.

MacDonald was thinking desperately. Thread was the translation for zwirn, but what the hell was nadel? He knew nothing about sewing and Hawkins was making noises behind the counter.

"We need seven yards from each. Can ye do that?" His voice rumbled out and it left no doubt that Hawkins best do it.

For an answer, Hawkins flipped the blue bolt and ran it the length of the counter. He then took the measure from the end and laid it to a mark on the counter. He made a slit with his knife and tore the material upward. He did the same with the white bolt.

"What else?"

"Mrs. Lawrence, what is the English word for nadle?"

She looked at him. "It's needle, und I need vhite thread, at least two spools."

"Ye heard the lady. Then we need a pair of trousers for her, a shirt, a pair of boots, and some socks." He was truly ignorant of the fact that scissors, buttons, thimbles, and thread wax were needed.

Anna believed that she could devise something for a button or fastener. She did not wish to owe any more money to this man.

By the time they left the store, their purchases were considerable for they needed another blanket and food. MacDonald insisted on two receipts, one for him and one for the Eighth Infantry Commander. There was no place to change into any of the clothing except the socks and boots. The lace-up brogans were too stiff.

"We will now go to their headquarters. I have an order for a wagon and mules. I did not think you wished to ride a horse." He remembered that Kasper had said Anna could drive a team as well as a man, but that she did not ride.

By late afternoon they were camped by Limpia Creek. MacDonald had driven down an incline that led to the river. The mules were staked and hobbled in the grass after the cart was half hidden by the willows growing up towards the low bank. "There is water and grass in this area. Once we hit the Pecos River, a ferry will take us across. There isn't much cover, but I would like to take a cleansing. Perhaps you do also."

Anna looked at him in horror and her words were rapid. "I cannot do so without cover. You may not see me without clothes. Do you intend violence?" Her grey eyes were ice and her mouth a tight line.

"Ye Gods, woman, I but made a suggestion to make us more comfortable. I twould stay on this side of the wagon until ye tell me all tis clear. Then we can exchange places. There are willow shrubs if ye stay low.

"If ye prefer, ye can pick up the wood and chips for the fire or start yere sewing. Ye can go first or nay at all. As for violence, my ranch tis in the vicinity of Schmidt's Corner and I twill live there someday. Ye are safe with me." He had reverted to his own language.

"I will wait until there is a better way to bathe privately." Anna could not think of the English words.

"Some of the country we will cross has less cover. They must have given you an old garment as there is a sour smell. Keep it on and bathe." He had returned to using German.

Anna blushed, but raised her head and looked directly at him. "Part of that is my ears, or lack of them. They cut them off when I did not do their bidding. They haven't healed."

MacDonald was left bug-eyed and opened mouthed. What a lassie. He had nay seen the like in this land.

Anna turned and began to gather buffalo and cow chips and stray twigs for the evening fire while MacDonald cared for the mules and his horse before taking his "cleansing."

As she returned to the area where they were camped, she chanced to look in the direction of the water. Was it curiosity or was it because it had become quiet? She never resolved that question, but his broad, muscular back was devoid of clothing, the water dripping down from his dark hair. She turned so quickly the load she was carrying almost fell. That he was a huge man, she had not doubted, but the muscles like cords on his back and arms were so unlike anything she knew from Mr. Lawrence it took her breath away. What is the matter with me ran through her mind. Her annoyance at herself lasted until he returned carrying a small tin.

"This tis," and he started again in German. "This contains a special salve. I keep some with me in case I pick up an infection or suffer a wound. It will help heal your ears." He wondered how he had missed realizing that the matted hair around that portion of her face was more than grime. Indians used water for bathing and washing. He had been too long in the company of men.

Anna's stare was defiant. She was daring him to touch her. He handed the tin to her.

"I suggest you at least wash your hair before applying it. I will start the evening meal, and you can start your sewing."

She considered and knew he was correct. The flesh where the outer ears had been were scabbed over and needed to be cleaned. "Do you have any soap, please?" Her voice was almost meek.

The half smile was back on his lips and amusement lurked in the dark eyes. "Aye, here it tis. Ye twill have but air for the drying."

Anna palmed the soap and marched toward the river. The view across the river was unrestricted. Round river rocks and sand lined the beach. The willows extended out into the water and the cottonwoods created shade. She could smell the smoke and grease in her clothes. Why hadn't she brought the trousers and shirt? She could have hidden behind the tree trunk. Because you are a stubborn woman, she thought. She turned and walked back to the cart. MacDonald was kneeling where the fire would be, piling on dry leaves and then the smaller sticks.

She ignored him and reached over the cart to pull out her bundle of clothes before returning to the water's edge. There she removed the socks and brogans as she did not want them wet, and began unbraiding her hair. Why hadn't she asked for a comb? Once her hair was wet the curls would become a mass of snarls within hours. She knew it had turned white, but at thirty-three it was doubtful that any man would look at her. Normal men wouldn't anyway. She was too tall; worse she had been in a Comanche camp for two seasons. She would be fortunate if Gerde even allowed her near little Hans. She smelled of the Indian camp and their foods. She knew it. What did it matter if the man raped her? She was already fouled in the eyes of the white man's world.

She pulled off the offending deerskin garment and plunged into the willow-protected water and used the soap to scrub vigorously at her body and her hair. Before walking back to dry ground, Anna looked around, but MacDonald was nowhere in sight. She moved swiftly ignoring the rocks under her feet and pulled on the man's shirt and trousers. The trousers were rough canvas and the shirt cheap cotton, but they covered her. Her hair she tried wringing out, but it was too thick, curly, and unruly and soon soaked her shirt. She turned away from the cart and as rapidly as possible put on the socks and boots before buttoning up the shirt and trousers.

The only thing to do with the hair was to run her fingers through it and braid it. She would need to use the rawhide ties for now. Once the hair was braided, she opened the small can and applied the salve. Maybe it will work and maybe it won't were her thoughts. She stood and returned to the camp.

MacDonald was sitting on the cart tongue whittling and glanced up.

"Those boots announce every step ye take." He stood, folded the jackknife, and smiled at her. "Ye look like a young, albino laddie. Ye need some weight on that skinny frame and then ye twould be magnificent."

There was admiration in his voice and Anna drew in her breath. Had she been insulted or complimented? It was difficult to tell.

MacDonald insisted on doing the clean up while she worked on her skirt. She had him cut a four inch strip off the side of the blue material and then cut the remaining piece in half before sewing the two large pieces together. At first her efforts were clumsy, but as time went on her stitches became her stitches: a close, small, neat line of white marching across a blue field. All too soon the light fled and nighttime held sway.

"I can let the fire burn a wee bit longer for yere sewing this eve as we are still close to Fort Davis. By tomorrow eve, I canna do so."

Anna looked up puzzled and then realized what he had said. "Thank du, Herr MacDonald. I vill this thread finish…" and realized her words were wrong. "I'll use the thread now in the needle and stop. Thank du."

He smiled at her and used her language. "I noticed the tips of your little fingers are gone. Did that occur before you were captured?"

She raised her head and tightened her lips. "No, they did that when they gave my sons to others. I tried to fight them. They cut them off to show that my boys were dead to me. They were not dead, and Daniel still lives. They are my sons. I was stronger then. They healed over." Her grey eyes were defiant as though defying him to challenge her.

Had he challenged everyone in this land when he first walked free? Did she fear he was going to bed her or argue that she should nay have fought? It twas a wonder they had let her live. Then realization hit him.

"Is that when your hair turned white?"

She looked down at the sewing and continued stitching while she spoke. "Yes, by the next morning it was completely white. They weren't sure whether it was magic or if there was something wrong with my mind." She tied off the thread and looked up.

"There, I have finished for this evening."

MacDonald stood. "I suggest ye sleep in the cart if ye still dinna feel safe."

She looked at the cart. It was perhaps four to five feet in length which meant she would need to sleep cattycornered. Plus, the boards would be rough and harder than the ground.

"Would it be all right if I slept under the cart?"

He smiled. "That should nay be a problem, Mrs. Lawrence."

Chapter 20

Across Texas

Anna awoke the next morning and realized that Mr. MacDonald had breakfast started. Then she realized her ears were not sore, but her hair was matted again, either from the salve or the drainage. She held her hands over her ears and pain did not streak through her head. She walked to the area they used for the latrine for nature was demanding. Then she washed her hands in the river. When the water settled, she lifted the braids to see if an image was reflected. There was none. Still it felt better and she walked back to the camp area.

"Thank you, Mr. MacDonald. The salve seems to be working. There is no pain this morning." She did not dare trust her words to English.

"Would ye like me to verify that?"

"No, thank you, Mr. MacDonald, but I am grateful. Will this deplete your supply?"

The half smile was on his lips and the amusement in his eyes. How could he tell her that on board the *Golden One* was a machine that extruded a stream into the tin upon command?

"No, I have a supply hidden away at home." He returned to cooking the fat back. "The coffee tis done and the biscuits from last night are in the box. Take a plate and we'll eat. I'd like to be on the trail ere full daylight."

They spoke very little while on the trail. MacDonald rode his huge black horse as he watched their backs, the sides, and checked for Indian sign while she drove the cart with their gear. He went on hunting forays to augment their diet with antelope, rabbit, deer, or an occasional grouse. He kenned that Zark, as he had named his horse, could outrun most Indian ponies, but the sturdy mules never. They could outlast a horse, require less water, and less expensive feed, but they weren't known for speed unless specifically bred for racing.

Evenings Anna would be busy with her sewing and MacDonald with tending the animals and cooking. She insisted on doing the plates and utensils whether it was water or sand they had for cleaning. She winced when she heard the ferry fee, but MacDonald was not concerned. He insisted the man give him a receipt.

"Tis the only way the Army twill pay me back."

Once, when they were near a town, MacDonald asked if she wished to stop and buy anything else.

"No, I will not go into town dressed as a man." Her face was set again. How did she tell him she had not finished the underskirt? She couldn't and didn't. Only married women talked to their husbands about such things. He did not ask again.

One afternoon found them near a river of goodly width, but not overly deep. MacDonald motioned to a stand of cottonwood trees and willows, and pulled up his horse beside her when she stopped.

"This tis a very pleasant place to camp for the bank slopes downward and ye twould be well hidden whilst ye bathe. We are about four days out of Schmidt's Corner. The river tis less clean and deep farther on, and the banks nay as high."

Anna stared at him. "So close?" Her voice was almost a whisper. She continued to use German.

"Aye, we've been on the trail for seventeen days. It's been a grueling trip for ye, but I thought ye wished to be back among yere relatives as quickly as possible." He noted that a bit of weight was back on her skinny frame.

She stared at the reins in her hands. "If I change now, my clothes will be dirty from being on the ground." She knew that Gerde would have no clothes her size even if they welcomed her. Her trail clothes were filthy. She drew in a deep breath.

"Perhaps it would be best to take me back to that town. I could find a job as a laundress. Then if Kasper and Gerde want me to come there, they can write a letter."

MacDonald's eyes widened. "Mrs. Lawrence, I canna go into Schmidt's Corner and tell them I brought ye all the way from the wilds of West Texas and then left ye in Arles. They twould be outraged."

"There are other people there where they live, is that not true?"

"Yes, but Mrs. Schmidt, Mrs. Rolfe, Mrs. Phillips, and Mrs. Hernandez are the only adult ladies. The other men do not have a wife. Mrs. Jackson died some years ago, and the other families live outside the town."

"I cannot go where I am not wanted."

"Mrs. Lawrence, if ye do nay go with me, Kasper will come for ye. Why put everyone to that trouble?"

"After all the trouble I have already put you through, is that what you mean?"

"Nay, that tis nay fair." His voice was rumbling out in anger and exasperation.

For a moment she was silent and then she smiled. MacDonald was awestruck. The hard planes of her face seemed to melt and her face was transformed. The smile brought a glow to her skin and to her eyes. It was as though she were a different person; someone you wanted to know and trusted immediately.

"Mr. MacDonald, that was not fair. I am sorry." She put out her hand. It was a gesture she regretted for suddenly his large hand had closed around hers and he was smiling.

"Ye twill be happy to ken that Kasper has told me that one of yere church men twill be coming through."

"Oh, I want to talk with one. I need to know if it is all right to divorce a man who plotted to have his family killed by Indians."

"Dear Gar, how do ye ken that?"

For a moment she tightened her lips. "Mr. Lawrence took his riding horse to do haying and he did not take Daniel with him. I had sent Daniel out to him. He also took the rifle and the shotgun. The Comanche did not kill him, but took Daniel. The first night we camped, Daniel told me that his father had spoke with their leader before riding away. He knew them."

"It will be difficult to prove in court, but I seem to remember something similar that Mr. Rolfe told me about his and Kasper's visit to Wooden. I shall ask them when we are there."

"Thank you, Mr. MacDonald. Would I be able to bath in the river tomorrow evening?"

"Aye, the river tis deep enough and there are willows. It does nay have the high shielding banks."

"Then I shall wait. Tonight I will wash out my hair and shirt. May I take the soap?"

"Aye, of course, ye can. Why do ye even ask?"

"Because the soap is yours." She was defiant again.

He handed her the soap. "The nights are getting cooler. Take my jacket and wear it till the shirt dries."

"I will use my blanket if the coolness bothers me." She took the soap before walking down the embankment.

At the river she paused and walked closer to the edge. The high banks on the other side waved brown grass and white clouds floated above, sometimes crossing over the path of the sun. Long shadows covered the Earth until the clouds moved forward on their journey. She knelt at the river, ignoring the water that seeped around her knees and removed the leather ties and stuck them in her trouser pocket. She shook out her hair, bent over and began the washing. When the water was clear of soap, she removed the shirt and washed off the surface dirt. Without hot water, a scrub board, or plunger there was no way to completely clean the shirt. At least it would smell better. Before putting it back on, she splashed water under her armpits, soaped them, and rinsed them off with the shirt. She then rinsed the shirt again before putting it on. By now she was shivering.

I should not be shivering. It is because I am so weak, she thought and began to button the shirt. It was a slower process with wet material. She ran her fingers through her hair, trying to unsnarl the curls. It was futile without a comb. Thoroughly exasperated she pulled the whole mass forward and braided it. She knew without looking it was a mess. Both ties helped to hold the hair, but there was no way to pull it up as a respectable woman would.

At least the effort distracted her attention away from the afternoon's coolness and she headed back up the embankment. Mr. MacDonald would be wanting his "cleansing." What a strange choice of words.

Chapter 21

A Truce

The next day was warmer as the heavy clouds had moved on. Soon it would be cooler and the rains would come. Anna chose a spot in the river that was as hidden as possible and bathed. She thanked God that no one came and Mr. MacDonald was true to his word. He did not approach. He was a big man and she had felt the hardness of his muscles when he picked her up at the Comanche camp. She had seen that pattern of muscles on his back and knew she was no match in strength. Her respect for him had grown; grudgingly, but grown.

It was a relief to don her slip and skirt. She had fashioned a loop on the band on the left of the open area and put two small ties on the opposite side. By threading one through the loop and tying the two together, the skirt would remain up. She strode back into the camp area.

MacDonald's eyes opened wider as he watched her approach. This was indeed a magnificent lassie. Her stride was long, her shoulders broad, and her head held high. He had seen few other women as tall and they tended to stoop and lower their heads. Not this one. The white hair was a plus in his eyes. In Thalia, this denoted authority, someone from a ruling House.

"I can tend to the cooking this evening, Mr. MacDonald." He had the two rabbits cooking in the Dutch oven. She knew the biscuits needed to be mixed and rounded before adding to the Dutch oven. Their flour was almost gone. Soon there would be nothing but meat.

He smiled at her and took the soap. “Ye look magnificent.” With that he trudged off with the water barrel on his shoulder.

He returned about thirty minutes later carrying the full water barrel. Anna was awed each time he had done this. No man was his equal in strength that she had ever seen. When the barrel was securely lashed inside the cart he came over to the fire.

“How tis the coffee holding out?”

“There should be enough for another day.”

He sighed. “It tis nay my favorite beverage, but it does wash things down. How long ere supper?”

“I think about five or ten minutes for the biscuits. Does Kasper have any way of getting fruits or vegetables?” She was thinking of her own gardens in Missouri and Texas. This ground seemed drier less like good farming soil, but it was late summer or early fall. She had not seen a calendar for almost two years.

“There are canned ones. I believe Mrs. Schmidt said something about a garden next year if Kasper could finish the fence. It seems the small animals feasted on everything.”

The evening meal passed in silence. Anna was thinking of her reception. Would she be welcomed? Perhaps at first, and then the doubts, the misconceptions, the accusations would begin. Was she really wise to return?

She finished her meal and stood. “I should do the cleanup this evening. You have been very kind in doing what I should have been doing while sewing.”

MacDonald swallowed the last of his meat and smiled. “I ate the food also. That means I’m responsible for part of the dishes.”

“Most men would not have done so.”

His smile was broader. “I am nay most men. We’ll each wash our own.”

Dusk was falling into night when they returned to the fire for the days were growing shorter. “I doubt if there tis anyone out there this eve, but I twould like to rest for a few hours as my sleep has been short on this trip. Tis it possible for ye to stay awake for a few hours and then wake me about midnight?”

Anna was struck with the realization that he must have had reasons for sleeping while she stitched at the material. “Of course, I can, Mr. MacDonald. I’ll sit here and walk back and forth.”

Amusement lit her eyes. “It’s too bad there isn’t a book to read or more sewing.”

MacDonald handed her his pocket watch, and then spread out his blanket before lying down. He pulled his hat over his eyes, held his rifle over his chest, and went instantly into a light doze.

How does he do that? Anna found the man puzzling. There was something more than size or politeness that made him different. Was it the rolling, rocking movement while he walked? It did seem his arms were set forward more than others, but that could be from the muscular structure. No, it was something else. She shrugged. She had no reason to suspect his intentions. If he had meant to harm her, he would not have waited so long.

She walked around the camp and then sat by the fire. Sometimes she added more fuel, but when she felt sleepy she would stand and walk again. By ten o’clock she began singing the hymns she remembered. She kept her voice low and only sang at the edge of camp or down towards the river. It was maddening how slowly the hours seemed to creep.

At midnight, she stood near his makeshift sleeping area and spoke. She did not touch him. That would have been wrong. “Mr. MacDonald, it is midnight.”

He took off his hat, sat up, ran a hand through his hair, replaced his hat, took a firm grip on his rifle, stood, and farted.

“My apologies, Mrs. Lawrence. Thank ye for waking me.” He stalked off toward the edge of camp.

Anna smiled. It was what people did when they awoke, but at least he was polite. Within minutes she was asleep.

The words, "Mrs. Lawrence, the morning fare tis prepared," seemed to buzz in her head within minutes. She opened her eyes and realized that dawn was streaking its gold and pink lines across the sky.

"Ja, Herr MacDonald," she answered and stood, quickly flapping the blanket as though to clear any grass and dirt, but in reality to hide the sound of her own morning air. She hurried to the latrine area after putting the blanket in the cart.

She returned to find her plate filled with fried potatoes mixed with the leftover rabbit meat.

"I fear our meals twill be mostly rabbit the rest of the journey. A stop at Arles would have enabled me to purchase some canned goods and more flour."

Anna bowed her head and then looked directly at him. "Mr. MacDonald, your meals have been bountiful. You have spent too much of your own money on me."

"Mrs. Lawrence, yere idea and my idea of bountiful do nay coincide. Some of the money I have spent will be reimbursed by the Eighth Infantry when I return the mules and the cart."

A slight flush filled her cheeks. "I, I forgot, it had been so long since I had a full meal. That was wrong of me. Is it too late to go back?"

The amusement was back in his eyes and that smile tugging at his mouth. "Yes, it is. Schmidt's Corner is closer." He began to eat and Anna bowed her head before taking her first bite.

"You will let me wash and mend your clothes for repayment before you leave, won't you?"

"I have a spare set of clothes at the Rolfe's, but, aye, if ye insist, ye may wash and mend them."

Silence reigned again, but it was a different silence. The tension had disappeared.

That evening they talked and gradually Anna's tale spilled out in response to MacDonald's gentle probing. She had "felt" something was wrong that morning and was packing necessities when the two boys began fighting. She had sent Daniel out to be with his father for an eight-year-old was capable of working in the fields. Plus, Mr. Lawrence had taken all the firearms. She felt he would protect his own son. Margareatha and Lorenz she had sent out to gather the early corn. She planned to take that with them when they left. Just as she was ready to step out of the door, Auggie needed to be changed. That's when the Comanche rode up. She closed her eyes for a moment and completely changed the subject.

"How long will we be on the road tomorrow?"

"We twill be in Schmidt's Corner tomorrow afternoon in time for supper."

Anna gasped air into her lungs and slowly let it out.

"Will you be eating with us?"

"I would nay infringe on yere reunion. My friend, Herman Rolfe, always has a place for me at his table."

Anna looked at the fire. In a way, she was disappointed. This was madness, but she respected this man, respected his strength and his kindness. It was a dream for she was still married and her children still lived. No man would be interested in her.

"Ye twere fortunate the Comanche did nay kill ye and just take the baby."

His comment made her snap her head up. "I grabbed the broom and knocked one of them down. I was going for the second man when the third came out of the cabin carrying Auggie by the heel. What could I do? He was going to bash my baby's head against the doorframe."

"Dear Gar, woman, do ye nay ken it tis a wonder they did nay kill ye then and there."

"Even men have enough sense to know the baby needed my milk to live." This time she looked away. Why was she being so bold?

MacDonald's shoulders were shaking. "And if the mither twas such a warrior, think what the son twould be."

"They laughed at the one I knocked down. I think he did want to kill me."

"Of course, he did. Ye humiliated him. He probably made yere life miserable."

Anna nodded her head. "His woman was the one that spit on me when they cut off my ears." She stood and walked with long angry strides toward the latrine area.

It was MacDonald's turn to drag in his breath. This lassie twas a warrior. Nay did he think he twould ere find such a counselor in this land. He must find a way to wed her. How did one court here? Friend Rolfe could give him pointers. He had already promised to help her find the proof to divorce her husband. That should keep them in communication. The idea that she might discover his two hearts never occurred to him. He took his rifle and stood.

Chapter 22

The Courtship of Anna

The morning clouds obscured the early sunlight and a cool, crisp breeze swept over the prairie when Anna returned from the latrine area. Her mind and heart were in turmoil. This would be their last day on the trail. Mr. MacDonald was hooking the harnessed mules to the wagon tongue. His horse was not saddled, but tied to the back of the wagon.

He smiled at her and held the reins as she climbed up onto the seat. He kept the reins in his hands and climbed up beside her. "We twill be at yere brither's place ere nightfall."

Anna turned on him and put her arms akimbo. "Mr. MacDonald, vhat are du doing?"

"I am driving today."

"I am not your horse riding."

His smile was broader. "Mrs. Lawrence, ye are excited about returning to House. One minute I can see the elation in yere eyes and in yere walk. The next minute, ye close up and will nay look at me or anything else. Those mules twill feel the agitation from ye through the reins. If they decide to stop, they twill nay be easy to start again."

She spoke rapidly in German. "Are you so eager to be rid of me?"

For a moment MacDonald looked shocked. "Mrs. Lawrence, I intend to adhere to all rules, but once ye are with yere brither, I wish to court ye."

"What?"

"I wish to wed ye, Anna Lawrence. I have nay seen any like ye in this land." He was pleading with his own words. "Ye are a magnificent woman. Ye fought like a Warrior when attacked. Ye did nay give in for two years. Tis an admirable display of courage. I am awed. Ye also are a Kenning Woman."

It was Anna's turn to be in shock. This strong, gentle man wished to wed her? Was he serious? Why would he joke now?

"Mr. MacDonald, du must know I am Christian and belong to a Lutheran church."

"Of course, Mr. Schmidt has mentioned it, but I dinna ken. What tis Lutheran? Tis that somewhat like the Methodists?"

"No, we are looked down upon by Methodists because we permit alcohol. We are Christian. My children will be raised as Christians and our beliefs taught. I have not seen you praying. Do you have a Bible?"

"Mrs. Lawrence, we are on the trail. As a scout, I must travel light, but ye are correct. I dinna believe as ye do; however, I twould nay interfere with yere beliefs or practice."

"And what if there are children?"

He swallowed. "I fear there twill nay be any. I, I had, how to say this, I dinna wish to offend ye." He hesitated and then remembered the men talking about a trapper who came down with mumps. The man had not remained in bed and the swelling had descended to his balls. The men had guffawed about the man never being able to have children and called it the swelling disease.

"I had the swelling disease. I am told that that takes away the ability to have children." It was the most plausible explanation he could devise.

She stared at him. "Not always." Her words snapped out. "So, the question remains, would you object?" Anger was in her voice.

The half-smile was back on his face. "I twould rejoice."

Her head was high and her mouth stiff. "You must know that you need to ask my brother's permission."

"Aye, I ken that, but I doubt if yere brither has that much control over what ye twill do."

A small smile appeared on Anna's face.

"Do you know me so well, Mr. MacDonald?"

"Mrs. Lawrence, I have told ye. Ye are a magnificent woman. If I twere nay driving this team, I twould kiss ye."

Anna drew in her breath. "That is not allowed until we are married."

"Are ye saying ye twill agree to wed?"

"I did not say that. A person should know what to expect from a suitor." She looked down at her folded hands. Then she lifted her head and stared straight ahead and her voice became fierce. "I will not make that mistake again."

"I can nay blame ye for that. Soon we twill be at the start of my land. I'll show ye where I have planned to build a home. We twill nay stop, but ye twill agree it tis a wise choice."

The morning had been sunny, but clouds covered the sky and the temperature began to slide. Shortly before noon, MacDonald topped a rise and pulled the team to a halt. He pointed at the prairie below where a spring could be seen sending a small rivulet of water towards the lowest area.

"I plan to build to a home just to the north of the spring where the ground tis higher. The spring can be capped..."

"And a springhouse built around it." Anna's grey eyes had widened.

"Aye, if that tis what ye want." His rumbling voice filled with enthusiasm. "The barn and stables twill be to the south where the land rises again."

"If and when I am granted a divorce, Mr. MacDonald, I will consider marrying you."

He wrapped the reins around his left hand and turned enough to pull her close and taste her lips. It was a kiss unlike any Anna had known. Mr. Lawrence rarely bothered. This one started soft and then she could feel the demand for more, the gentle moving back and forth over the mouth, and finally firm, hard against her lips. And she was matching his every movement, wanting more, liking the smell of him, his touch, and the demand was in her lips.

She came up gasping for air. "Mr. MacDonald! That is not allowed."

His smile was broad, his white teeth gleaming. "Of course, Mrs. Lawrence, it nay happened."

He unwrapped the reins from around his hand and snapped them against the animals' backs.

"Schmidt's Corner tis about three hours from here. We twill be there in the late afternoon. Let me know when ye wish to stop. If ye twould fish out some of that jerky we can have a bit of sustenance on our way."

Anna reached back and pulled up his possible bag. She was still panting. Part of her wanted to slap his face, the other part wanted to tell him to stop and kiss her again. The latter, she suspected would be a sin or would become one. Her prolonged separation from her family, her children, from her known world had left her yearning for human contact. Anna would forever damn the Comanche for taking her children. She opened the bag, extracted the jerky, and handed him two strips.

"Ye should eat."

"I am not hungry." She stared straight ahead. Three hours he had said. What would Kasper and Gerde say when they saw her? Would they be horrified? What would their reaction be to Zebediah's request that he be allowed to court her? It struck her that she just thought of him by his first name and she clasped her hands together in a prayer. *Forgive me, forgive me, I am a silly woman.*

MacDonald seemed to realize that she had withdrawn again and remained silent for many a bumpy mile. There was a trail of sorts here from people and freight wagons coming from Arles going toward Schmidt's Corner and the German settlements further north. The prairie grass was shorter, the ground cut into ruts in places when the wagons came through after a rain. Wheels and horses helped to pack the ground. The prairie grass was brown from lack of rain, drooping in places, and waiting, knowing the rains were soon to blow in from the south.

They pulled up near a scrub oak and MacDonald stepped down and tied the mules. They immediately began to munch at the grass. Anna was grateful as they had not stopped since morning. Both went separate ways to attend to nature's demands.

He was leaning against his side of the cart when she returned. He heard her step, turned, and smiled.

"Shall I come around to the other side to assist ye up into the cart?"

"You know that isn't necessary." The fierceness was back in her voice and she bounded upward.

He shrugged, untied the mules, and resumed his seat. "Up Jennies, ye'll soon have a rest and a cool drink of water."

He turned towards Anna who was once again sitting with hands clasped while staring straight ahead. He decided to speak in German as she looked truly lost. "Just think, you'll soon be with your brother's family and have your Bible to read again."

Her shoulders relaxed and her eyes closed for a prolong moment. "Yes," she agreed. "Does Kasper still have other books?"

"He has a great many books—for out here. He kept some of his textbooks and is teaching me Latin."

Anna stared at him. "Why Latin?"

"I chose it as the language to help me understand the other languages of this world." He winced inwardly. He had let down his guard and referred to Earth as "this world."

"But you already know German."

"I know enough to read it also, yes, but not to write it."

"Which other language are you learning?"

"Well, like others out here I'm familiar with Spanish, but someone told me they were using a dialect, not Spanish.

"Do you read other books, Mrs. Lawrence?" It was a fair question as many women did not unless their family was wealthy.

"Yes, I used to read the textbooks that Kasper brought home. My father could not see any reason for a girl to advance beyond eighth grade. I was lucky. Some of those older Germans thought that fourth or fifth grade was enough for a woman." Once again she looked straight ahead and clamped her mouth tight.

Chapter 23

Refuge

Anna was white-faced. Her fingers were knotted together, her eyes dry, and her back and shoulders held as straight as a soldier at attention. MacDonald had ceased all attempts at conversation when she had grown silent. The road had brought them into Schmidt's Corner.

They had seen the smoke rising from the different chimneys. She was tempted to tell him to turn around, but did not trust her voice. She did not move as they drove past a two-story house and then a cabin that looked like it had four rooms, a blacksmith shop was set at one side of the cabin, but further back on the property. Next was a small tavern. A wainwright shop set directly across from the blacksmith and corrals were at the side. A house was being built behind the shop. The prairie was gone from the road through town.

Ahead Anna could see another two story building with a long porch overhang and a sign was positioned high between two of its side posts. She could see the lettering proclaiming "SCHMIDT'S CORNER." She saw that the clapboards had been whitewashed as they drove between the tavern and the general store. In the back she could see there was a stable set a few feet north of the store. A garden was between the store and the river.

The garden didn't look too large and the fence was a strange combination of posts, wire, and rocks.

MacDonald pulled the mules to a stop and yelled. "Hello the house." This would bring either Kasper or Gerde to the door. He was afraid Anna would bolt if he swung down and left her with the cart and mules.

Kasper appeared within a few minutes and looked at them with puzzlement. He could not understand why Mac wouldn't just bring a visitor into the house. Disbelief began to spread across his face when he realized the woman beside his friend was extremely tall.

"Anna," he whispered. His beautiful sister was white-haired and not moving. He jumped down the three steps and ran towards the left side of the cart.

"Anna!" This time it was a full-throated welcoming roar.

Anna turned to look at her brother running towards her and the tears welled up. Suddenly, his arms were there to support her and she found herself on the ground hugging him and being hugged.

Gerde appeared in the doorway holding the hand of four-year-old Hans. She had heard Kasper's yell and at first the name had not registered. All she saw was Kasper holding an ill-clad woman, and she turned a puzzled face to MacDonald. He was grinning broadly at her as though he had just achieved something grand.

Like Kasper she realized the woman was tall, taller than most men, and her eyes widened. How could it be Anna? How could she have white hair? She swallowed. She knew them both well. That meant Anna would be staying with them and sleeping in the bedroom that was meant for Hans. It would not matter to Kasper how much his twin had changed or been changed.

Kasper and Anna were walking toward the porch, their arms still around each other as if afraid the other would disappear if they lost contact. At the steps, Kasper halted as Anna grasped his arm.

She had been reciting, "They took my babies, they took my babies," in a broken voice. Now she took a deep breath.

"You owe Mr. MacDonald money. I am sorry, but he bought the material for me to make clothes." She choked unable to say more.

Kasper turned toward MacDonald.

"Mr. MacDonald, may God bless you." His voice was ragged and he took a deep breath. "Will you give me a few minutes with my family before I thank you properly and repay you." Tears were on his cheeks.

"Mr. Schmidt, please, take all the time ye need. I shall visit friend Rolfe or Owens. Tis there room to stable these Army mules in yere livery?"

"Yes, there's no charge. Thank you." He choked the words out. Kasper and Anna stumbled up the stairs and then Gerde was hugging Anna.

Chapter 24

Celebration

The little saloon was packed. Jesse Owens was behind the bar, happily pouring drinks and taking bets. Kasper celebrated the return of his sister by buying a round of drinks for those present and inviting his neighbors to a Texas barbeque in three days. He had stayed long enough to drink two filled mugs without commenting how much better his own brew was. He had even bet on the outcome of the evening's poker game. Most of the men had snickered at Kasper betting on a fellow Dutchman. Rolfe had bet that he would win, but the others believed differently. MacDonald was the one to pick. Look at the size of the man. He had to have a larger capacity. He would be able to sit and drink longer than Rolfe without going outside to piss.

Jesse, as owner of the saloon, held the bets. He would collect ten percent no matter who won. The pot was to keep growing by one cent as long as the players sat there. Any man that went outside to piss lost his winnings, his place at the table, and the chance at the pot. Another was eligible to take the empty chair if they had five cents and had not gone outside. If they lost their money, they would still have a chance at the pot as long as they didn't take a trip outside—for any reason. Every man had to drink the same amount of beer.

Both Tilden brothers were here and one hand from each ranch. The Jacksons, both Ben and Tom, had drifted in early and were sipping their beers. Tom was really too young to drink, but if the old man didn't give a damn, neither did Jesse. Profit was profit. Malcolm Phillips, the wainwright, had his hat pushed back and a frown on his lean face. He was determined to beat both Rolfe and MacDonald.

The Blue Diamond mule train had arrived just before twilight and unloaded Kasper's cargo before delivering to Jesse. They'd stacked his beer kegs along the wall behind the bar and stayed. Some of them paid Consuela for a plate of the beans she had cooking outside. Jesse needed to consider having that available more often. Consuela and her husband, Cruz, might be without dinner occasionally, but they were using his place of business to make money. They had also moved their shack onto his property. Where they had been was part of Rolfe's land, and Jesse didn't charge rent. Consuela cleaned for him and Cruz did small jobs.

The game had seesawed back and forth. Rolfe had won an early pot, and then Phillips pulled in a bunch of chips. The cost of the ante wasn't high. These were friends and neighbors and they valued the chips at a penny each. No one could afford to lose big in these times. The Tillman's hands were young and had dropped out early. Malcolm played until his last two nickels. He kept them for more beer if the game ran much later. He was frowning at the men playing.

It was well after the midnight hour and MacDonald and Rolfe were the only two left playing and the only two who had not been outside. Jesse kept filling their mugs whenever they both were empty and each laid a nickel on the table. All of the men were sipping slowly to forestall running out of money for beer. The late crowd was seriously depleting his delivery, and Jesse was wondering if he'd ordered enough beer for the month.

Rolfe dealt another hand. "Tell du vhat, Mac. Ve drain these fast and order another."

"Go to hell, Rolfe. I'll bet two pennies." A strained look came over the broad face and he stood, leaned over the table, and glared at Rolfe.

"Friend Rolfe, ye are nay human!" He stomped out.

Rolfe grinned at the retreating back and pulled in the pot. He stood, stuffed the coins into the bag hanging down from his belt, lifted his mug, and drained the contents.

"Vell, boys, dot ends this evening's play. I'll be back in to collect my vinnings." He followed the big man out the door.

Jesse considered running after him. If some of those freighters hadn't slipped into a drunken sleep he might have for it was Rolfe's and Kasper's money that he held, plus his own ten percent. Anger and bafflement were on every face.

"What the hell? Was that planned? Did those foreigners make fools of us?" Malcolm was bitter. He didn't trust those men. They weren't true Texans or Southerners. Buchanan was a shit poor president, but he was too weak to do anything about the South.

Leighton Andrew, head Blue Diamond freighter, placed his empty mug on the bar. "I doubt it. I've dealt with Kasper since he's been here. If he has a fault, it's being too damn honest." He nodded at Jesse and turned to his crew.

"Let's go. We're rolling out early. Somebody kick McPherson and Kincaid awake."

Rolfe was still emptying his bladder as they left the saloon. MacDonald was buttoning his flap. The deep rumble of MacDonald's voice was heard.

"Twould ye care for another drink, friend Rolfe?"

"Hell, no, Mac, Clara's going to be on a warpath tomorrow. Let's go collect my winnings."

Chapter 25

Quest for Truth

Rolfe and Kasper pulled up their horses at the O'Neal plantation. They had been on the trail for three weeks. Before he left, MacDonald had offered to pay for their grub and any expenses. Kasper wouldn't hear of it as Mrs. Lawrence was using her portion from their grandparents' estate. It was a small amount of cash since she was female and not male, but Kasper had carefully put it aside. Somehow he knew his twin lived. He had been surprised when MacDonald approached him.

"Mr. Schmidt, in the ways of yere land, I need to request yere permission to court yere sister when I return."

Kasper had stood speechless for a moment and almost answered in Deutsche. Then a huge smile lit his face and he clasped MacDonald's hand. "Of course, Mr. MacDonald, of course, I give my permission and my blessing; if Mrs. Lawrence will agree to it."

It was MacDonald's turn to smile. "She has already done so. That tis why I am anxious to see the divorce settled. I wish I could attend ye, but I must return the mules and the cart within a specified time. They can be small minded about such things, and there tis a matter of them reimbursing my receipts. Twill probably take them months." He had left the next morning and Rolfe and Kasper two days later.

Both Rolfe and Kasper took time to shave and put on their clean clothes before approaching the O'Neal ranch. Neither was sure of their reception as O'Neal had not been overly civil the first time. It was as though he had begrudged them every moment, but felt obligated by moral law to show them the grave sites.

A Mexican man held their horses while they went up the porch stairs and knocked at the door. A Mexican woman responded to their knock and directed them to wait in the foyer. Out of courtesy, they removed their hats. If there were slaves, Kasper didn't see any. That seemed strange on a cotton plantation, but felt it better to hold his tongue.

O'Neal appeared with the servant girl and narrowed his eyes. Southern hospitality vied with open dislike.

"Why have ye two returned?"

Kasper remembered that O'Neal had been annoyed with Rolfe's heavy accent, although the Irish lilt still sang in his voice.

"My sister, Mrs. Lawrence, has been rescued. She told us that Mr. Lawrence had taken his rifle, their shotgun, and all their ammunition. He also took his riding horse to the field rather than the workhorse and handed their oldest son over to the Comanche. She would like to bring charges against the man for attempted murder. When we were here previously, you mentioned that someone had seen him ride away when the Comanche attacked and that they had not followed him. Perhaps you could tell us who that was. Then we could secure a deposition from the man to present to the authorities."

Rolfe had cautioned Kasper not to mention divorce. "That man is Catholic. He is against all divorces unless the Pope grants them."

O'Neal's eyes brightened. "Yes, that is possible. Meet me in Wooden at the Justice of the Peace this afternoon. He functions as the Notary Public. I'll have the man with me. Lawrence needs to be on a handbill as a wanted man. He was a despicable neighbor and a despicable man." He turned and walked back down the hall towards a far room.

Rolfe jerked his head toward the door, stifling an itch to toss his bowie knife into the man's back. They mounted their horses and rode down the long lane past white fences holding riding horses and cattle. Wooden was but a two hour ride from here.

As they rode, Rolfe unfolded his plan. "We can ask him about the dead children again when we have someone else listening." Rolfe disliked O'Neal. He was too hate-filled and vindictive—and for what? Mrs. Lawrence or Clara had not enlightened him if there was a reason.

"O'Neal hates everything about your brother-in-law. I can't figure out why unless they were in a fight and he lost."

Kasper ducked his head and his mouth twitched.

"You know the reason. What the hell is going on, Herr Schmidt? I need to know if there's going to be a fight."

Kasper swallowed. "It seems Mr. Lawrence might have fathered a son with the current Mrs. O'Neal."

Rolfe put out his arm. "Ve stop now and jaw." German words seemed inadequate.

The men dismounted and stood next to each other letting the horses crop at the grass. "Why didn't you tell me?" Rolfe's voice had risen. "And how do you know?"

"Some laundress or like person whispered as much to my sister after O'Neal made sneering remarks about poor, white trash while she was in the store. It seems the son looked exactly like Mr. Lawrence."

"Did she see the son?"

"No, he had left the area. Anna does not know where he went."

"If that's true, why would Lawrence come back here?"

"He was unaware that such a birth had occurred. He had been wounded in 1836 during the war with Mexico for Texas's independence. Anna didn't think he'd been a participant, but someone nursed him back to health. When she confronted him, he admitted it was Mrs. O'Neal. Lawrence had left soon after he recovered. He owned land in Texas, and wanted to return here after he and Anna were married for several years. He had no idea that the woman who nursed him had married someone else and lived in the vicinity. At least that is what he told Anna.

"Anna never understood why he wished to return to Texas as he was not a farmer."

Rolfe shook his head. "He doesn't sound like much of a man. What else did Mrs. Lawrence say about the Comanche attack?"

"She suspects Mr. Lawrence may have taken personal things, but can't be certain."

"Why?"

"She said two of his books were gone from the chest in their bedroom when she was packing to leave."

Rolfe considered. "We'll head towards Wooden, but we aren't going into town until this afternoon. It's run by O'Neal. Did you notice that the General Store, Feed Store, and livery stable are all owned by an O'Neal?"

"Yes, I did." Both men had remounted.

"There could be a lot more of them. If his whole family came here, they'd pretty much stick together, no matter who was right or wrong. Don't say anything to upset O'Neal. We don't want him to change his mind."

It was not difficult to find the Notary's office. It was located beside the small bank next to a lawyer's office. The buildings were wooden, but only the bank had the false front to give an impression of a higher, more substantial building.

"Ve vait outside." In town among Southerners, Rolfe spoke his brand of English as German upset their sensibilities as much as a Mexican speaking Spanish.

O'Neal and another man rode up after they had waited about fifteen minutes. O'Neal's horse was a Tennessee Walker and he wore a grey suit topped by a white hat. The man accompanying him was dressed as a typical hand, canvas trousers, cotton shirt, boots, and an older, wider brimmed hat. His clothes were dusty, dirty, and trail worn. His horse was a mustang, with shorter, wider hindquarters for making quick turns when chasing cattle.

They dismounted and walked into the Notary's office. Another man sat chatting with the man behind the desk. He saw who it was, stood, and grabbed his hat.

"So long, Hollister, I'll see y'all tomorrow."

O'Neal looked at the man. "On your way out, get the Sheriff over here."

"Yes, sir." The man hurried out as Rolfe's blocky form was about to fill the doorway.

Hollister stood. "Mr. O'Neal, it's a pleasure to see you. May I be of service?"

"Yes, I want you to take a deposition from Mr. Allen regarding that Comanche raid a couple of years ago. Because of the woman's brother, we are finally able to prove that Lawrence is a contemptible renegade, or at least a white man working with Indians to kill his family."

Rolfe and Kasper were in time to hear the exchange. Kasper was about to comment when Rolfe nudged him and shook his head.

Hollister looked at Kasper and Rolfe. O'Neal must have realized he was neglecting form. "Mr. Hollister, this is Mr. Kasper Schmidt, the brother of the unfortunate woman held captive by the Comanche. The other is a Mr. Rolfe, his guide."

Once again Kasper received a nudge to remain silent. Hollister nodded "hello."

"Mr. Schmidt wishes to be able to press charges and save what is left of his sister's reputation." The words implied it was futile, but family loyalty overrode reality.

"Shall I wait for the sheriff, Mr. O'Neal?"

"No, he can read the document."

Paper, pen, ink, and the seal appeared from the desk drawer. Hollister nodded at Allen. "Go ahead. Write down the date, your name, and what you saw that fateful day."

"I cain't write more than my name." Allen's voice was sullen, angry at having to admit this in front of men that could read and write.

"Very well, I'll write down what you have to say. Proceed with your name first."

Allen told of how he had seen Thomas Lawrence hand a heavy bag and a rifle or shotgun to one of the Comanche warriors. Mr. Lawrence then rode away. He had left his son standing in the field and an Indian rode over and picked up the boy. Then the Comanche rode towards the Lawrence cabin.

The sheriff walked in and introductions were performed again. It was with profound relief that Kasper and Rolfe were finally outside with the signed, witnessed, and stamped deposition. They wasted no time mounting their horses.

"Shouldn't we stop for supplies?"

"Hell, no, we're getting out of here before he changes his mind. Maybe that Allen saw something, maybe not, but it won't matter in a court. We'll ride slow and steady for a mile and then we'll trot a bit."

When they finally reined in their horses, dusk was falling. Rolfe had selected a spot by one of the creeks that were in this wetter part of Texas. They could hobble their horses in the grass after watering them, and they would sleep beneath the trees.

"I'm going to get one of O'Neal's cows. We may be on his land and he owes us a meal." Rolfe rode off.

Kasper shook his head. He wasn't sure who had done the most sinning. Himself for not protesting the whole procedure when Rolfe said Allen and O'Neal might be lying or not protesting when Rolfe said he was going to steal a cow.

Chapter 26

Marriage Plans

It took one year for the divorce decree to become final. During this time, MacDonald arranged for his home to be built. By Thalian word usage, his House was his family, his abode his home. The barn, washhouse, and springhouse were also constructed. A cistern was installed just outside the springhouse so that Anna would not have to labor so hard for water. Cruz Moreno, from Schmidt's Corner, had been hired to build a rock fence around the garden plot behind the washhouse.

Three crab tree seedlings had been ordered through Kasper's store. When they arrived, the trees were transferred to larger containers, but left behind the Schmidt's Corner's general store. Cruz had installed fencing around the trees to keep the jackrabbits out. Anna had watered and tended them. Real apple trees would not do well here, but crab apples could grow almost anywhere and they made wonderful apple butter and apple jelly. She would transplant them after their marriage.

The barn and the springhouse went up first. Then the fences were built around the sides and back of the barn to create barnyards. MacDonald took to sleeping in the barn loft. He could keep an eye on the construction while he was there. Most of the time, he and Rolfe were out on the range branding and checking the cattle. Martin was old enough that he spent the weekends with them or anytime that Kasper was not conducting classes. They had driven another herd up to Chisholm, the Indian Agent in the Indian Territory.

"Too damn dangerous to go to New Orleans now, Mac. Some of them Southerners really hate Yankees, and me, they consider a Yankee. They ain't sure about du, but if du answer the question wrong or refuse to drink to sechees they ain't going to like du any better."

"What the hell is 'sechees'?"

"Dot's vhen they leave the Union."

"Ye Gods, it twill nay go Secession."

"Don't bet on it, Mac. Some are ready to do it now. Vhy do du think all that killing in Kansas?"

Anna worked with Kasper in the store, the stables, and with either Kasper or Gerde in their garden. She helped with Gerde's cleaning, laundered MacDonald's clothes, and spent any spare moment sewing clothes for both of them. She refused to take any money from MacDonald. This was her way of paying him back. MacDonald smiled. Her stubborn pride amused him, but the clothes were a better fit than his other clothes during his sojourn on Earth.

He courted Anna in accordance to the proprieties of the 1850s' mores. He did not touch her, hug her, or kiss her. At times his body would quiver whether from desire or restraint was difficult to tell for Thalians touched, they stroked, they hugged, and he was physically so close to her. The longing at times was overwhelming and sleep fled from his brain. The years of isolation at the Justine Refuge had nay been as difficult. Kreppies and Justines were nay desirable beings.

A year had passed and they planned to leave for Arles in the morning to procure the license and to be married. From there they would take the stage to Houston and a boat to New Orleans. Then they would ride a steamship up to St. Louis.

"It costs too much money, Mr. MacDonald."

"Don't ye wish to see yere fither and introduce yere new husband?"

"Of course, I do." Anna stamped her foot in frustration. "But you have worked so hard for your money and it will cost more to finish this place."

"That tis all accounted for, Mrs. Lawrence. If I canna give ye pleasure and the things ye deserve as mistress of my heart, what good tis money?"

Anna shook her head. "You might need it for something important on this ranch."

He had brought her to the ranch to see the almost completed kitchen and great room. He grabbed both of her hands in his.

"Mrs. Lawrence, how long has it been since ye have seen yere fither?"

"Almost four years."

"And how eld tis he?"

Anna winced. "He is almost 60."

"There, ye see. We may nay have this opportunity again. While we are in St. Louis, ye can see about buying a sewing machine and I twill see about one of those pumps I heard about from the freighters. That way ye twould nay need to pull up water for anything."

Anna stared at him and shook her head. The man was mad.

"Now we shall go inside. I have a surprise for ye in the kitchen."

They walked through the back door and Anna stopped.

"Mr. MacDonald, the cabinets—they—they are for my height." For a moment, all Anna could think of was the backache that resulted every time she did dishes in Gerde's kitchen. "How did you know?"

Anna ran her hands over the wooden cabinet top, marveling at its newness and the correct height. Here she would not need to stoop for kneading, for stirring, for washing dishes. If she looked to the right, she was looking out onto what would be part of the front yard. If she turned to the left, there was a corner cabinet and another small set of lower cabinets. Then came the window that looked out onto the springhouse, the fence that ran from the edge of the house, and followed the springhouse around to where one of the crab apple trees would be, and then on to the washhouse. She turned to MacDonald, her grey eyes shining, "Mr. MacDonald, I could kiss du."

It was too much for MacDonald. All the years of longing, needing the touch of another being, of holding someone close, the need of a caress all overcame his good intentions, and he gathered her into his arms, his lips finding hers with a pent up demand.

At first Anna was too startled to object and then she found herself returning the kiss, her own loneliness and loss meeting his. It lasted until she could feel the heat coming off of his hands and his body. His hands and kiss demanded more and she wasn't sure she had the strength to refuse him. Just as suddenly the kiss stopped and he held her close, swaying back and forth, and murmuring.

"My Anna, my love, I ken I must wait."

And he broke away as he almost ran for the door. "I twill get the z…horses."

She was left gasping, unsure, what should she do now? Dare she confront him? It was too improbable, too cruel, and yet he, like Mr. Lawrence, had said there would be no children. Silent tears ran through her heart and she knew what she must do. To be safe she would wait until they were back at Schmidt's Corner for Anna knew her children lived. What was inexplicable, she had seen them all in this house opening Christmas presents, but that was in the early days of her captivity and she was half mad. When a vision was true, she would have more than one. She had not seen Mr. MacDonald in that dream, nor had she ever dreamt that scene again.

Chapter 27

The Quarrel

Anna saw him coming with the buggy and hurried out, closing the door behind her. As he pulled up she climbed onto the seat and sat with her shoulders straight, her hands folded in her lap.

"Mrs. Lawrence, if I may apologize."

"Vhy? I should not have encouraged du so." She clamped her mouth shut.

"Ye did nay, but if ye prefer, I twill remain silent." Beneath his calm, MacDonald felt an unease grow. This was not the animated woman he loved.

"Ja, that vould be gut for now." She looked straight ahead not daring to look at him.

By the end of the three hour drive, MacDonald was clenching and unclenching his teeth. His futile attempts to speak, to apologize, or explain had been rebuffed; sometimes with words, but mostly silence.

At the back of the general store, MacDonald pulled up with a, "Hello the house." Before he could leave the buggy and tie off the reins, Anna was up the steps and at the door. She turned before entering the kitchen to face him.

"Mr. MacDonald, I cannot marry you. You lied to me. All of it was lies!" She clamped her lips together and dashed into the house banging the door behind her.

For a moment MacDonald could not move. Then he mounted the steps and raised his fist to pound on the door. To his surprise, Anna, shawl in hand, opened it.

"I have the right to ken why ye think I lied." He was roaring. His voice filled the house and the outside world.

"Really, Mr. MacDonald, I should not need to explain." Anger rolled through her words.

Kasper's dark head appeared in the hall doorway. Gerde was looking at them, her eyes wide.

"Ye owe me that much. I have nay kenning of what ye mean." He had managed to get control over his voice and it was back to a deep rumble.

"That cannot be true, Mr. MacDonald." Anna's teeth were almost clenched in her anger.

"Then tell me."

"I cannot in front of other people. It might put you in danger."

"Then put on yere wrap and we twill talk out here. There tis light enough for them to see us. I have pledged ye my troth, my heart, and my House. It binds me to ye. If ye continue to refuse me, everything that I have here tis yeres and I twill go elsewhere."

A solemn Anna regarded him. "I cannot take what is yours. You cannot be serious." She hesitated, knowing full well he was serious.

"Very well, Mr. MacDonald, we will talk outside."

She turned towards Kasper and Gerde. "I will return soon. He will not do anything in full view of everyone." Her comments left the couple puzzled. They could not conceive that gentle giant hurting anyone.

Anna swung the shawl over her shoulders and stepped outside. Twilight was beginning to throw a grey mantle around the world and the sun was slowly leaving the sky. She held her head high and her shoulders straight.

"We will go over by the cottonwood. If you start to yell again, everyone will hear you." She did not wait for him to grasp her arm, but marched down the three steps.

He was beside her within seconds, his long legs easily keeping pace with hers.

She stopped by the tree and looked up at him. Her grey eyes were calm, her face betrayed nothing.

"When did I lie to ye?"

"The lie was the reason you gave for not having children. I knew when you hugged me in the kitchen. I heard your two hearts. I will not marry another man with two hearts. One who says there will be no children and when there are children the man hates us and tries to kill us." Determination was in her voice and brightening her eyes. "Why didn't you tell me the truth?" The last words were hurled at him.

For a moment MacDonald stared at her, his mouth open, until he remembered to draw in a breath and speak. To Anna's surprise, his voice was a low, awed whisper.

"Yere Thomas Lawrence had two hearts? Dear Gar, woman, ye twere married to Toma."

"I was married to Mr. Thomas Lawrence."

"If he had red hair and copper colored eyes with gold rings around the pupils, his name tis Toma." His voice was back to normal.

Anna's lashes blinked over the grey eyes, and she drew in a deep breath. "What else is a lie? Have you told me your real name?"

He hesitated. "I have nay. Like Toma, I was hiding my true identity for my name makes nay sense in this world. I am Llewellyn, Maca of Don." He gave a slight bow.

"This world? Don't you mean country? Where are you two from?"

Bitterness was in his voice as MacDonald explained. "He tis a Justine from the planet Justine."

"That is nonsense."

He continued. "My fither twas a Justine and my mither a Thalian from the planet Thalia. The Justine on the ship I came in planned to abandon me here on Earth, but his plans went awry. While we searched for Toma, the inhabitants of this planet killed him. I twas left in control of the ship. I can take ye to it and prove everything I have said."

Anna was shaking her head. "Mr. MacDonald, that is worse than a fairy tale."

"Does it sound so foolish if I tell ye that in addition to his two hearts, yere husband could control certain people with his mind or that he had the ability to go into other people's minds and know what they were thinking?"

The anger left Anna's face and she was silent for a moment. "He tried to go into my mind, and I wouldn't let him," she whispered.

"How did you know?" Her voice was strong again on the last phrase.

"I told ye. He tis a Justine, and ye are one of those that he could nay control. Why did ye go to Texas with him if ye kenned what he could do?"

Anna stamped her foot. "I was being a good Frau. Now do you see why I won't marry you? I will not go through years of no love, no conversation, except suddenly the thought occurs and then there is another baby, and silence grows in the house because you are certain that the baby can't be yours. Then when you realize that the baby is yours, you will view it as a monster; something to be destroyed. You fear that if people know you have two hearts they will not understand and try to kill you."

"My darling heart, if the Justines are wrong about the abilities of a mutant being able to fither a child and there tis a baby, I twill be the happiest man in Texas. Yere reasoning that I twould stay away from the marriage bed tis wrong. Thalians are known for their, uh, frequency in pursuit of happiness." He was almost stuttering. How to put the Thalians' enjoyment of sex into words that would not offend Anna eluded him.

"I twill seek ye in the bed every evening if that tis yere desire." He blurted the words in his own manner.

"What?" Anna's eyes widened. "Mr. MacDonald, how can I believe you?"

"Anna, Mrs. Lawrence, I have nay lied to ye. Ye twill be part of my House and all that I have tis yeres. If ye dinna marry me, I twill sign over my land and home to ye and ye twill live in my heart forever. All that I ask is that I be allowed passageway to the foothills."

"I do not want your land or your money…" Her voice stopped. "Why the foothills?"

"That tis where I have hidden the vessel that brought me here."

She stared at him. "Mr. MacDonald, do you realize how dangerous your position is if that is the truth?"

"It does nay matter, if ye believe me."

"Mr. MacDonald, I do not want your land." She stamped her foot in exasperation.

"Then what do ye want?"

"I want a husband that loves me, cherishes me, attends church…"

Instead of waiting for her to finish, MacDonald swooped her up into his arms and kissed her, pulling her closer, tasting her lips, her neck, and then again on her lips. Anna forgot to fight him and suddenly she was kissing him back, feeling the warmth of him, the hardness. This is my man ran through her mind and she tightened her arms around him. Finally he released her and set her down, and then he did a surprising thing.

He laid his head on her right shoulder and made a "tsk" sound in her ear, and then his head was on her left shoulder and the same sound in her left ear.

"That tis one of my traditions." He was smiling broadly.

"Mr. MacDonald, we should not be kissing until we are married and even then not in public."

She took a deep breath and continued. "Not telling the truth is very much like lying. Why didn't you tell me?"

His hands still rested on her shoulders as though fearing she would run from him. "I did nay tell ye about the two hearts for fear I twould frighten ye away. If ye told Kasper, he twould tell Mrs. Schmidt, and she twould tell someone else. The world twould ken and there twould be those who twould wish to lock me up or put me on exhibit. That twas the fear that stilled my tongue. I did nay ken how to tell ye that we canna have wee ones. According to Justine biology, I am a mutant; like a hybrid, a mule. There tis nay seed."

"Mr. Lawrence made some ridiculous statement about not being able to have children, but we had children, and three of them still live. What will you do when we find them?"

"If we are so fortunate, they twill be part of my heart and my House. If they wish, I twill be fither to them and adopt them. The inheritance of my House twill be theirs."

Dusk was upon them, twilight having fled. The night was becoming grayer and soon the moon would begin to cast silver light through the clouds.

"This thing, this vessel that you came in, what is it?"

"It tis a spaceship, a craft made for transport among the stars, but for now it remains hidden."

Anna was shaking her head again. "How can I believe you? I want to, but it all sounds—sounds like magic, like the work from the hands of God. That cannot be."

"It tis nay the work of God. It tis the work of beings using their intelligence. Thalians are not as advanced as the Justines in their knowledge, but we too had spacecraft."

"If they are so powerful, will they not come again?"

"They canna. My mither destroyed their planet and most of the Justines."

Anna's eyes widened. Stamping her foot conveyed nothing to this man and did not stop his strange tale. "See, the story grows bigger and more, more… reason says I cannot believe you, but I want to believe you."

Llewellyn drew in a deep breath. "Aye, but if ye twere to go with me, I can prove how true everything tis that I have told ye.

"I love ye, Anna Lawrence, and I wish ye by my side as my counselor, my wife. To ye I have pledged my heart."

"You tell me the rest. Then I decide if I will go with you and see if what you say is true." Neither one seemed to realize they were facing each other, gripping the other's hands as though fearing the other would let go.

He let out a sigh and continued. "If ye twill let me explain without interrupting, I shall try to tell ye everything.

"There twas a war waged by the Justines and their allies, the Kreppies, against Thalia. We had the Brendons from another planet as our allies. The Justines destroyed our war fleet and killed over a million Thalians. Then they attacked Thalia and Brendon. More of us died. In my land, women fight as Warriors the same as men. My mither twas one of the best. They exiled her to a barren asteroid. She managed to beguile her Justine guard, kill him and the Kreppie guards before escaping in a Justine vessel. She then had to teach herself the finer points of handling the Justine spaceship. While she did so she realized she was pregnant. I dinna ken how she managed, but she was able to birth me alone and take me to her brither on Thalia along with a crystal explaining everything. Then she drove the spaceship into the Justine planet. Most of the Justines died that day, but enough survived that they established a colony on an asteroid and put the Kreppies in charge of guarding Thalia and Brendon. When I was twenty-one, I fought in the dinner arena and won. They discovered I had two hearts. The Justines condemned me to isolation from Thalia and then abandonment when I was mature. That tis why I twas on that ship. I twas to be left here to die."

"But why? If you could not have children, how would your being there matter?"

A small smile twisted one corner of his mouth. "In their science, beings from two different planets canna exist. That I existed twas an abomination to them."

"Mr. MacDonald, have you told me everything?"

"Nay quite, for if somehow we could return to Thalia, ye twould be Mistress of Don and help rule my land."

"Now you are going to tell me you are King of Thalia, yes?" Scorn was in her voice and she tried to extract her hands, but he stepped closer.

"Nay, I am nay a king. The land of Don tis a continent, but I am the last of Don's ruling House. I am from a line of kinemen; that tis cattlemen here. All Thalians are considered Warriors."

It was Anna's turn to breathe in deeply. "And your king would welcome you back?"

"There tis nay king. Thalia tis ruled by a Council of the Realm, but that too tis under the control of the Justines. I canna return till I learn to handle the spaceship."

"And if I don't want to leave here, then what? Am I to be abandoned?"

"Nay! Ye are my heart." MacDonald's voice started to rise in irritation. With effort, he brought it under control.

"Let me explain. It twill take seventy-five or eighty years for me to learn the math and the system. There tis much I have to learn and there tis nay here to teach me. Kasper has taken me as far as he tis able with the math that he kens.

"If ye still doubt my words, my offer to take ye to the *Golden One* and show ye everything that I have said tis true still stands. In truth, I twould like for ye to see it and see how we lived."

"Mr. MacDonald, who would be with us on that—that *Golden One*?"

"Mrs. Lawrence, nay twould be with us."

"Mr. MacDonald, I do not trust myself alone with you. I will trust that you have told me the truth."

"What made ye change yere mind?"

Anna looked straight at him, her chin lifted. "Because, Mr. MacDonald I love you. I will go with you after we are married."

Once again MacDonald swept her up into his arms. This time Anna was quick enough to put her hands on his chest.

"Mr. MacDonald, you are taking liberties with me. The world already thinks me a shameless hussy. When we are married, then we can do that."

A wide smile lit his face. "Mrs. Lawrence, do ye ken what ye just said? Does that mean we are going to Arles in the morning?"

"Yes, Mr. MacDonald, I will be ready at four o'clock."

"May I at least hug ye?"

Anna's eyes lit up. "Yes, Mr. MacDonald, and then you may walk me to the door."

Chapter 28

Marriage

"Mr. MacDonald, you are supposed to let me undress and then return to the room."

"My love, why twould I leave?"

They were in the newest and biggest hotel in Arles. The hotel boasted of its large rooms and comforts, but MacDonald doubted it. Anna, however, did not wish to spend their wedding night on the ground. To her it would be like the Comanche. That the Comanche had a comfortable bed with coverings never impressed her.

The wedding ceremony had been preformed by the Justice of Peace, Vincent Mallory. The Rolfe family and the Schmidt family attended them. Mr. Jackson and his son Tom were keeping watch over Schmidt's Corner.

MacDonald paid for the meal afterward and listened patiently to all the well-wishes and blessings. He wanted to be alone with Anna and now that they were, he was not going to adhere to the moralistic standards of this Earth. He doubted if all men did that anyway. It did nay sound natural.

She stared at MacDonald in surprise.

"Mr. MacDonald, it is not proper."

"Bah! I have waited too long for this. The courtship twas yere world's rules, but here we have a room and privacy. We should be able to bed by my world's customs even if there tis nay a proper cleansing room."

Anna swallowed. She wasn't sure she wanted to know his idea of a proper cleansing room, but he was right. They were in the privacy of their own room. What difference did it make if she were without clothes?

"We have waited for over a year, Anna, and ye should call me Zeb, or Llewellyn, or Maca, anything but Mr. MacDonald."

Anna was debating in her own mind how to address this issue. If she called him by his given name, she might slip and call him that in public.

He stepped forward and his arms were around her. "Lassie, dinna make me rip the clothes off ye." He bent his head and found her lips, his huge hands trying to work the buttons of her dress. He almost gnashed his teeth at the delay. Anna pushed at his chest.

"Zeb, I can do that a lot faster."

"Aye." He began throwing off his clothes. Anna tried to reach over and put them neatly on the chair.

"Woman, I twill hang them. Ye get out of those horrible, restricting clothes." The word horrible brought Anna up short.

"I will have you know I am an excellent seamstress. There is nothing horrible about my clothes."

"Ye Gods, they cover ye completely and there are layers of them. It should be a one or two piece form-fitting suit."

"Mr. MacDonald!"

He grinned at her. "Remember, I am Zeb." He sat on the bed and pulled off his boots.

"Yere buttons are too much for me and those buttons on yere shoes look even more frustrating."

Anna sat in the chair and used the hook to undue her shoe buttons. It wasn't as rapid as MacDonald pulling off his boots, but once she was finished she stood. She still had three petticoats and hose to remove. She turned her back as a last attempt at modesty. It was futile.

Llewellyn was wed and this was to be a Thalian evening. He began slowly, but found the long years had built up both fire and desire. Anna felt his arms around her, his hands on her breasts and then he turned her to him, pulling her close, his tongue licking at her neck, and she felt his hardness against her, pressing, demanding. How could the man be so rock hard? She felt his hands slip down to her back cheeks and fit around them as he lifted her up against him. Then he turned towards the bed and she could feel the independent movement from below. She almost expected him to throw her on the bed, but it was a gentle lowering, his right hand moving down below, touching nerves she didn't know she possessed. A musky smell rose off him, beguiling, heady, yet unlike anything she had ever experienced.

The first time went far too rapidly and she heard his ragged breathing.

"Wait, my darling, I twill be back. I did nay give ye pleasure that time."

Anna ran the words over in her mind. What was he talking about? Mr. Lawrence never was with her more than once and it would be years in between the next time he exercised his rights as a husband.

Zeb was running his index finger down her face, over her lips, and then he began to touch all the other areas, and Anna found herself responding as he slipped inside of her again. This time it culminated with a loud "aaaAAAHH" coming from deep within Anna's most inner self.

MacDonald clapped his hand over her mouth. "Ye Gods woman, ye twill have people in the entire county thinking I am killing ye."

Anna was shaking and gasping as he pulled his hand away. He kissed her cheek, then her shoulder, holding her body up against his. At last she quieted and touched his face with wonder.

"Is that the way it is supposed to be?"

"Of course, my counselor."

"Why do you call me that?"

"Tis what we twould call our wedded mate on Thalia." They were whispering in case other guests were now on this floor or in the other rooms.

"I have been so lonely, the ache inside twas, at times, nay bearable. Thalians need to touch, to bed, and nay could I do that here."

"What? You are a man. They go…" Anna paused, "to certain places. Are you saying you did not do that?"

"Nay, but the times were few, and most lassies there are too small. In the first years here, I tried to stay away from too many Earth beings. I needed to learn more about the land and the way the beings here live."

He was stroking her face, her arms, her legs and suddenly, she realized he had revived for yet another time. Anna stared at him in wonder as his hardness plunged into her.

* * *

She was exhausted as he pulled her upward. "Come, sweet one, we must use their idea of soap and water. In the morning I twill get more ere we leave on the stage."

Chapter 29

The Journey

Both MacDonald and Anna were aching from the bumps and jolts of the stagecoach when they stepped onto the street in Houston. MacDonald was again consumed with wanting, but nothing, absolutely nothing would have induced him to use one of the small rooms at the stage stops. Anna was bleary-eyed from lack of sleep. She did not trust the other passengers and there was so little time to run to the outhouses and eat. The water for washing hands in the basins was none too clean. She had gritted her teeth and used it anyway on the theory that at least the soap was strong.

MacDonald had been to this city before and he hailed a small cart pulled by a black horse that looked like he had been worked too many years. The black man driving the horse looked about the same. His white hair poked out of holes in his hat creating a halo. The man looked at MacDonald, Anna, the steamer trunk, and decided to be honest. He wasn't sure he could lift that trunk or if his horse was capable of pulling such a load. Those two people were not normal size. Giants, his mind told him.

"Sir, y'all best hail another cab or first check into the hotel."

"We are but going to the waterfront to purchase tickets to St. Louis."

"Yus, sir." The man alighted to heave the trunk into the back. MacDonald had already placed it in there.

They had just enough time to go from the stage line in Houston to the waterfront and book passage on a steamer to New Orleans. MacDonald hefted the steamer trunk and guided her up the gangplank to the main deck. She barely noticed the smell of the sea, the piled up bales of cotton and the oil smell coming from them. Once they were in their cabin, Anna revived.

"I've never been on a ship. Does everyone get seasick?"

"Nay, but then this tis nay really the ocean. We are in the Gulf of Mexico and twill go directly to New Orleans. If a storm twere to come in, the waters could be rough, but that does nay happen this time of the year."

"How did you find that out?"

"Herman and I twould travel to St. Louis with our furs. He and Mrs. Rolfe lived there and the people in St. Louis kenned the way of the Mississippi and the Gulf."

"Ach, ja, I had even met Mrs. Rolfe at church before they married. I did not know then we would be neighbors."

A horn blew, then a whistle, and they felt the movement of the ship. "We have some time ere they serve the supper. This tis nay one of the fancy steamers we twill board in New Orleans, but, Mrs. MacDonald, twould ye care to take a turn on the deck or a turn in bed?"

She smiled at him. "Mr. MacDonald, I did not know you were so formal."

"Formal be damned woman." His white teeth flashed and he began disrobing. "This shall be a trip we remember."

Anna could not argue with him. Work would be waiting for them when they returned and his work might take him away for long periods of time. Once they were in New Orleans they would take a riverboat up to St. Louis. There Mr. MacDonald planned to rent a buggy and horses for the drive to Papa's farm. She felt MacDonald was spending too much money, but she wanted to see her father. It would probably be the last time in her life. Letters from Kasper and Gerde to various family members were packed in their trunk. For them it was a trip that would never happen.

That night after the love making, MacDonald had started to roll to the side and Anna rolled with him. She put her head on his chest and hugged. Somehow she had to convey how much she loved him and how safe she felt with him. That in this marriage they were truly one flesh.

His arms tightened around her. "Anna, my love, do ye ken what ye have just given me?"

She raised herself enough to look at him. "What?" I've done nothing different she thought.

"Thalians can transfer emotions between each other by hugging or touching. Just now I felt yere love for me from here," and one forefinger touched her forehead, "and from here." This time the forefinger touched the area of her heart. "Tis a sensation denied me all these years."

* * *

The pier in St. Louis was crammed with goods and laborers scurrying to unload or load. The smells were different as the bales and bales of cotton were absent. The odors of corn, oats, wheat, hops, wood, coal, iron, and hemp predominated. Farms and factories from states in the Midwest and those in the Northeast had sent their merchandise to be distributed southward. The grain, goods, and people were loaded unto all types of river craft to make the trip down the huge river. Once again MacDonald hailed a vehicle to take them to a hotel.

"Shouldn't we just rent a buggy and go to my father's home?"

"Nay, first I wish to show ye some of St. Louis, and mayhap, ye can order that sewing machine ye want." He smiled at her.

"And I wish to be someplace where it tis nay so crowded. Dinna ye say yere fither had five children?"

"Ja, but they are expecting us." Anna was already calculating the cost in her mind. There was no controlling this man.

"We twill go tomorrow or the next day."

The steamer was placed in the back of the buggy. "Once we are checked into the hotel, we shall go by the American Fur Company's mart. It tis something I wish to show ye. There are cobblers located in that area to make decent boots and shoes for the two of us. They twill be ready for us when we leave."

The room was much larger than the cabin and MacDonald gave a huge sigh. "The bed tis nay large enough, but at least we twill nay be twisted up like a coiled rope."

Anna realized that he meant the beds were small for her also. They had ordered a special bed frame for their bedroom in Texas. She planned to make the mattress with heavy cotton batting. Until then, a straw tick would do.

For MacDonald the fur trading market was a disappointment. The smells of oil and tanned furs, woolen blankets, gear of all kinds made from leather, cotton, twine, iron, wool clothing, bolts of cheap cotton were there, but he no longer knew any of the clerks running to and fro and somehow they did not seem as frantic as a few years ago.

"Come, we twill visit a cobbler, find a place to order a sewing machine, and dine before retiring. That way we shall be able to leave early in the morning." He paused.

"I forgot that ye lived here too. Is there ought that ye wish to see?"

"No, nothing except the church, but we'll attend that Sunday."

They passed out into the bright sunshine. A drunken man reeling down the street stopped in front of them.

Tasker Thomas had been on the sidelines of the fur trade. When it ended he had become a laborer on the docks and continued to blow any pay on booze. His pate was bald and his teeth few. His clothes showed that he spent far more on drink than on them. He took one look at MacDonald and bellowed.

"Hey, Mac, where yu been? Aint seen yu in a coon's age." He swayed back and forth grinning at them. "Hell, beggin' yore pardon, ma'am," for he had seen the annoyance cross MacDonald's face, "I heered yu and Rolfe either got killed off by the Injuns or were still huntin' fur in Mexico. It's me, Tasker Thomas. Used to do some packin' on mules into the rendezvous. Yu couldn't spare a few coins for the old days, now could yu?"

MacDonald didn't remember the man and the rum smell was almost overpowering, but he smiled and pulled out a couple of coins to drop in the man's hand.

"Aye, that I do for an acquaintance from the eld days. Friend Rolfe and I are now ranchers. Good day to ye." With that he grasped Anna's arm and they marched to the nearest cobblers shop.

Thomas stared after them and shrugged. Damn trappers. They always did have a high and mighty opinion of themselves. He stared at his bottle. Damn, almost empty. He stared at his hand holding two half dimes. Just enough for another drink. He staggered down the street in the other direction and almost ran into a woman charging out of a store with a bundle wrapped in brown paper and tied with string. Only someone this big couldn't be a woman, could it? But it wore skirts.

He stepped down into the street to take a better look. For a moment his eyes cleared and it was like looking at Mac. Straight dark hair, 'course hers was covered by some hat that didn't fit right, the same square face with the straight nose, the upper lip thin, but the bottom lip full. Her upper body was outlined by the tight blouse. The woman had biceps on her like a man. Hell, bigger than a man's.

"Hey, lady, I just saw somebody who looks just like yu, but he had on trousers. Bet if yu had 'em on, yu'd look just like a man." This was so funny he began laughing and slapping his knee.

The woman brought up her free left arm in a huge sweeping arc and swatted him to the side like he was an annoying insect. He landed in the mud rutted street, scrambling for his lost bottle, hiccupping and cursing.

For her part, she stepped to the wagon, placed her foot on the board, and boosted herself up on the seat with the driver.

"To home, Charles."

"Yes, Missus Gordon."

This was the finest job he and his wife Ruth had ever had. It didn't matter that his name was Charlie and not Charles and that Mrs. Gordon referred to a house as home or rolled her r's. She could use any words she wanted. She paid decent wages and provided a house to live in. He and Ruth had saved enough to buy a small home and rent it out. If Mrs. Gordon ever quit running a fancy place for men to bring women, he and Ruth would still have a house to live in. Mrs. Gordon could talk as strange as she liked.

Chapter 30

Memories

It had not taken long for MacDonald to haggle with the stable man over the cost of a buggy and two horses for one week. They were on the road to Papa Schmidt's place before seven o'clock. Anna still remembered the route out of St. Louis. She kept up a running commentary on the people she had known, pointing out the different trees and flowers growing by the roadside and tales of where she had grown up before arriving in this country.

The miles clopped away. The nearer they came, the less Anna spoke until she became silent for her memories of her early years were rushing back and overwhelmed her mind.

Papa had cleared the land in 1839. She had become the de facto woman of the house for her father and brother just as she had been in the homeland. To her horror, Papa married the twenty-year-old Johanna Polzien early the next year. There was an immediate clash as to whether Anna still ran Johann Schmidt's household or Johanna. Of course, Papa had sided with his young wife.

Anna had been studying from the books Kasper brought home from school: Latin, algebra, novels, and English. When a handsome, red-haired teacher at the St. Louis University proposed, she had not hesitated. No one thought there was anything wrong with a seventeen-year-old woman marrying someone who claimed to be thirty-five. Anna was puzzled when she heard his two hearts, but said nothing. She was unprepared for his cold, icy fury when he learned she was pregnant.

It was a shock when she felt him probing her mind. She stood stunned as he pointed his right index finger at her and intoned his words.

"Tell me who you committed adultery with so that we can divorce. You will not pass off a primitive Earth being as my child. Who was it?"

His mind clashed with hers and she felt arcing points of pain within her head. Anna wet her lips. "How can you say such things?" She shook her head and her hurt was replaced with a raging anger. It was like she threw him out of her mind and threw up bricks to block him.

"I have been with no one else. Don't you dare try to do that to me again! It's foul. It's wrong and it hurts."

For a moment Mr. Lawrence stared at her and then slammed out of the house.

He had not returned until well after midnight. Anna was not sure where he slept, but it was not in their bed. She had prayed for God to forgive her temper, but she had felt so violated. How could someone go into another's mind and try to command them to speak? Did it have to do with the two hearts? When they first married, she thought it was a flaw like the calves with two heads. Now she wasn't sure. What had he meant by primitive Earth being? Is that how he thought of her? She had been puzzled that he had been with her but once since they wed. She knew her father and Johanna had used the marriage bed more than that. Her room had been right above theirs. She was not certain, however, how frequently man and wife should be together like that.

The surprising thing was that she had enjoyed it. This was something else she wasn't sure should be, but there was no one to ask. Her mother had died in childbirth when Anna and Kasper were seven.

The next morning, Mr. Lawrence did not speak to her and did not again until after the child was born. Divorce was not an option. He could not prove she committed adultery and there was no other reason the law would grant a divorce. Anna spent her pregnancy banging things around. She would berate him for not speaking and he would leave for most of the evening. She never knew what he did or where he went, but he did not return reeking of liquor.

He did hire a midwife. The delivery took but seven hours.

"What a beautiful little girl you have, Frau Lawrence."

Tante Bertha's round face beamed as she laid the baby in her arms.

Margareatha Louise Lawrence was baptized one month later. Mr. Lawrence did not attend. She had been horrified to find out he was an atheist.

"I do not give credence to superstition by attending primitive rites."

He was just as horrified to hear the two hearts in Margareatha's chest and see the golden circles around the pupils of her copper eyes. For months he walked around with a frown on his face, deep in thought. His habits changed and he did not leave the house at night.

It wasn't until Margareatha was three years old that Mr. Lawrence returned to their bedroom. He had resumed teaching Anna mathematics and English grammar. He considered German too guttural. "English is completely devoid of reason, but at least it does not grate on one's ears." Anna no longer cared about his opinions, but she wanted to learn.

His reaction to her second pregnancy was one of bewilderment. The coldness of a loveless marriage descended upon them. He spent more and more time at the college and library studying and writing notes in his cryptic language. Anna didn't care. She had enough friends now to realize this was not a marriage. It was not like those where women were beaten, but there were marriages where women and men loved each other. Anna was too proud to admit the loneliness in her marriage to anyone but her twin.

She gave this baby the name of Daniel Anson Lawrence. "If du do not claim him, at least he knows he is the son of von of us." Mr. Lawrence insisted she use English to speak in their home. When he was gone, Anna ignored the edict. Daniel had dark hair and his eyes remained grey like hers. There was but one heart in his chest.

Their marriage remained the same as before. He refused to communicate with her and spent his time studying manuscripts and heavy tomes. Kasper was taking the last of his courses to prepare him for Concordia Seminary. She rarely saw him. At times it was a relief to return to her father's farm with the children and help with the planting or putting up the vegetables. The yard around her house was not large enough to produce anything. Mr. Lawrence insisted they were not to live like the lesser beings. It frightened her when he spoke in those terms. She did defy him by having Daniel baptized and attending church with the children.

She could name each time Mr. Lawrence behaved as a husband. The winter cold of late 1849 and early 1850 necessitated his return to their bed for shared warmth. A sudden warm snap brought forth his manhood. In April, she had an announcement.

"Mr. Lawrence, I am pregnant again."

His face became immobile. "Are you certain?"

"Ja, three months it has been now."

"Learn to phrase your sentences correctly." He rose and left the house.

Lorenz Adolph was born the last week of October. He and Daniel looked alike, but in his chest beat two hearts.

Mr. Lawrence became white-faced with the news. He did not return for two weeks.

The children and house kept Anna busy enough that his coldness and absence was not bothersome. Lorenz was the amazement. He spoke and walked at nine months. His temper tantrums (according to Kasper) were on a par with hers as a child. His hair remained black and curly like hers and his eyes remained a grey color. By the time he was three, he was trying to beat Daniel at games and loved playing the game War with his Uncle Kasper. Mr. Lawrence once again visited their marriage bed.

The inevitable occurred.

"Mr. Lawrence, I am with child."

He spun on his heel and remained absent for three weeks. When he returned, he made his announcement.

"When you are strong enough after bearing this child, we will leave for Texas. I have land there."

That night, Anna had written to her brother. She sealed the envelope and on the outside she wrote: To be opened upon verification of my death.

Chapter 31

The Schmidt Farm

"My beautiful little girl, you have suffered so much. Your hair is whiter than mine."

Johann Schmidt had returned from the fields and enfolded Anna in a bear hug. The man stood six feet four and had the stocky farmer's build. At sixty-three he was still solid and could see without glasses. His hair was grey, but abundant.

For a moment they stood with arms wrapped around each other. Then Johann bent and kissed her cheek and Anna rose on tiptoe to kiss his cheek.

"Come, Papa, you must meet my husband."

MacDonald was standing just behind them, his amused brown eyes surveying the scene.

Johann looked at MacDonald's chin and then lifted his eyes upward.

"Papa, this is my husband, Zebediah L. MacDonald. Mr. MacDonald, this is my papa, Mr. Johann Schmidt."

The two men shook hands. Anna performed the introduction in German and Johann used German also. "It's not often I have to look up at a man."

A smile broke MacDonald's face. "And it is not often that I meet a man that is almost as large as I."

"You are a farmer?"

"Rancher."

"And what is the difference? You raise cattle. You have to grow crops to feed them."

"They are range cattle, longhorns, they eat prairie grass. Anna is insisting we purchase a milk cow so for that we will need to raise hay."

"Don't you fatten them before driving them into town?"

"Longhorns aren't that good for tallow and there is no market for meat in the closest town, as other ranchers live closer. My neighboring rancher and I have driven herds as far as New Orleans and up into the Indian Territory for the reservation. The cattle eat grass on the way."

"How can you get a decent price for them?"

"The price is decent enough. The ones we sell in Texas are for bones. The ones we drive to the reservation or New Orleans are slaughtered for meat. The U.S. government has a set price, but longhorn meat is lean and it goes to the poorer butcher shops in New Orleans. That city is so big they need meat. They're not too fond of Yankees, and that is pretty much what Friend Rolfe and I are considered. We don't stay. It's probably just as well, for then our money isn't wasted on high living."

Johann smiled. "Come in, come in, and meet my Frau and what children are there. Emil is putting away my team, and then I must finish chores."

The Schmidt's dinner table was huge and piled with food from the garden. Chickens had been butchered for the occasion. Meat was rarely eaten except at winter butchering time for there was no way to keep it other than salting, making corned beef, or canning. Ice was too expensive. Pigs were used more for meat than beef. Pork could be smoked, made into sausage, and pickled. The sausage kept best deep in crock jars, and sealed with rendered lard or in winter stuffed into the intestines and strung in an unheated room.

Johanna rang the bell for dinner. She was displeased when Anna had appeared to help the last half-hour. Part of Johanna was relieved to see her alive, but alarmed that once again someone other than her children would make claims on the Schmidt farm when Johann died. She was twenty years younger. The man was in his sixties. He wouldn't live much longer.

She and Johann had six children, five of them living, and she was expecting the next one. Anna was acting like she ran things, exclaiming over her mother's dishes. Johanna's lips were compressed as she rang the bell again.

"Dinner."

Everyone trooped into the dining room. The table was heaped with the chickens, gravy, mashed potatoes, sliced tomatoes, corn on the cob, butter, homemade dark bread, pickled onions and cucumbers, two pitchers of milk, one smaller pitcher of cream, three different types of jams and jellies, and a desert made with mulberries, crumbs, and sugar.

Johann led the family in prayer and the passing of food began. Each one began talking about the events during the years they were separated.

"Kasper's store is prospering. There are more people in Schmidt's Corner now and the neighboring ranchers also buy supplies there."

"Trinity Evangelical has a new Vicar. He needs to mature." Johann was surprised that the man was thirty years his junior. It was unsettling. "He preaches if Pastor Walther is gone. I can read just as well as he does."

"But you can't read in Latin, Herr Schmidt." Johanna had nothing but reverence for the Vicar.

"Or Greek, Frau Schmidt, but if Kasper were still here, he could do that."

"Kasper decided to get married instead of becoming a pastor and waiting to marry." Johanna sniffed. The implication was clear. Kasper had erred. She still resented the money spent for his education.

"They are very happy." Anna would tolerate no aspersions against her twin. "And Hans is growing rapidly."

"Do you think you will study to be a pastor?" MacDonald asked the young man seated across from him.

Emil was tall, gangly, and sour-faced. He'd spent his time eating as rapidly as possible and ignoring MacDonald and Anna.

"No, I don't waste my time like Kasper."

"That was not wasted time. He even lent me his books."

Emil glared at Anna. "Why? You're a woman. You don't need school."

"Emil, that is enough." Johann raised his voice to his son. "Everyone needs to know how to read God's Word and stop the shopkeepers from gouging them."

Emil looked doubtful and spooned more potatoes onto his plate.

Anna helped with the dishes when the men left the dining room. MacDonald had a set look to his face.

At three o'clock Anna walked out to the field carrying a wicker basket filled with sandwiches, cookies, and water. They were putting the sheaves into stacks. First two were stood upright and leaned together, two more leaned against their sides, and another spread out over the top to shed water if it should rain or sprinkle before the thresher arrived. The horse drawn thresher was due Monday morning. Neighbors would come to help bring in the sheaves to feed them into the machine.

MacDonald did a quick calculation. He was hot, dirty, sweat-drenched, and itchy from the oat chaff. If they stayed, he and Anna would both work physically harder than they would on the ranch. Emil's animosity had not abated. He had skimmed Johanna's mind enough to know that she resented Anna and anything that Anna said or did. The dislike between the two was almost palpable. He had not realized this situation would develop when he agreed to stay overnight. Baths for everyone might not be a Saturday night ritual here.

He smiled at Anna and gratefully swallowed the water before passing it to his father-in-law.

"I did nay expect ye."

"Ach, Johanna was fussing with tonight's meal, and preparations for church tomorrow. I thought it might be best to give a hand this way." Her mouth was barely moving and her eyes were hard.

"I think we should go into town this evening and rent a hotel room. The church tis in St. Louis. I could take everyone to dinner at a restaurant."

"Mr. MacDonald, wouldn't that be very expensive?"

"There twill still be enough to buy ye that sewing machine." The smile was back on his face. "We twill order baths for this evening and bathe in privacy."

He turned to Johann and switched to German. "Would you like to accompany us into town and dine there?"

Johann stared at him. "A very kind offer, but we must be up early in the morning for the chores." He was thinking that Anna had married a spendthrift. She was apt to be back with them in a few years and then how would he placate his Frau?

Anna was thinking almost the same about Llewellyn's spending habits, but the thought of being away from Johanna was appealing. Being alone with her husband was also a pleasant thought. At least they would not be paying for everyone's dinner.

Chapter 32

Home

"There it tis." MacDonald pointed to the two story house on the prairie. The springhouse and barn were also completed. A wide smile split his face. "We shall stop and look before going into Schmidt's Corner for our supplies."

They had arrived back in Arles on August 20, 1858 after a six-week honeymoon of visits, shopping, and traveling. Their first stop had been at the lumberyard in Arles to settle for any work done beyond what he had paid for. Elias Clifford, the owner, explained they had hit a snag and could not bring in anymore doors or lumber for the upstairs until September. Influenza across the nation had slowed deliveries. MacDonald decided to wait until then before ordering any more work. He and Clifford did not get along, but business was business in this land. He wanted to ascertain what work still needed to be done. Clifford was in a foul mood as the lumber and other materials should have been freighted in at the first of the month. Influenza had struck some of the townspeople here. The heavy, early rains were making the situation worse.

MacDonald had recalculated his funds and decided that more fencing around the barn and a place in the barn for the milk cow Anna wanted was more important than buying doors for unfinished bedrooms upstairs. Anna needed the milk cow for her baking, butter, buttermilk, and clabbered milk.

"What if we have children? We will need it then."

"My love..." and he stopped when he saw her lips tightening. Anna won. He had purchased a milk cow in Arles. Delivery of the fencing was set for seven days in the future and the cow for a week later.

As they topped the rise to the Rearing Bear ranch the sight of their white two-story home, washhouse, springhouse, their own barn, and corral around the east side of the barn brought smiles to their faces. They tied the team to the porch rail, and MacDonald used the skeleton key to unlock the door. Hand-in-hand they wandered through the downstairs.

"Oh, look, the cabinets. They are perfect." Anna was beaming. "I cannot wait to put my dishes up there. And look, look, Zeb, the stove has a reservoir for keeping water warm." She was twirling around, almost dancing when MacDonald pulled her in close.

"This makes me wish we had the bed made now. Are ye sure the floor will nay serve?"

"It will not." But in her happiness she smiled at him. "We must make Schmidt's Corner before nightfall, and then bring all our things from their storeroom here."

"Ye, my love, are a slave driver."

A quick check showed that it was the upstairs that still needed the doors. Everything was framed and the rooms of the downstairs walls were plastered. All the windows had been installed. He would need to talk with Rolfe about bringing in more funds.

The trip into Schmidt's Corner took three hours. They had expected Martin to come running as he always did, but he must have been doing chores. MacDonald pulled the horses up behind the store, and Anna stepped down from the buggy.

"Ye are supposed to let me help ye."

"Ach, when do I need help getting out of a buggy at my brother's house?" She ran up the steps and knocked at the door.

"Kasper, Gerde, we are back."

A smiling Kasper opened the door as she was speaking. "We heard you pull up." He waved at MacDonald.

"Please put the horses in my stable. Herr Rolfe is not well."

Anna's eyes widened. "What happened?"

"The freighters came through. One of them had influenza. He's buried in the graveyard. Jesse was down for a month, but is back on his feet. Then Herr Rolfe came down with it. He is recovering, but Frau Rolfe is exhausted as Olga has it now."

"What about the two boys?"

"So far they have shown no symptoms, but who knows. I've tried to help, but Gerde's afraid that Hans will come down with it. She has been sending food over since Olga became ill. I just returned."

Gerde voice came from behind him.

"Come in, come in. There should be enough for all."

"I'd better Mr. MacDonald tell." Anna would use English whenever her sister-in-law showed off her better command of the language.

They heard his footsteps behind them.

"I heard enough of the conversation that I shall see Friend Rolfe for a minute. Dinna worry, I twill nay go in, but I thought we had a deal with Mr. Chisholm for cattle delivery this fall. I shall be back as soon as I put the horses up. After we eat, I twill load up what we have stored here, pay ye for the merchandise shipped in, and then we twill return to our ranch and nay bother ye."

Anna turned to him. "Does that mean du are soon leaving, Herr MacDonald?"

"I could nay bear to tell ye, but it twill bring in the money we need for winter supplies and furnishings. The U.S. government doesn't pay that much for beeves for their reservation, but the money tis guaranteed."

Anna mentally counted the weeks. No, it is too early to be sure, she thought.

MacDonald appeared for supper in less than thirty minutes.

"Friend Rolfe tis well on the mend. Young James tis now coming down with the sniffles, but Mrs. Rolfe gave us her blessing. She wants a new rug for the living room." He ladled gravy over his mashed potatoes.

"This can be bad, Herr MacDonald. Remember the papers in St. Louis and New Orleans all spoke about this disease." Anna had worried that they might catch it, but so far neither exhibited any symptoms.

He smiled at her. "I'm sure this tis isolated enough here. Jesse has recovered too. That means people can fight it off."

Gerde shook her head. "It hit three men already. One died, Jesse almost did, and I heard the Phillips both are feeling poorly."

"How did you find that out?" Kasper was puzzled.

"When Consuela was in here buying flour and sugar for Mr. Owens. It seems Mr. Phillips was over at Jesse's and complaining about his wife not being able to do much."

"Herman and I twill nay leave for another week. That should be enough time to see if anyone else succumbs."

Chapter 33

Influenza

Gathering the herd took a few days. Rolfe had returned to his usual state of health. When MacDonald and Rolfe left, they were confident that all was right in their world. The influenza epidemic he and Anna had read about in St. Louis had spared them while they were there, and the entire Schmidt family—if you didn't count the baby's runny nose.

Two weeks after they left, Anna was wishing she had told MacDonald about her suspicions. There was no doubt in her mind. She was with child. She went about singing while she tended her house, the cow, and the draft horses for pulling the buggy and any farm work. She cut prairie grass with her scythe and raked it into a pile. She wondered where Kasper was as he had promised to check on her every few days. The last time he came he was brimming with news.

"The Rolfe boys are running around like Indians, but both Mr. and Mrs. Phillips have come down with high fevers. It must be more of the ague. Strange, it seems to hit one family at a time."

"How is Jesse?"

"He's fine. Ben Jackson and his son, Tom, both had it after you left, but they were barely sick."

"Your family seems to have avoided it."

Kasper grinned. "Gerde plies us with tonic on the chance we might. You and Mac avoided it while you were gallivanting around the country."

"We did not gallivant! We only went to see Papa and then stayed in St. Louis four nights, plus some time in New Orleans and Houston."

"Wouldn't you feel safer if you came into town while your husband is gone?"

Anna's eyes widened. "Mr. MacDonald left his shotgun with me. If any Comanche comes, I will use it. I do not want to leave our home. I still have curtains to make for the living room and bedroom."

She grew pensive. "Winter will be here soon. Mr. MacDonald said to order what we will need. Do you have a bolt of blue or white flannel?"

It was Kasper's turn to stare at his twin. They had been friends while growing up. Anna matched his studies and would outrun and out-climb him. Sometimes he felt like he knew her better than his wife.

"Anna, are you—I mean, I know men and women don't talk about that, but are you?"

Anna put down her cup and laughed. "We never could fool each other could we, Kasper?"

"Does Mac know? When?"

"No, I wasn't sure when he left, but now I am. It will be another five months." To herself she thought and it will be a boy.

He swallowed the last of the coffee. "I'll be back in another week."

Kasper was a few days late when he tied his horse to the porch rail and ended Anna's worry as to where he was.

"Come in, come in, that wind is sharp today."

"There isn't time, Anna. Mr. and Mrs. Phillips were really ill. Mrs. Rolfe has fallen ill and Olga isn't well yet. Gerde is afraid to go anywhere near them because of Hans." Kasper swallowed before speaking again. It was difficult to bring Hans into it, but Hans had been frail since his birth; not really a blue baby, but he could not run any distance without sitting down and wheezing.

"If you could come to town and help the Rolfes and the Phillips with cooking, it would be a big help. Mrs. Tillman can't come in from the ranch because Ben was just in to buy something for her ague complaints. The other Mrs. Tillman is too close to birthing to go anywhere."

"But somebody has to milk our cow."

"I'll come back every day."

"Don't be ridiculous. We will tie the cow to the back of the buggy. Maybe the Phillips and Rolfe families will give you the extra feed. We can share the butter and cream."

"They will. Everyone is pitching in to help the other person. Jesse is fine, but the Mexican family behind him is down with it now and he is cooking their meals. The elder Mr. Jackson has been coughing again, but so far he isn't as sick as the rest, plus his son is taking care of the work and the animals."

"I'll pack a bag."

Kasper's face and grey eyes showed relief. "I'll hitch up your buggy and bring up the cow."

"Oh, and there is fresh milk in the springhouse. We should take that with us."

After packing, Anna put on her coat. The morning was cool and the wind was still blowing. They were mostly silent on the way into Schmidt's Corner. They turned toward the barn as they neared the Rolfe home.

Kasper turned to her. "Are you sure you want to do this, Anna? If something should happen, I mean, well you've had a rough two years, and Gerde was always so sick." He was almost blushing and realized his sentence was badly framed, but how else does one ask what normally wasn't mentioned between the sexes? They had been extremely close as children. He felt he had a certain right to intrude where normally only the husband would.

Anna turned to him. "I would not be here if I were not sure. Even if Mrs. Phillips were well, she would be of little help. She doesn't like us and Clara doesn't really speak English."

"I'll put the cow in Rolfe's corrals. The horse shouldn't bother her, and she can forage there. It is Martin's riding horse and accustomed to humans. Then I can go over every morning to milk her."

"I should be able to do that." Anna grabbed her bag as she spoke.

"You may have enough to do taking care of Mrs. Rolfe. You can send Martin over to tell us how things are going. It will not take long to put up the horses. Thank you, Anna. Mr. Rolfe was very generous when he let me purchase land for the store and livery."

Chapter 34

Bereft

"Tante Anna, come quick. Mama can't breathe."

Anna turned from the pot she was stirring and saw the frightened face of thirteen-year-old Olga. Her raspberry lips were still cracked from the high fevers, but she had recovered. Clara had never regained any strength and her coughing and fevers remained. Keeping the children away from her or Clara away from the children had been impossible. Three-year-old James would cry or sneak into her room and Olga had tried to help. She would minister to her mother or carry out the thunder mug. Martin would try to watch James, but he was less than attentive at keeping a three-year-old away from their mother.

At one time, Anna had all three as patients. Olga still had the remnants of the flu when Anna arrived. Young James had been next and then Martin. The children recovered in the same order. The Phillips' had gradually recovered. Clara was up and better. Anna had been packing to return home when Clara Rolfe appeared flushed with fever.

Anna kept the house, did the washing, ironing, and cooking. She was now in her fifth month and showing. She was trying to sew clothes for herself and a layette in any spare time. She had thought Clara's fever a bit lower and taken a moment to check on Olga's cooking. She then started to ladle a bowl of beans for herself; anything to be away from the sickroom. Anna moved the pot over to the register and followed Olga into the bedroom.

She prayed that Olga had exaggerated, but she did not hear the heavy wheezing or deep coughing that could be heard all over the house. Olga was on the floor, her face on her mother's chest sobbing.

"I shouldn't have left her. Ach, Mama, I'm sorry, I'm so sorry."

Dear God, thought Anna. Poor Olga. She will have to care for two younger brothers. How do we explain this to Mr. Rolfe? She could smell the fluids that had somehow been in Clara's fever-wracked body.

"Olga, will you send Martin to my brother's house and ask Mr. Schmidt to come here? We need to think of a way to tell James and Martin. Perhaps, Mr. Schmidt with his Pastor's training will do better than you or I. I'll find a nice dress for your mother and fill a basin with water."

Olga sobbed harder. "Mama, I loved you."

Anna gritted her teeth. Olga had been so grown up in helping. She sank down beside her and put her arm around the child-woman.

"Olga, your mother is with God. Your brothers need you now and so will your father when he returns."

"What if he blames me?"

"Why would Mr. Rolfe do such a thing?"

Olga sniffed and then hiccupped. Anna handed her the handkerchief from her apron pocket.

"He won't. I just miss Mama. She taught me everything." Olga wailed again. "She taught me how to play the organ and how to bake. And she taught me to sew and crochet."

"Of course, she did, Olga. She loved you. She loved all of her children and now the younger ones need you. They will not realize this. They may even resent you, but they need you."

Olga swallowed. "I'll go get Uncle Kasper. Young James is probably there."

"Do you want to say a prayer first?"

"Won't Uncle do it better?"

"Much better, go now and bring him."

Anna remained on her knees for a moment to say her own prayer for strength. She would need to wash Mrs. Rolfe, dress her in clean clothes, and comb her hair before they could put her in the coffin. She assumed Mr. Phillips would be hired to build the coffin. First she needed another sheet for the bed. She prayed there was a clean one. Gerde had been doing the laundry, but Anna couldn't remember putting one in the basket. She was exhausted and longed to return to her own home.

Chapter 35

Death Stalks Schmidt's Corner

After they buried Clara Rolfe, Anna had started to pack, but Gerde realized she had a fever. Kasper pleaded with Anna to stay. Gerde was afraid to let Hans come near her. In 1858 no one knew that the flu germs were distributed before the start of the fever if someone touched or used the same item. The water bucket in the house was for all with one tin cup hung on a nail beside the bucket. They did not use a glass for each person. Gerde recovered two weeks later, but Hans took ill during the first week of his mother's illness.

Anna tried everything: steaming under a tent made from a sheet, plasters on the chest, extra bedding and hot coffee to bring the fever out of the body, but nothing broke the phlegm in Hans's thin chest. Upon her recovery, Gerde began to care for Hans, rocking him when he cried and trying to force broth down a swollen throat.

It was a relief to let someone, anyone, take over nursing the sick. "I'll leave tomorrow," Anna told Kasper. "I think Gerde is strong enough and Mrs. Phillips has been quite neighborly for a change."

Kasper had nodded. He was too distracted at the thought of Hans being ill. Gerde had had miscarriage after miscarriage after Hans. How the sickly child had lived, Kasper did not know. The fourth time Gerde miscarried, the doctor's words had given him another cross to bear.

"Another pregnancy will probably kill her. I suggest you find another, ahem, outlet for your manly vigor."

Kasper could not, would not commit adultery. It was not in his nature. That would be sinning and men sinned sufficiently without deliberately breaking one of God's commandments. He wasn't as outwardly as passionate as Anna, but he loved deeply and he loved Gerde. He could not hurt Gerde anymore than he could deliberately hurt anyone else. That Hans had survived was a miracle when so many healthy children succumbed before the age of two. It wasn't until Hans had reached the age of five that they had begun to breathe easier. Now this. Perhaps he would ask Mr. Jackson to take the cow home for Anna.

He made a sandwich of mashed beans and poured a cup of milk for Gerde. He knew she would not leave Hans, but she would rest while he took over any nursing duties. As he turned from the counter it felt like a knife entered his head. Gerde's wail of grief and agony rang out again and again. Kasper ran for the stairs.

Anna emerged from the living room where she had started packing for the journey home, ran up the stairs behind Kasper, and followed him into the room.

"Please, God," she whispered, "don't let it be what I think it means." It was the wail of agony she had screamed over and over for her lost children.

They found Gerde bent over the bed sobbing, her shoulders heaving up and down as she tried to breathe, cry, and speak. "Hans, my angel, my Liebling." And the agonizing cry went out into the night again.

Kasper went to his knees beside her, laid his head on Hans's chest, and tried to feel a pulse.

"Anna, a mirror, please. You'll find it on our chest of drawers."

"I'll need a candle or the lamp to find it."

"There's a candle in the top drawer of his chest." Kasper barely got the words out of his constricted throat.

Anna retrieved the candle and used her apron to lift the hot lampshade. Once the candle was lit, she gently replaced the shade and slipped into the bedroom on the other side of the hall. She knew exactly where the mirror was. She had nursed Gerde in this room.

It took but moments to retrieve the mirror and return to the death room. Kasper almost tore the mirror from her hand and held it over Han's pallid face and opened eyes. There was no breath. Kasper put his other arm around Gerde and held her close. Anna closed the door behind them and went to the Phillips to tell them of the need for a new casket.

Chapter 36

One More Grave

Anna looked at the assembled townspeople. Gerde's and Kasper's white faces were a stark contrast to the black clothes they wore. Gerde's face was like stone and Kasper's gentle eyes were totally bewildered. He had been unable to read God's Word at the grave and Phillips could not read Deutsche. Anna had read from the gospel of St. John. Now a hymn should be sung, but Kasper was unable to lead them. The death of their only child had stricken them both mute.

Anna began the prayer from the Lutheran funeral service that ended with, "Into your hands, we submit his spirit and our lives." It was two days after Hans had slipped away. Kasper had tried to lead the service, but his voice cracked and he buried his face in his hands. Anna wondered why she felt so warm when the blowing wind was so cold.

The group at the grave included the Rolfe children, the Phillips, Jesse Owens, the two Jackson men, both Tillman families, and Cruz Hernandez, his wife Consuela, and their daughter Olivia. What they thought of the Bible reading and prayers in German, Anna did not care. It was bad enough that she, a woman, had to take over the service. Didn't God say women had no authority over men? But Kasper was not able and Mr. Rolfe and Mr. MacDonald had not returned. At the close of the service, Anna decided that something should include their neighbors.

"We should say The Lord's Prayer and then sing a hymn of your choosing." She was not really capable of smiling, but she looked directly at Ben Tillman.

Ben, a lanky, rawboned, straw-haired man nodded and led the group. They ended by singing an Isaac Watts hymn that the Phillips's and the Tillman's as good Methodists knew, "Why Do We Mourn Departing Friends."

Anna had stayed in Schmidt's Corner for the funeral. She had done most of the cooking and baking for the people that would be at the Schmidt's home after the burial. For a moment her eyes closed and she felt her stomach lurch. She was desperate to return home before she became ill too. Everyone was dabbing at their eyes and looking at her. She swallowed and straightened.

"Von't du stop by, please? There is plenty for all."

There was more than plenty as Mrs. Phillips and the two Tillman ladies had brought cornbread, cookies, and yeast rolls. Anna took a deep breath and started to walk back across the ruts that served as a road through town. There was no doubt now, she was feverish. A dry, hacking cough erupted. Dear God, she couldn't be sick. She was almost six months pregnant with Zeb's baby. She knew it was a boy just as she had known what sex her other children would be. Surely God would let her have this one after losing her other four.

Her steps became more erratic as they neared the General Store. Ben Tillman stepped up to her. "Let me help y'all, Mrs. MacDonald. Yore as white-faced as a hooty owl."

Anna desperately wanted to retreat to the living room where she had slept during the ordeal of nursing Gerde and Hans, but that was where the ladies would be sitting. The men might sit long enough to eat, but most of them would be outside passing a bottle to strengthen the coffee. Somehow she managed to get through the afternoon and wave goodbye to everyone. She was shivering as she tried to do the dishes. Kasper came in from tending the horses and milking the cow.

"Anna, you are ill."

"Just a bit..." a wracking cough nearly doubled her over. Then she realized she needed to vomit. She pushed past him and out through the kitchen door. She made it to the porch railing before losing her lunch and her breakfast.

Kasper was beside her. "Anna, you're shivering. Come in. I'll bring the bucket into the living room and get the bedding; unless you want to sleep in Hans's room."

"No, I can't sleep there." She let Kasper lead her inside and to the sofa. Her head was pounding and every bone in her body ached.

She vaguely remembered Kasper tending to her for two days. Then it was Gerde still dressed in black and unsmiling. On the fourth morning Anna felt weak and her stomach muscles were cramped from the vomiting and the diarrhea, but the headache had miraculously retreated. I can sit up now, she thought, and eat the oatmeal this morning. And the contractions began.

Anna drew a deep breath of air into her lungs and a moan escaped from her mouth.

"No, not now, not Zeb's baby." Birthing children had never been difficult. She had Margareatha in less than eight hours, and the boys had been swifter. Her screams had been limited to one or two, but this was different. The pain drove her to her knees when she tried to stand. She wanted to summon help, but all she could do was pull the bedding underneath her to keep from staining the floors. An oilcloth was needed, but there was no time.

She grunted as the next wave hit her. Bearing down was involuntary. It was what the body did to rid itself of something that needed to be gone.

"Kasper, Gerde!" Anna was able to yell on the third contraction. She could feel the head emerging now and tried to hike the gown upward. It was difficult with the long material and the way she had landed on the floor.

It seemed forever, but then Kasper was kneeling beside her.

"Do you need help getting up?"

"Don't be foolish, Kasper." It was Gerde, her voice harsh and hard. "She's having the baby too early. Go bring some water from the reservoir and some clean rags. I need a scissors or a sharp knife."

Gerde had been full of resentment that Anna was with child when she could not, but this was different. The birth was too soon. The child was probably dead or soon would be, and Anna could die too. The thought of losing another family member in this wild place was too much. Small in stature, practical, determined, Gerde could do the work of three and now work needed to be done.

She shifted Anna enough to get the clothes out of the way. The baby's head was there and the scalp covered with black down underneath the coating.

"PUSH!"

Anna grunted and complied, knowing this was wrong—too soon, too quick.

As Kasper walked back in the room he saw that Gerde was holding a small bundle nestled in part of Anna's skirt.

"Did you bring the water?"

"Yes."

"Quick, say the words. He's still alive."

Kasper shot a quick look at Anna. Her eyes were closed and she was still bearing down. The room reeked of blood. He knelt beside Gerde and dipped his hand into the water and sprinkled the water on the baby's head.

"In the name of the Father," he dipped his hand again and sprinkled.

"And the Son," once more he brought up water in his hand and splashed over the baby's head as he intoned, "and in the name of the Holy Ghost, I baptize thee…" he hesitated and looked at Anna.

"Llewellyn Gephardt MacDonald." Anna was watching him, tears flooding her eyes.

"Llewellyn Gephardt MacDonald." Kasper ended.

"Now give me the scissors and bring more rags and an oil-cloth. There will be more blood for a while. We need a small box for the baby and other things." Gerde would not say afterbirth in front of both a man and a woman, but she was still giving orders. She took the largest, cleanest rag from Kasper and wrapped it around the baby.

"Please, let me hold my son."

Gerde's stone face softened. "Are you sure? He's having trouble breathing." She did not need to say, "He will die in your arms."

"Yes, give him to me."

Anna took the small, frail body and looked at the heaving chest and perfect little face, head, and hands before holding him close. It did not take long for the small body to quiet and remain motionless.

Anna closed her eyes. "I have killed my son. I should not have worked so hard. I was arrogant and thought I was strong enough to do it. God in Heaven, forgive me."

Gerde looked up from her tasks long enough to command in a sharp tone. "Stop that. You had a high fever for three days. It's a wonder you kept the baby this long and you know it. There was no way to avoid the flu. Only three people in this community had avoided it; one of the Tillman's, Kasper, and Tom Jackson."

Anna lay back completely exhausted. "It's almost more than I can bear. First my other babies, now this one." And the tears would not come.

"Ja, it's hard." Gerde choked. She had been crying for days and there was no hope of another baby. If Anna were smart, she would follow the same path. After all, the woman was thirty-five, almost to the end of her childbearing years.

Kasper returned with a handful of rags, a newly cut oilcloth, and an empty crate. "This is all I could find."

"It will do. Put the oilcloth on the sofa and help Anna back up there. I'll see if one of these blankets is still usable." It better be, she thought. There isn't another clean one in the house. She took the stilled baby from Anna and placed it gently into the crate. She could not help but touch the cheek with her finger. How rapidly the body grows cold, she thought.

Anna found she was still shaky and let Kasper support her. The oilcloth was slick and cool, but it helped when Gerde put the blanket over her.

"I'll see if you don't have a clean nightgown in your bag."

"I don't. It's dirty. I haven't had time to wash clothes."

"It will be better than this one." Gerde's voice was grim. "Kasper, turn your head."

Gerde put the rags beneath Anna's buttocks and spread the rags outward. "Try not to move until I can get some safety pins." She looked at Kasper and inclined her head toward the box.

Kasper swallowed and nodded to Gerde. He picked up the box and walked from the room. He had to take everything to Malcolm for another coffin. It would be a very small one.

On his way back home, he almost stopped at Jesse's for a beer, but decided against it. Anna was still too much of an invalid to drink any, but she would need it to gain some weight. At least Anna could try to have another baby, he reflected. He was not bitter as he had heard Gerde's tears too often. The ache in his heart for Hans was almost unbearable. At times he felt so tired he did not even wish to move. Poor little Hans had survived a bad birth, chicken pox, and measles when other, healthier children in St. Louis and Arles had died. He had always blamed himself for Hans's shortness of breath. He had been the same way as a child. Then the enormity of Gerde's words hit him. He was one of those that had not taken influenza. There was no point in pursuing the whys. Kasper knew that he was one of the weaker specimens of manhood. Being spared a serious illness could not be because he was less sinful; he wasn't.

Gerde was soaking one of the sheets as he entered their kitchen.

"She is crying now."

"You didn't stay with her?"

Gerde turned to him. "Why? She wished to be alone. There is a great sadness when you lose a baby." Her tone became harsher, her face whiter. "Better to cry and get it over with."

"But the comfort of God's Word, wouldn't that help?"

"No." Gerde punched the sheet down into the salt water. "I'll let that be for an hour."

"We can hold the service tomorrow. The baby did live more than a few minutes." The need for something to do, to make things right, drove Kasper.

Gerde looked at him. "She will not go. She is too weak. It is best to have it then."

Chapter 37

To Live Again

"Mac, look at that." Rolfe pointed to the three fresh gravesites where the town had decided the graveyard would be located. "What the hell happened?"

"I dinna."

They had intended to be back at least a month ago, but they had to wait for the government payment and then Rolfe was asked to help in translating for the army and a band of Kiowa.

"It's an adult grave and it looks like two children's graves." Rolfe slapped his horse with the reins and galloped for his house.

MacDonald stared at the graves a bit longer and turned to follow his friend. Young James and Hans were the only children in town. The two Tillman families each had wee ones, but none of the crosses had names. Perhaps someone was still working on the boards with names and dates.

He held his horse to a walk as he wanted to give Rolfe a chance to recover if the news were bad. Both parents had declared that James would be a pastor. The thought that they could determine the future for a three-year-old amused MacDonald.

"Hey, Mac, you should go to Schmidt's place. Yore woman is there." It was the elder Jackson. He had emerged from behind his house.

"Are things all right at the Rolfe's?"

"They're under control. Mrs. Rolfe died of the ague."

MacDonald sat mute.

"Yore woman almost died taking care of everybody and losing her baby. We gave everyone..." He was talking to air. "A right nice funeral," he finished to himself.

MacDonald wheeled his horse and cut through the back way past the tavern and pulled up at the porch. He did not bother yelling a greeting, but took the three steps in one bound.

Gerde opened the door for him. "She is in the living room."

MacDonald removed his hat. "Mrs. Schmidt, Mr. Jackson just said Anna had my baby."

His brown eyes were worried, puzzled. "Do ye ken why she did nay tell me?

"Ja, but I will let her tell you."

He turned towards the small hallway between the store and the living quarters. At the door he turned back. "Yere Hans?"

Gerde's voice and eyes were hard. "He is with God."

"I sorrow with ye, but I must go to Anna." Two quick steps and he was at the door.

Anna was struggling to sit up when he appeared in the doorway. Any anger he harbored for her not telling him evaporated when he realized she had lost weight again. Her cheek bones were protruding and the grey eyes filled with fear. Dear Gar, how could his Anna be afraid of him?

Four steps and his long legs carried him across the room. He swept her up into his arms and pulled her close.

"Mr. MacDonald, I am still bleeding. I should remain on the sofa with the protection of the oilcloth." Her voice was muffled. "I don't want to make Gerde more work."

"Will ye call me Zeb." It was a demand, not a question, but he lowered her back onto the sofa and stroked her hair.

"Mr. Jackson said ye nearly died taking care of everyone."

"No, but it did weaken me. That was why I became so ill, and Zeb, I'm sorry, so sorry. I lost our little boy." And she buried her face in her hands.

"Anna, are ye all right now? And why, why did ye nay tell me? I would nay have left ye."

She raised her head. "I did not know for sure until you were gone for two weeks." She swallowed, and then whispered. "There had been some spotting the month before, so I wasn't sure. But I couldn't stop nursing the people. There wasn't anyone else and then Mrs. Rolfe died. Poor Olga, she was so heartbroken." She swallowed. "Mein Gott, Mr. Rolfe, did he, does he know?"

"He does by now. He rode for home when we saw the graves. We twere afraid one of the wee ones twas Young James."

Anna closed her eyes for a moment. "So much sickness, so much death. Gerde was like a stone statue and then I, I went down and lost our baby. Oh, Mr. MacDonald, I, I cannot tell you how sorry I am, but I didn't know how to do it differently. If you want to leave me, I will understand."

Her face, her eyes were full of misery and for a moment MacDonald looked at her before pulling her close again.

"Why twould I leave ye, my love? Ye have given me the greatest gifts possible. I have yere love and ye have proved that I, Maca of Don, have seed. "We have proven the Justines wrong. I can replenish the House of Don. When I leave, I twill have my own House to defeat them."

"Leave? When are you leaving, Mr. MacDonald?"

"Leave? Woman, I have told ye, I am nay leaving my own true love. Why canna ye believe me? And stop calling me Mr. MacDonald."

Anna smiled at him for the first time since his arrival. It was like a jolt of electricity transforming her face and eyes.

"We are in someone else's home. It is proper to be so formal, but Zeb, thank God you are home and safe."

"We twill leave as soon as I can arrange everything. Mayhap by tomorrow."

"We, I mean, I—I can't leave, Zeb. I shouldn't be moved. Poor Gerde and Kasper have had to look after me."

"What tis wrong?"

A slight tinge of color appeared on Anna's cheeks, but she answered. "I thought you would understand, but you don't have any other children. I lost the baby. There is always bleeding during and after a birth or a miscarriage. Usually it is slower than this… "

She got no farther.

"Tis there any pain?"

Anna coughed. "I'm sorry, but it is the after effects of the flu. Please, I need my handkerchief."

"Ye have an infection. I twill tend to my horse and be back with my bag. There tis something there that twill cure ye."

He bent his head first on one of her shoulders and then the next, making a "tsk" sound in each ear. "That tis my way." He grinned at her, rose to his feet, bent and kissed her.

"It was a little boy, Zeb. He would have looked like Daniel and Lorenz. I named him Llewellyn Gephardt MacDonald and asked Kasper to carve the name on a board until we can afford a tombstone. Is that all right?"

Laughter shook his shoulders. "Oh, aye, my love, tis a fine name. He twould have been a mighty Warrior from all of his childhood battles."

Chapter 38

Anna Meets the Future

Anna was still weak from losing the baby, but the coughing and aftereffects of birthing had ended. Whatever was in MacDonald's tins had worked.

They had ridden double on his horse to the cave. The surprise of seeing a light come from a palm-sized gadget had been bad enough, but this—this thing was impossible to put into words. She stared stupidly at the huge machine in front of her wishing to be back out in the air again.

MacDonald stepped forward to place his hand on the side of the *Golden One* as he called it. She forgot to exhale as the panel slid back into the ship and revealed a huge interior. A ramp large enough for two wagons abreast was lowered and MacDonald turned to her with a huge smile on his face. The smile faded as he realized that Anna was about to topple.

"My love, are ye all right?" He was beside her, his arms around her.

Anna found she could breathe in and out again. "Yes, it is such a…It is so huge."

"If ye canna enter this time, I ken, but I really wanted ye to go to the Medical Room. The systems there twill tell us exactly what ye need. I can create something that twill stop the seed of either of us."

"Why would you do that?"

"Because ye should nay have another till ye have regained yere strength. Too many die from childbirth in this land."

"They don't die in your land?" The idea was amazing. Anna thought of all the graves of women that she had known and that had died during childbirth. Her own mother was dead from having miscarriage after miscarriage. Other women could have a dozen children or more. Not all of the children would survive, but many of them did. Could there really be a land that most women gave birth and survived?

"Nay, they dinna die, nay do the wee ones die, but then a House Thalian has nay more than three children. Sometimes, tis said the Ab females twill bear four, even five, but I nay kenned any."

His words were totally perplexing. He had explained that House meant the ruling families and their members. A House was family or a clan, but a home was their living quarters. He had not mentioned anything about Abs.

"If you will give me your arm, I can walk." Anna held her head high. She would not appear a weakling beside this strong man. It was the same type of rivalry she had felt when younger and she and Kasper played at climbing trees, (forbidden but ignored), building houses with blocks, and playing War or Chess.

He tucked her arm securely under his arm before guiding her steps up the ramp. Inside he touched a circle and the ramp and panel slid back.

"This tis the compartment for the other machines. There are the Scouts." He pointed at two smaller machines that looked like they had the same strange windows as the spaceship, but she couldn't see through them. The Scouts were about the size of stagecoaches without a place to hitch a team. She couldn't imagine their purpose.

"They are used to fly over a planet's terrain, record the landscape, and as a vehicle to go from one base to another ere returning to the *Golden One*." His voice was rumbling in her ear. "The other machine is for moving earth if needed in a small area or precision is required."

She turned to him, her eyes wide and bewildered. "Do you mean people ride in them? But how? How does this," she waved her hand in a circular motion, fly? It is huge. How can you get it off the ground?"

MacDonald smiled. "It tis a technology based on the storage of the sun's energy into specialized treated crystals. There are also fuel cells infused into the inside of the walls the length of this ship. In less than two hundred years, I twill need to take it up into the sunlight for recharging."

Anna clung to his arm. "Zeb, how can that be? You cannot live that long, can you?"

He smiled down at her. "My love, right now I am about eighty-five of yere years. Thalians live to somewhere twixt three hundred forty-five to three hundred seventy-five years. The Justines live thousands of years. Since I am both, mayhap I twill live that long."

She closed her eyes. This was a problem she had not anticipated. She untangled her arm and stood in front of him. "And what do you intend to do when I grow old?"

"I twill dye my hair grey, then white. Nay fear, ye are my counselor, my wife. I twill nay leave ye."

Anna swayed toward him and he picked her up. "Ye are still weak. We are now going up to the Medical and find out how to make ye strong again."

He carried her to the wall, at least it look like a wall to Anna, and put his finger on a circle. A smaller door slid open.

"This tis the lift. It twill carry us to the second floor."

She closed her eyes as they went inside and she opened them in time to see the panel slide shut. There were four walls surrounding them in a place not much larger than a small shed. It was almost impossible to breathe and she was not sure she heard a humming or if her ears had stopped up like when she had a bad cold.

Once again Llewellyn touched something and the door slid open. Anna's eyes widened. This was a small area. To her left was a wide shiny door that emanated a faint bluish glow like the glow coming from the floor. To her right was another wide door made from what she assumed must be glass. She could see elevated tables of grass, plants, and huge forms that looked like trees.

"What is that?" She pointed at the door displaying the vegetation.

"It tis the horticultural, air, and water cleansing facility. The controls are set on low occupancy. I dinna ken how to do the maintenance and just keep pressing the auto maintain command. So far that has worked well." He smiled at her.

"The Medical is to our left."

"Zeb, put me down."

Llewellyn looked down and saw that the color had returned to Anna's face and she was growing testy. He set her down.

"After we leave Medical, I shall show ye the Command Center, and introduce ye to the cultures of my world."

"What do you mean by cultures? Are there more than one kind of people on your world?"

"On Thalia, nay, we are all Thalians just as the beings on this planet are all humans." Anna blinked. Surely he didn't consider the Comanche human, and then she remembered God's Word said they were all one. It was a hard thing to accept.

Llewellyn laid his palm on the wall and the door slid open for them. This room seemed barren. Two slim beds with white linens and flat pillows were protruding from the walls, banks of what looked like metal drawers decorated with strange symbols and without handles lined one wall. There was a chair of golden hue set against that wall, but Anna could deduce no reason for it. A large circle was on the floor on the other side of the room with what looked like a matching circular metal frame above. The golden light still glowed around them. Anna had tried, but she could not detect any visible source of light.

"This tis the Medical facilities. Ye twill need to stand on the circle." He pointed to the floor beneath the frame. "It twill weigh ye and then scan yere body. Ye need to remove all yere clothes."

"I will not."

"Anna, we are married. I have seen ye without clothes."

She clenched her teeth. "I have no idea what that," and she went to an English word, "contraption ist."

He grinned at her and began to pull off his shirt. "I twill show ye."

Once disrobed, MacDonald stepped onto the golden circle. A whitish grey essence seemed to surround him from floor to the ceiling. For once Anna was too upset to admire this muscular man that was her husband. The muscles rippled down his back, his arms, his stomach area, the buttocks, and down through the legs. A strange, deadened voice came from the wall panel directly in front of him.

"This is a male Justine-Thalian mutant with two hearts, superb muscular development, and weighing two hundred and ninety pounds." A flexible tube snaked from the wall and touched his shoulder.

"He is in need of vegetable matter minerals which will be dispensed in Unit Two. Is there anything else?"

"Nay." Llewellyn stepped out of the circle.

"Now tis yere turn. It canna give yere correct weight if ye are clothed and it twill be confused at first. It has nay ere scanned an Earth being.

He moved toward her and unbuttoned her skirt. "It twill nay harm ye." He bent and kissed her cheek.

"Zeb, I, I am not sure this is safe."

"This is so ye twill be strong again. There tis nay to fear. Please believe me."

"There is someone looking at us. I am not stupid. That voice came from someone."

"Nay, it comes from a manufactured unit that can put electronic readings into an automated voice."

Anna took a very deep breath. Should she believe him? This birth had taken something out of her. Perhaps it was because she had been so exhausted. She had sworn an oath with this man and so far he had not betrayed her.

"Very well, but I want the clothes close. I am so skinny now. It's embarrassing for you to see me, and I am still weak." All things she hated to admit. Her words trailed to silence.

"I shall steady ye as ye take off yere garments and then I shall turn my back." He knew the pallor of her skin was not natural and she was still far too slender. For a few brief weeks after their marriage he had bedded a vibrant female. Her wit and intelligence had astounded him, and her courage made her magnificent. That moment when she transferred her emotions had brought a comfort he thought gone. He could nay bear the loneliness of Earth without his counselor. If turning his back because of modesty made her well, he would turn his back.

"Very well."

The clothes took several minutes to remove. She had used his arm to steady her while removing her shoes and cotton hose. When she was down to the last underskirt, she commanded, "Now turn." She waited until he faced the door before slipping the skirt downward and stepping onto the circle.

The strange, hollow voice began again. "This appears to be a female being of the same species as the description Ricca gave us with a blood sample. The body configures closely to that of known beings. A blood sample will determine any replacement. It may or may not be adequate. More information on these beings would be helpful." Anna almost stepped backward out of the circle, but the snaky appendage was too rapid for her and it tapped her shoulder. Silence descended upon the room. She wasn't sure, but she might have heard a hum coming from the walls.

"This primitive has just had a child less than sixty sun cycles of this planet. Weight is one hundred thirty-five pounds. Like the other being, she is devoid of certain minerals and elements. The iron level seems to be significantly low. Her blood is a match to the Justine-Thalian mutant. More data of these primitives is requested for further testing. They should be unconscious but alive.

"Remove the container from Unit Two and the nutrients for this being will be dispensed. Return in thirty days. If still deficient, a blood transfer can be administered to her. Ricca should be notified prior to that."

Llewellyn walked to the other side of the room and withdrew a vial. Another replaced it. The hazy gauze-like air surrounding Anna disappeared.

She looked at Llewellyn. Her face and eyes betrayed her bewilderment. "Who and what is Ricca? Is this Ricca watching us?"

A huge grin split Llewellyn's face. "Nay, he tis the Justine that..." he hesitated for a moment, "that twas named the commander of this expedition. He tis nay on board right now as I explained."

Anna's face cleared. He had warned her that saying the Justine was dead might override all the controls he had taken.

"We twill visit my quarters and use the cleansing room before we dress to return home, my love. We'll return as soon as ye regain yere strength. Then we shall bed here and romp in the cleansing room."

"I will not walk around naked." Anna picked up the first undergarment and slipped it over her head. She reached for the second one when MacDonald stopped her.

"My love, just put the dress on over that and leave it unbuttoned. There tis nay to see us."

"Aren't you going to dress?"

"Nay, I twould just need to take everything off for the cleansing."

"We can walk on that strange floor without shoes?"

"Aye, that we can. It does nay bite or grab at ye."

He handed Anna her shoes and picked up the rest of her clothes. Then he picked up his. Anna stared at him for a moment before pulling her dress on.

"Now we go to the lift again. My quarters are above."

Chapter 39

The Cleansing Room

To Anna it was like a miracle how rapidly they could be at the top of this huge machine. Llewellyn was touching the panel that opened on the Command Center.

The space in front of the lift was open and wide. There was a huge round table that looked like molded wood with chairs set around it and half-circled by those strange windows that were not windows. She should have been able to see the rock wall, but it was not there—just those dark, smoke-colored panes.

"Why can't I see through the windows?"

"There tis nay to see but rock and those are nay really 'windows.' They are viewers that the scanners can put images on. It can be a panoramic view of the heavens or the terrain below."

Anna gritted her teeth. "Zeb, I have no idea what you are talking about."

He took her by the hand and led her to one of the chairs.

"Sit there, my love, whilst I show ye."

He touched something on the circle enclosing smaller circles and the "window" in front of her showed darkened rock.

Anna gasped. "It's magic."

"Nay, Anna, tis the technology of the Justines. Twould ye like to see and hear about my world now or after we have used the cleansing room?"

Her back was rigid again. She was practically nude, sitting at some strange table in a strange chair, and nature's functions were demanding that she find a thunder mug on this strange craft.

"I need to use the outside. Give me my clothes."

"I told ye my quarters have what ye need as tis part of the cleansing area."

"How can that be?"

"Come, tis quicker than trying to go outside."

Anna stood. She was ready to demand they go outside anyway when he picked her up and carried her. He went down the hall away from the lift as he called it. The same blue floors were illuminated by that golden light.

The first room she saw was large and open with more of the strange furniture. There were chairs and sofas that were covered with rich material. The tables were sleek, rounded, and gold, burgundy, or green. They looked like they had been molded and were set between some of the upholstered chairs. She wondered why golden globes were embedded in the walls of this room. He walked so fast there was no time to discern more. Then she noticed smaller glowing ovals on the walls.

"What are those strange, little, glowing things on the walls?"

"They are name plates. If there twere a crew, each twould have an assigned quarter and their fingers or eyes twould open it. As tis, I've set them all for my command." He touched one of the small oval plaques and the door slid open to reveal a bed covered with a golden colored sheet and a flat pillow.

"The Justines dinna bother with frills." The door slid shut at his touch and they were inside. He walked to another door that seemed to be glass, but she couldn't see through it. Once again his touch opened a door that slid into the wall. This room was as wide as the other, but separated by a two panels decorated with etched suns and planets orbiting them. The back panel went halfway across the room. This side held a basin that looked like black rock had been fused with white. Three black stems protruded from the wall and pointed downward into the basin.

"That tis for washing yere hands after using the facilities." He set her down and held his hand under one of the stems and water ran down onto his palm. It went downward through an opening in the bottom. "One tis cold water, one tis warm water, and the right one tis the cleansing agent. They dispense whenever ye hold yere hands underneath one."

There was no answer for this folly, and Anna was gritting her teeth.

"I cannot use that."

A quick smile lit his face and he led her around the panel that jutted one quarter of the way across the room. He lifted a lid from a square shaped blue box that was made of the same material as the walls of this utterly overwhelming, impossible place.

"There tis where ye sit. When ye are finished, here is the material ye use." He lifted the lid of a smaller box set into the wall. Later Anna would realize it was not a moveable box, but the cleansing material, as Zeb called it, would automatically refill for any used.

By this time Anna had no choice. She would have rather been outside where she could have hid someplace. She felt exposed even when he stepped back behind the golden panel.

When she finished, she emerged red-faced and flustered. She wanted to leave immediately. Llewellyn was standing there as naked as when they walked in here, waiting for her, and a happy smile spread across his face.

"And now, my darling lassie, we shall use the cleansing room. Ye might wish to take yere hair down as the water and cleanser twill hit yere head area too."

"What are you talking about? There isn't a tub here or any way to heat water."

For a response, he stepped closer, tugged her dress upward, unbuttoned her slip, and took as many pins as he could from her hair.

"Zeb, I am not sticking my head under that—that thing." Her voice was strained and she tried to point at the basin.

"Come, Anna, ye twill see."

He led her around the other panel and touched another oval. A door slid to the left and revealed a space as large as the springhouse. Other stems came from the wall and ceiling. These stems were wider and had what looked like knobs at the end. The knobs were punctured with little tiny holes.

"When we step inside, this door twill close. I twill press another oval and the water and cleansing agent descends. It twill then switch to pure water to rinse us totally clean. There are pads on the ledge," he pointed to one side, "for the, er, more intimate areas. When the water stops the warm air begins. Ye can stay as long as it takes yere hair to dry."

Anna was looking at him with disbelief.

"Please take all those things out of yere hair. I dinna wish them to wash down into the system."

Anna knew this was insane. Nothing like this could possibly exist, but to humor him, she removed the hairpins. She suspected it was the only way she was going to be able to leave this machine. She could not think of it as a spacecraft.

Llewellyn put the pins on the ledge with the basin and they entered (in Anna's mind) the chamber. He pressed an oval and the water and soap sprayed out over them.

He reached out and took the pads. One he handed to her and demonstrated their use with a wicked grin on his face. Anna was so startled she could not move. Then the sensation of the water, the soap, the clean smell of it all brought her back to normal. Llewellyn demonstrated using his fingers to work the cleansing agent and water through his hair and then he was against her massaging everything through her hair. She leaned into him. It had been so long, so very long, and she felt the maleness of him.

When the clean water stopped warm air came down through those strange stems. Anna tried running her fingers through her mass of curls.

"Wait, I twill retrieve a comb."

He stepped out of the chamber and returned in less than a minute. "It tis one of the things that tis the same on all four planets. They are necessary for the beings that have hair."

Anna shook her head. "What are beings?"

Llewellyn's smile was back; the amusement in his brown eyes. "I mean those that inhabit a planet and till the land or manufacture the products. In yere land, ye call yereself humans or people. We all did at one time, however, the Justines, the Brendons, the Kreppies, and the Thalians are nay completely alike. We canna say they are people like us, yet they exist and have the ability to go out into space."

"And we don't." It was a snapped reply.

"Oh, but ye twill, my love, ye twill. Look how rapidly yere technology advances. It should have taken yere world another century to produce a steam engine to run ships on the seas and in trains on the land." He smiled at her and started for his clothes.

Anna was busy working at the snarls and lifting her hair to the warm air. For some reason she felt better than she had in months.

"Zeb, that, ah, the medicine you gave me, how long does it last?"

He turned back to her. "It twill last for over six months, or it should. It depends on how depleted yere system twas." And he turned again to hide the fact that he wanted her now. Then he felt her hand on his shoulder.

"Zeb, do you think you could hold me now?"

It was too much. His Anna was his again. His resolve to wait until the next time vanished.

Chapter 40

North and South

"You all ain't welcome here no more." Malcolm Phillips's anger pushed him back to his younger days before his schooling and entry into the ownership class. His wainwright shop had prospered enough that he had purchased a slave to help him with the heavy lifting, gardening, haying, and caring for the milk cow and chickens his wife had insisted upon acquiring.

"The great state of Texas has seceded. We are at Wah!"

Kasper and Gerde were shaken. This was their home. Their livelihood was here. Surely, this man had to be mistaken. It was the beginning of April and the prairie was filled with green waving grass again. Gerde's garden was planted and completely protected from the rabbits, occasional stray chicken, or any other four or two legged marauder.

"If you haven't pulled out of here in three days, this place will be burned. Your place and Rolfe's! Too damn many Dutchmen have defiled our glorious Cause. The real men of this place will be joining the army." He turned and stomped out of the store, banging the door behind him.

"Our other neighbors can't be involved." Kasper looked down at Gerde. "I'm going over to Jackson's place and then over to Rolfe's. I refuse to even bother Jesse with this. The man cannot change that much overnight."

The people in Schmidt's Corner knew that the Texas legislature had voted to secede on February 1, 1861. Texas had joined the Confederacy on March 2, 1861 and kicked Sam Houston out as governor when he refused to respond to the roll call. The one paper from Austin that they had seen railed against the Congressmen from the German settlements who had voted to remain with the Union. It called them traitors, scum, and warned them to leave the fair State of Texas.

Kasper found Benjamin Jackson at his blacksmith shop pounding on a horseshoe that was on the anvil while Ben Tillman waited with his horse.

"Howdy, Kap. Iffen y'all need any work done, it'll be awhile. Ben's horse needs shoeing."

"No, I don't need any ironwork. I'm here because Malcolm has just issued a threat. He said that my place and Rolfe's would be burned in three days. I was wondering if that was the sentiment of everyone."

"Stupid ass," grunted Jackson as he looked up. "Why burn the one place that has supplies when there could be interruptions in deliveries? His folks must not have talked about the War years at all."

Ben and Kasper looked blank for a moment and then remembered that Jackson's people had migrated down from Maryland. He was talking about the War of 1812.

"And," continued Jackson, "I sure as hell ain't going to get someone like Rolfe or MacDonald coming after me for revenge."

"Well, he did imply that everyone would be leaving to join up with the Confederate Army."

"Bring that horse around here."

Kasper stood out of the way as Ben backed the horse toward Jackson.

Jackson looked at Kasper long enough to say, "Tom's leaving to join up, but I'm too old. They don't need old men running up to Washington. Ain't going to be that long anyways."

"Malcolm's just got a hair up his butt." Ben Tillman chimed in. "He's mad 'cause he don't have fifteen slaves to avoid going to war. His missus is going into Arles to wait it out, and brother Dooley's woman is goin' down to San Antonio to be with relatives. She figures it's a nice way to visit 'cause Dooley's sure to be back in a couple of months. I'll be leaving too, but Janey's staying here with the young 'uns. Keep the place tidy and all. I sure don't have time to burn other folk's places down before I leave. If Rolfe lived, he'd kill us before we even got to Arles. He ain't been in a good mood since his wife died."

By this time, Jackson had measured the iron shoe against the hoof and held it over the forge and worked the bellows. He then laid the horseshoe on the anvil and banged away with his hammer.

"Steady that horse," he yelled at Ben.

Kasper nodded at the two men and walked over to the Rolfe homestead. The house was set fairly close to the road. He figured it would be best to ask Olga where her papa and Martin were. He was never certain whether they were after cattle, horses, or hunting. As he angled across the open space, he saw Martin riding his horse, practicing with a lasso. The youngster's skill was impressive. Thirteen-year-old Martin was blonde, blue-eyed, and stocky like his father; yet, he was more often found working with horses and cattle than Rolfe. Rolfe could find any excuse to go hunting and be gone for days.

Martin waved and turned his horse sharply and sent the lasso twirling onto a post. He must have signaled his horse, for it slowed and braced its hooves, giving Martin an opportunity to pull the rope taunt. He grinned at Kasper, dismounted, and patted his horse on the neck before retrieving the lasso.

"Hullo, Uncle, y'all look worried." He did not have his father's accent. He could speak, read, and write Deutsche as well as English due to Kasper's teaching, but his speech was forever a blend of Texas and occasional German syntax when upset.

"Do I?" Kasper tried to look reassuring. "I just wondered where your father might be."

"I think he's hunting." Martin shrugged. "If he ain't back by tonight, I'll go check over at Uncle Mac's and Tante Anna's place tomorrow. They might need me to help with something."

Kasper considered. Jackson and Ben Tillman had not been threatening. "Thank you, if he does come back this evening, please tell him I would like to speak with him.

"Is everything all right here? Do you, Olga, and Young James have enough to eat?"

"Ja, we're fine Uncle. Y'all sure nothing's wrong?"

"I'm positive." Kasper hurried away. He decided a stop at Jesse's was necessary. He was beginning to think a mug of beer might be good since it was a warm afternoon. Gerde rarely drank. It was as though all the pleasures of life had died with Hans.

Jesse looked up as he walked in.

"Howdy, come to jaw or do y'all want a drink?"

"Both, thank you." Kasper laid a nickel on the counter.

"Has Malcolm been here, Jesse?"

"Oh, he's been here. He wanted me to ride with them to Arles and sign up for the glorious South."

"I see. Are you leaving?"

"Who me? I've got a place full of beer that somebody has to buy. Young Jackson is leaving from what the old man said, but he's smart. He plans to ride all the way down to San Antonio before joining. It still won't do no good."

"I don't understand."

"Hell, y'all are from the North."

That brought a wry smile to Kasper's face as he took a sip. "Most people don't consider Missouri the North."

"Yeah, but the iron and steel is shipped from the North through there. What do we ship? Cotton, sugar, hides, and tallow. That don't make much in the way of guns and bullets. Besides, I've been North. That's where I was before I wandered in here. I'd been to see where my grandparents lived and maybe take up a trade there. Y'all have any idea what a place like Cincinnati looks like?" He paused briefly as Kasper lifted his mug. It didn't do any good, Kasper sipped set the mug down.

"No, but St. Louis was definitely growing when we left."

"Well, sir, St. Louie can't even compare. Leastwise it couldn't about ten years ago. And y'all know what else? I met some of my Yankee cousins. Farmers they are, not a tradesman like me."

Kasper took a larger swallow to hide his smile. The world considered Jesse a tavern owner—not the more respected tradesman.

"Them boys were tough, and they warn't no slouches when it came to firing a rifle. Maybe they ain't fancy gentlemen riding fancy horses, but that ain't what wins a war."

"Well, Malcolm and Ben both seem to think one Southerner can whip ten Yankees."

"What if they did? The North can replace those ten, but the South ain't got that many people."

Kasper realized that he had misjudged the man. Jesse observed more than people realized.

"Did you, ah, by any chance hear Malcolm's threat?"

"Yeah, he wants to burn you out. I told him if he started a fire here and put us all in danger, he better run damn quick. Besides, the last thing I want is someone like MacDonald coming after me. Hell, Rolfe would join in just for the fun of it."

"Thank you, Jesse, but all the same I intend to keep watch the next few nights."

"Tell you what, I'll send Cruz over to give you a hand. Y'all can pay him a quarter a night. He'll think it's big money and that way y'all get some sleep."

The sound of a team of horses racing into town drew their attention. They both moved towards the open door as the windows were too small and filthy to see through. Kasper recognized the MacDonald's rig and handed his mug to Jesse.

"It's Anna, it's her time!" He raced out the door, all other worries forgotten.

The dust was settling as Kasper rounded the corner and ran to the buggy. MacDonald was wrapping the reins around the rail. He nodded at Kasper and hurried to the back of the small wagon. Five quick steps and he dropped the tailgate. He reached for Anna who was scooting towards the edge.

"I can walk."

She might as well have talked to the sky. MacDonald picked her up and headed for the steps.

"Would ye open the door, Herr Schmidt?"

"Ja, how long?"

Anna looked at him. "Soon, the first one was two hours ago. Now they are very close together."

They had plotted this last month. Han's bedroom had been turned into a delivery room. The oilcloth was already on the bed and baby clothes, blankets, towels, and a spare nightgown for Anna were in the chest.

As soon as he entered, MacDonald headed for the stairs.

"Mr. MacDonald, I can manage."

He ignored her and took the steps two at a time. Kasper followed behind to open the door. Then he returned to the kitchen.

Gerde was already filling a basin with warm water from the stove's reservoir. She looked up as Kasper entered. "We'll need one of the buckets filled too."

"Do you need your bag?"

"It's already there. Is Anna really sure? I don't hear her screaming."

"If I remember correctly she didn't scream when her others were born. Johanna thought she was unnatural."

Gerde just nodded. Her face was set, but she carried the water up the stairs. It was like a knife cutting into her to enter Han's room, but there was no other space and Anna was family.

Anna had hung her skirt, blouse, and one of her slips on the chair. She was busy working her shoe laces when pain wracked her face and she gritted her teeth.

"Lie down, Anna, I'll take off the shoes." MacDonald was exasperated, worry etched his face. Why had he let her carry this child?

"Mr. MacDonald, you will need to leave." Gerde had firm ideas about such things.

"He can't just yet." Anna gasped the words out. "He has to support me while I use the mug."

"That's just a natural feeling, don't you remember? You had five others." Gerde could not keep the bitterness out of her voice.

"And each time I had to use that thing." Anna was gritting her teeth again. "I don't want to dirty this oilcloth and then need another one." She stood.

Gerde hurriedly put the basin down and left. The woman was incredibly headstrong. What if she had the baby that way? She could hear Kasper coming up the steps. Why, she wondered, had Clara Rolfe died? She could have done this. This hurt and hurt, and she could not have another baby.

MacDonald appeared in the doorway. "She says the baby tis coming now." He carried the enameled thunder mug by the handle. "It seems my Anna kenned what she twas doing. I'll clean this for ye and return."

"Not in here," muttered Gerde. The man was as impossible as Anna. She let Kasper in long enough to deposit the bucket and then shooed him out.

Chapter 41

The Maca's House

Kasper met MacDonald coming up the steps to the porch. "We really need to stay out here and not disturb Gerde and Anna."

"But what if she dies this time?" MacDonald's view of birthing on this planet was set in the realities of the age. Women and babies died during the birthing process. Even if there were a doctor present, the man was often worse than none as strips of pus could be on his hands or coat. Nay seemed to ken the danger of infections.

"Don't worry, my friend. Johanna served as midwife when Anna had the others. Johanna insisted there is something abnormal about Anna. She has no problem, doesn't scream more than once or twice, and the babies arrive healthy and hale."

It was enough to make MacDonald grit his teeth. Why had he agreed to this madness? Was it to prove that he, Maca of Don, truly had seed and could start the House of Don again on this planet? Anna had been insistent.

"I want to give you a baby, Zeb." She had smiled that glorious transforming smile and he was swept away with her plans.

"I never have any trouble," Anna had continued. "The last time was because I was exhausted and then I became ill. Now I am healthy again. This will be like the others; an easy pregnancy and four to five hours for delivery."

Her prediction about the pregnancy was correct. There was no morning sickness. She did not show until the fourth month and did not slow her work that much.

In the fifth month, she had looked at him and said, "I am sorry, Mr. MacDonald, but this baby will be a girl."

"What tis that to be sorry about?"

"I thought all men wanted a son."

"All I want tis my counselor safe. A lassie or a laddie makes nay difference. Either twill be part of my House."

In the ninth month Anna slowed down much to MacDonald relief. One unsettling event did occur.

"I'm sorry Zeb, but we can no longer be husband and wife until after the baby is born. Then it will be two to six weeks before we can be together again."

"Why?"

She had looked at him puzzled. "Because, well, it, it hurts inside to be a wife to you now."

"Dear, Gar, why did ye nay tell me?"

She had blushed before looking straight at him. "Because I like being your wife."

That had brought a smile to his lips and he had stepped closer and put his arms around her.

"And why so long afterwards?"

Anna had let out an exasperated sigh. "Because nature cleans out the womb."

"Ye Gods, woman, I should be able to get something from the *Golden One* to stop it."

"It is necessary to...." once again she had colored. "If it doesn't clean out, a woman can become infected. Then you can't nurse your baby and it is very dangerous."

"And if it tis longer?"

"Then something else is wrong and once again, it is dangerous for the woman." MacDonald lost the thread of his memories as a scream from upstairs made both men stand straighter.

MacDonald gritted his teeth, his muscles were bunched as though ready to knock Kasper out of the way and run upstairs. Silence descended and only flies buzzing around could be heard.

Kasper had a quizzical look on his face and shook his head no. "You can't intrude now."

"What tis the matter with ye? That twas my Anna screaming in pain."

Kasper looked at MacDonald. "You are the most upset father I have ever seen. Most women carry on like that for hours. According to Johanna, Anna usually screams when it is pretty well over. Anna has her babies more rapidly than others." He decided a change of conversation would do the agitated father a good turn.

"Either way, it will be a long night for me."

MacDonald swung his head to look at Kasper. "Why?"

"Oh, Malcolm is now threatening to burn us Yankees out."

"Are the rest of the men in town joining him?"

Kasper found himself looking at a very angry MacDonald. "No, Tom Jackson has left to join the Confederate Army and Benjamin isn't interested. Neither is Jesse." The next thing Kasper saw was MacDonald heading towards the Phillips's place.

MacDonald found Phillips loading the wagon with his wife's trunks.

"Phillips!" The name came out in a full-throttled roar.

Malcolm turned to find himself confronting a Thalian Warrior. The dark eyes were hard and unrelenting, the throat and chest expanded, and a strong musk odor exuded from MacDonald's body.

MacDonald grasped the man by his arms and slammed him up against the wagon.

"Ye threatened my brither-by-marriage with fire. Ken ye that my wife and child are there? If any harm comes to them or the Schmidt's, I twill hunt ye down and break every bone in yere body. If ye are foolish enough to burn Rolfe place, Mr. Rolfe twill hunt ye down faster than I and take yere scalp. Do ye ken?"

Malcolm tried to put on a brave, angry face, but his body betrayed him and piss ran down the front of his britches.

"Answer me!" And MacDonald slammed him into the wagon again.

"Yes, yes, put me down. I…I was just talking—no harm meant—me and my missus are leaving tomorrow."

MacDonald released him. "If ye think ye can burn my place on yere way to Arles, dinna try it. I twill be following and I care nay if yere wife tis with ye. Dinna forget." He turned and walked towards the Rolfe home and upon arrival banged on the door with his fist.

Olga opened the door, her brown eyes sparkling, her brown hair pulled back severely into a bun, and her raspberry mouth smiling. "Hullo, Uncle Mac. Has Tante Anna had the baby?"

"Nay yet. Where tis yere fither? I need to speak with him."

"He's out hunting, Uncle. He should be back soon."

"When he rides in, tell him to come see me. If he does nay return by this eve, I twill need to speak with Martin." With that he ran back to Kasper's place.

"Anything? Any news?"

Kasper smiled. "Gerde waved a towel out the window. That is our signal that the baby is here." He quickly reached out and grasped MacDonald's arm.

"You can't go up there yet. Some other, ah things need to happen."

MacDonald was staring at him. "What things? Oh…" and he remembered the animals always had the afterbirth. Earth beings were probably no different.

"Yes, and, of course, Gerde and Anna will want to have things cleaned up when they let us mere men see what God has wrought."

Jesse appeared carrying three mugs of beer. "I thought you gentlemen might need this while waiting."

"We probably could have used it more when my sister screamed." Kasper gratefully accepted one. Jesse was not generous with free drinks. "I had to assure Mac that most women would have been screaming for hours."

"That's true," said Jesse. "At home all the men would retire to the woodshed and drink from a bottle my pappy had stored there. Course, I don't carry anything that strong. If y'all want anymore, I'll have to charge." He smiled and looked at the untaken mug.

"I surely do suggest y'all wet your whistle."

Gerde's head appeared in the upper window. "It's a girl. I'll let you know when we're ready."

Jesse look startled. MacDonald gave a huge sigh of relief and reached for the mug. He drained half of it before stopping.

Kasper shook his head and laughter edged his words. "Mac, calm down."

"Aye, but tis a vexing situation when there tis nay I can do."

Thirty minutes later, Gerde appeared at the doorway. It looked like she was smiling, but the effort to turn away the bitterness of her own loss defeated her attempt.

"The father may go up first and then the rest."

She stood aside as MacDonald bolted past her and up the stairs. Gerde had wisely left the door open when she carried the box containing the afterbirth down the stairs. She handed the box to Kasper and returned to the upstairs to fetch the bedding.

MacDonald was oblivious to all the details. All he saw was Anna in the bed, holding a blanket-wrapped baby, and looking weary yet smiling that wonderful smile at him.

Within seconds he was on the floor beside the bed pulling them both into his arms. He kissed Anna and released her. His hands began unwrapping the blanket and clothes covering baby.

"Zeb, what are you doing?"

"I wish to see my wee one."

"I told you it would be a girl and she is."

"Anna, ye have given me the greatest gift possible. I am Maca and my House twill be renewed. In my land, the baby tis always presented to the Maca; his own and all newborn House members."

"But not without proper covering."

He smiled. "They are always nude. Then ye can see the formation."

Anna's teeth were gritted. "She'll catch her death of cold."

"The beings of this world wear too many clothes." The booties Anna had so carefully knitted went the way of the blanket and MacDonald gazed with wonder on his child.

"Dear Gar, she tis such a wee mite." He gently took the baby up in his arms and touched her face.

The eyelids with four lashes each went upward revealing brown eyes and closed again.

A smile went across his face. "See, she kens it tis her fither."

He handed his wee one back. "I think ye can dress her more rapidly than I." And he beamed at Anna and picked up the booties to hand to her.

It took a few minutes to put the booties, diaper, and flannel gown on, then position the small square of oilcloth before wrapping the blanket around the child. When it was done Anna nodded at him.

He opened the door to the group standing outside. All of Schmidt's Corner's populace entered except the Phillips. Rolfe had appeared and nodded at MacDonald as he stepped into the room. Olga managed to reach the bedside before the others.

"Oh, is it a little girl?" Not waiting for an answer she looked at Anna. "Oh, Tante, she's so beautiful. Look, she even has fuzzy hair."

Kasper was next and he smiled at his twin. "Have you picked a name?"

"Aye, she tis Wilhelmina LouElla MacDonald in honor of our mithers."

"It is a suitable name for her. Have you considered letting us baptize her before you return to your ranch? With the war going on, it may be a long time before a pastor will be able to get here."

"Ja, it would be a good thing." Anna answered for them both. MacDonald held his tongue. He wasn't entirely sure what that entailed, but didn't wish to show his ignorance.

"Y'all baptize them that young?" Benjamin Jackson was puzzled. He thought only Catholics, Episcopalians, and Methodists did that. 'Course Methodists called it a Christening, but, hell, there wasn't any difference that he could see.

"Yes, we'll probably do that in two weeks when Mrs. MacDonald can walk again." Kasper was hoping that this time Anna would stay down the prescribed two weeks.

MacDonald looked puzzled. Why would a new mither nay walk for two weeks? Anna had other ideas.

"Don't be silly, Kasper. You know very well I won't stay down that long, but I would like some rest now." She looked at MacDonald and smiled.

"I should be able to ride home in five to seven days, Mr. MacDonald."

Gerde stepped forward. "Everyone out now. Miss Rolfe has brought an angel food cake. Please stay for a slice and coffee." Inside Gerde was seething. How dare that upstart child outdo her? But then she had been busy.

Everyone went downstairs and dutifully had the cake (which to Gerde's disgust was amazingly good) and a cup of coffee.

"This may be the last time we get anything like this cake. That war will keep supplies short." Jesse remembered his grandpap telling what it was like in 1813.

"Naw, it ain't going to last that long." Jackson was confident that the Yankees would run at the sight of a Southern force. Everybody knew the folks back East were too squeamish for real killing.

"I forgot to tell Anna something. I twill be right back. When I return, it tis a round of beer for everyone at Jesse's." He ran up the stairs with Gerde glaring at him.

Anna looked at him as he came in the door.

"I had nay time to tell ye, but Phillips has made threats against Kasper and this town. Rolfe and I twill need to follow him and be certain he does nay burn our places. Also I've had a letter from the last Captain I served under. He wishes me to rejoin the troops. We'll discus that when I return, but I…I… Ye ken that I am a warrior. Ye may wish to stay here whilst I am gone."

"I will not!"

His smile broadened. "Ye are truly a Mistress of Don." He bent and kissed her forehead before he left.

Anna took a deep breath as the door closed. Now she would rest a bit and then have something to eat. She smiled down at the baby, and for a moment her stomach cramped. Dear God, where were her other babies?

Chapter 42

Margareatha

"Mr. O'Neal is here to see you, Margareatha. Put on a clean apron and go to Mother Superior's parlor. Cover that wild red hair. Do try to control your tongue. You will be without the evening meal if you insult either. And hurry. They are too important for the likes of you to keep waiting."

Sister Agnes frowned at the young woman washing the dishes. She was a disgrace; a heretic. Sister Agnes would be happy to see this one depart, but Mother Elizabeth was not to be disputed.

Margareatha glared at the woman. Why would she want to see him? He had refused to help Mama and the boys. He had knocked her down and locked her in that shed. Then he drugged her to get her on that stage to the nunnery. If she threw one of the dishes the Sisters would drag her into that basement room again, and withhold food for two days. She wouldn't have to see him then.

"Why would I want to see that old man? He's the reason I'm here."

Sister Agnes gasped. "It is not the elder Mr. O'Neal, but the younger, and why they bother with the likes of you I'll never know. They are truly sainted." She turned and hurried away. There was no other explanation than witch for a woman so tall with red hair and strange copper eyes with gold circles around the pupils. The disgusting girl never became ill like normal people; not once in the nearly five years she had been here. Sister Agnes had been certain of it when Sister Carla had said there was something else wrong too, but was forbidden to speak of it other than it had to be the Devil's work.

Margareatha stared after the departing black skirt. Younger? What younger? Then she remembered. Mama had said there was a son, but he had been sent away to school. The son was the reason the older Mr. O'Neal hated them. It didn't make much sense to her twelve-year-old mind, but Mama had not explained anything else.

"Not until you are older," Mama had snapped.

Well, I am older, and I am not going to do anything to please anybody here. She slammed another dish on the table, not caring whether it broke or not. I'll go as I am, she thought and marched to the parlor.

No one paid any attention to her. Some of the younger sisters averted their eyes, sure that she was a witch or a heretic and probably both.

She knocked on the door and opened it when she heard the Mother Superior say, "Come in."

Margareatha walked in with her head held high. "Always be proud of your height," Mama had said. She would not droop or lower her head for the nuns no matter how many times they beat her. Neither would she curtsy to that woman. Her profession did not make her holy and she glared at them both.

Mother Superior Elizabeth's eyes widened. The disgusting Lutheran had not even put on a clean apron, but that was the Germans for you. Filthy unbelievers.

Jeremiah "Red" O'Neal set aside the cup he was pretending to sip from and smiled. Once cleaned up, Margareatha Lawrence would be a beautiful, imposing asset. He had gleaned enough to suspect she would also be very, very grateful. At twenty-two,

Red was six feet tall, two hundred and twenty pounds, broad shouldered and slim flanked. His clothes were tailored, his boots were cobbled, and in his chest beat two hearts.

"Hello, Miss Lawrence, it is a pleasure to finally meet you. I was gone when that horrific attack took place on your home."

The sharp words Margareatha had planned to say were stilled when she saw his eyes. How could that be? The sisters said that hers were unnatural and no one had eyes like that. This man looked like her father.

O'Neal smiled and stood. He had been able to enter her mind and confusion filled her eyes and face instead of the defiance that had been there. He doubted if she had the same ability as his hadn't been there until he was nineteen. According to his mother's letter Margareatha was now about sixteen or seventeen. Perfect for his needs and she was beautiful despite being tall.

"Mr. O'Neal, I apologize for her rudeness.

"Margareatha, you are to acknowledge Mr. O'Neal."

"Why? His family forced me here and my mother and brothers died because of them."

Mother Superior rose to her full height of five feet. She looked like a child among giants.

"No reprimand is necessary, Mother Superior." Red smiled at her and turned to Margareatha.

"I can't blame you for being upset. Why don't you go fetch your coat and then we'll leave here."

For one moment wild hope surged through Margareatha, and then she realized that she could not live on the outside without shelter or food. The hell with it she thought. I'll do anything to get out of here.

Mother Superior turned on Red. "That is impossible, Mr. O'Neal. Your father's instructions were to keep her here until she is eighteen; longer if she repents and becomes one of us."

"I'd have to see that letter, Mother Superior, for my instructions were to bring her back to Texas."

The Mother Superior stared at Red. To Margareatha's amazement, the women said, "Very well, give me a moment, please." She turned and walked out the door Margareatha had entered.

Red swung around to Margareatha.

"Quick, we have to leave now."

"They'll stop us."

"No, they won't." He grinned at her and took her arm. "Hurry, I can't hold them all."

Margareatha found his words puzzling, but they were stepping out of the other door of the parlor. This door led into the entry hallway where visitors to the nunnery could enter if given permission.

Red nodded at the woman sitting behind the lightly veiled cubicle and took his coat and hat from the wooden tree by the door.

"Good day to you, Sister."

And they were out in the fresh, wind-nipping air of Houston.

Red slung his coat around Margareatha's shoulders. "There wasn't time for you to get your wrap. Hurry, they'll be after us in a moment."

Questions rolled through Margareatha's mind. How had this happened? Why did that Sister in the hallway let them depart without questions, but sat there mute?

Margareatha's long legs matched his hurrying steps.

"Why did they let us out? Me, that is?"

"Because I held them with my mind; it's an ability that you may one day possess."

"That's not possible."

"Didn't you feel me brush your mind?"

They had turned the corner and Red saw the conveyance he had arrived in. The man's jaws were working his chaw. He spit out a brown stream on the board sidewalk and mounted to his seat.

Once inside the cab, Red drew the curtains.

"Where are we going?"

"You, Miss Lawrence, are going to a safe house where you can get cleaned up and hide while the police search for you. I've already made arrangements for new clothes to be tailored for you as I figured whatever you had in the nunnery would not be suitable outside. I just didn't realize it would be so bad."

Margareatha set her lips. How dare he?

"Why not stop and let me out now? We can end this charade. I have no idea what you are planning, but, I, sir, am not part of it."

Red settled back against the cushion. "Oh, cut the melodramatic crap. Didn't you notice we have the same type of eyes? Don't you wonder why that is?"

His words made Margareatha draw in her breath. She hadn't heard such words for the last five years, but this was a man from the outside world, not a nun.

"Why?"

"Because, Miss Lawrence, we have the same father and in all probability share another one of his strange anatomical traits."

"And that would be?"

He grinned wickedly. "We'd have to listen to each other's chest to prove it, but I have two hearts. I'm guessing that with those eyes that you have two hearts also."

This time the intake of breath was much sharper. Her two hearts had been discovered when the nuns were binding her chest because she was growing (according to them) an enlarged bosom. She and the three nuns in the room had all been sworn to secrecy.

"And just what, Mr. O'Neal, are your plans?"

"I'd rather not say at this point. If the police are called, which I doubt, I don't want them questioning this driver. I can assure you it is nothing illegal and you will not be expected to, uh, be with men alone. Right now, why don't you just enjoy the ride?"

"Will there be food?"

Red looked at her and realized she had very little weight on her, but that wasn't unusual for people in poor circumstances.

"Of course, Miss Lawrence, although it may not be fancy at first, I'm sure it will be better than what they had at the nunnery."

After about twenty minutes the driver pulled the team to a halt.

"Don't be alarmed at where we are, but it is the safest place I could think of. Everything is ready for you and you will be treated like a queen until all the clothes are ready. It's just that it would be better that you not walk in this, ah neighborhood."

"You mean I'm a prisoner again?"

"Oh, hell, no, but this is colored town."

"What precisely is that?"

It was Red's turn to be puzzled and then he realized that all those years in the nunnery meant the girl was probably as innocent as the nuns.

"It's the section of town where the results of the father's sinning live." He saw the blank look on her face and continued. "They are the ones who had white fathers and were given money or set free to stay far away from their white fathers."

He grinned again. "This lady has fallen on hard times. Her father passed away, but she sews quite well and will make sure that you are decently quartered and fed. I've paid her well to do that."

"You can't expect me to believe the O'Neal family is paying for this."

"They are not. I am paying for it. I'm a gambler, and you, my dear are going to be my edge."

"I have no money to repay you." The teachings of her mother and der Pastor were still etched into her mind.

"When we start working together, you'll receive a percent; let's say five and then ten. We can always adjust it."

“And what will I be doing, Mr. O’Neal?” She suspected this was not normal. The nuns had hounded her with the fact that there was no employment for females like her other than cleaning, being married, or becoming a nun. All of them were occupations that she rejected. She was too young. What if her mother still lived? Grandpa Schmidt or Uncle Kasper might still be alive, but she had no idea how to get to St. Louis from Houston. Margareatha rightly assumed such a journey would cost money and she had none.

He smiled broadly. “You are going to be my eyes.”

Chapter 43

On Being A Woman

Margareatha was safe in that run-down house where O'Neal had taken her. Her bed was a cotton mattress unlike the straw pallet she had slept on for five miserable years. It was covered by a quilt with embroidered birds in each square and the pillows were stuffed with feathers.

Erlene Blevins was the owner of the house. The first day Erlene let Margareatha sleep and when she arose informed her she was not to go outside as someone might see her. She insisted Margareatha sit at the dining room table while she served her.

Margareatha studied Erlene's bustling form. The woman might be about forty. He skin was a coffee-with-cream color, her dark eyes intelligent, and her hair was braided and twisted into a bun. She was wearing a short shift for working and bustled in and out of the kitchen

"Once y'all finish eating, we'll choose what fabrics y'all want for day wearing and night wearing. 'Course your nightshift will probably be cotton, maybe with some lace. Is that all right?"

Margareatha set the cup of coffee down. "Erlene, I have no idea about the different fabrics unless they are cotton or muslin. I know Mama had a dress out of some different kind of fabric, but I can't remember what it was."

Erlene sank down in the chair on the other side of the table. "Where y'all been? Oh, I'm sorry, I'm not supposed to ask questions."

"That's all right. I think Mr. O'Neal is too over concerned, but I guess we can humor him. Why don't I fix the meals and bake things while you are doing the sewing?"

"La, Miss O'Neal, your brother done paid for everything. Y'all shouldn't be in the kitchen."

"Why not? It's boring with nothing to do."

"Miss O'Neal, y'all are white folk."

"What does that have to do with it? We did our own cooking at home. I hate sewing. I'd rather bake something. I can't just sit here. You don't want me to go outside for fear of losing the money he paid you, but that isn't fair to you. I should at least be able to go to the outhouse."

"No, ma'am, y'all surely cain't. Then people would ask me what was going on."

"I should think they are asking already. Can't they tell there is someone here?"

"If someone ain't showing their face, folks around here will keep mum about it. They don't want no trouble."

"Erlene, I'll make a bargain with you. While you are sewing, I'll bake or make the meals. That way I won't snap your head off and you'll be rid of me a lot sooner."

Erlene put both hands on her hips. "You're not to do none of the cleaning up. Mr. O'Neal said he wanted your hands looking like a gentlewoman's. That soap would make them red like a crayfish. I carry in all the wood and get that fire started. If y'all start breaking nails, y'all cain't put the wood in the stove and I cain't be running back and forth."

"Oh, for heaven's sake, I'll be careful. This is all so silly anyway. I'll cook and you sew. Tell Mr. O'Neal to bring me some books if he shows up again."

Erlene looked dubious. She just knew one time and this white woman would want nothing more to do with the kitchen. To her delight, Margareatha's meals were good, but rather plain.

"Y'all need to add some spices."

Erlene opened a cabinet door. "See those tins, Miss O'Neal? That's what makes cooking good."

"I know they do. Mama had some, but they were so expensive she rarely used them for everyday meals."

Erlene shook her head. This young woman didn't talk like white trash, but she certainly had some of their ways.

"Y'all can use them. Mr. O'Neal won't mind paying a tad more if y'all put on some weight. I'm going to allow for that on your clothes."

The dresses were made from expensive material and they were beautiful. The under garments were soft cotton or linen. A cobbler came to fit her for proper shoes.

After five years of drab clothes, inadequate food, little schooling, and the brutal treatment from the nuns, Margareatha felt alive again as she whirled around in each new outfit. She found that she loved beautiful clothes; their color and their feel, and the sweep on her body. The image in the mirror proclaimed, "You are a beautiful woman." It was a shocking, breathtaking surprise after all the years of the nuns pointing out her physical, mental, and spiritual shortcomings.

Six weeks after he left her at the house O'Neal returned and paid Erlene for the sewing. He also inspected each dress and handed over a steamer trunk.

"Pick one for traveling and pack the rest. Let me know when you've finished."

Rita took a deep breath. "I don't think that work that you mentioned will pay for all of this. My grandfather won't have that kind of money either."

"This will be a very lucrative calling for both of us. I'll explain more when we're on the steamboat headed for New Orleans. When we arrive at St. Louis, you can decide if you want to continue and earn your own wages or go to your grandfather's farm. Remember, you are my sister." He grinned at her before departing to the parlor to sip whiskey with Erlene.

Margareatha's mind was in a complete whirl. Did he mean it? She could not believe there was any way she could help him win at a gambling game. Erlene had taught her the basics of different card games while she boarded here.

"Men like it when y'all can offer them a diversion." There was a slight smile on Erlene's face and scorn in her voice as she continued. "They cain't really spend all them hours in bed with a woman no matter what they want to claim."

That statement left Margareatha baffled. "What do you mean by that cryptic statement?"

"Lawd, Miss Lawrence, y'all mean y'all ain't ever been with a man?"

Erlene's revelations about men and women were difficult for Margareatha to process. Erlene was convinced that Margareatha would be destroyed by the world out there.

"Y'all get home to your folks as quick as y'all can. 'Course there's always the chance that they ain't going to want you. It's best to have a stash put away if it comes to that."

Margareatha tucked all this information away in her head, but it wasn't until they were on the ship to New Orleans and the steam trunk deposited in her room that she asked O'Neal again how she was to repay him. I'll kill anyone that tries to touch me like that, she thought.

He closed the door. "I don't want people overhearing this."

"Remember when I went into your mind. Was that a bad sensation?" He was curious as he had not met anyone that could enter his mind.

"No, but I certainly didn't want you there. You have no right to spy on me in that manner."

"I wasn't spying. I was just testing. If I hadn't been able to do so, this scheme wouldn't work."

"And what scheme is that Mr. O'Neal?"

"You'll be dressed in one of those two ball gowns and serving liquor to all of us seated around a poker table; that, and looking beautiful and smiling while you move around the room. You'll do this right after the hands are dealt and you can see the cards." His brogue had disappeared. "Then you'll picture those cards in your mind. Erlene has taught you what constitutes a good hand. I'll look into your mind to see what they have and base my bids on that. I figure, even with the odds in the dealer's favor, I'll be up about seventy-five to ninety percent in my winnings. And by the way, call me Red or Jeremiah."

"Why do you need me? Why not go into their minds?"

"Because, darling girl, it would make them uneasy and there are some I can't go into. This way, they stay relaxed, and we win."

Chapter 44

New Abilities

"What do y'all mean, y'all won't introduce me? I just lost two hundred dollars to your damn cheatin' ways. A night with her would soothe my temper!"

Margareatha whirled around. She had been at the sideboard pouring drinks, but there was something in the tone of his voice that told her this was more than an ordinary challenge. It was almost a full year since Red had rescued her from the nunnery.

They were on the Belle of St. Louis and smoke hung like clouds in the room where men gathered after dining to play their games of chance. The tables were occupied by four or five men talking or intently staring at their cards, sipping whiskey, and enjoying their cigars. Margareatha had been circulating the room, smiling at all when the man's voice intruded. She turned to see Red raise his eyebrows.

"You, sir, owe my sister and me an apology."

"Apology my ass! Not to somebody who talks more like a damn Yankee than a true son of the South." The man rose to his feet. He was heftier than Red, but only about five feet seven inches tall, and his face was flushed from the whiskey.

Red stood. "You really are intent upon a fight, aren't you?"

The man turned to Margareatha. "How about it, Missy? Y'all go with me right now and I'll forget this son-of-a-bitch cheated."

Margareatha felt the red rage boil through her system and sent her left fist into his soft belly and her right against his jaw. Her mind screamed hateful invectives into his.

'Crawl out of here, you spoiled brat. Keep telling me you're sorry.' She was using mindspeak and didn't realize her commands were silent.

The man began crawling to the door. "Ah'm so sorry, Miss O'Neal. Please forgive me, Miss O'Neal."

Red was standing, first looking towards the man and then at Margareatha who was panting while she continued to stare at the crawling man as though he were some sort of insect.

Red gathered up his coins and bills and stuffed them into his pockets. His drink he left on the table with true regret and walked over to Margareatha.

"Let me walk you to your room, Sister Dear. I know this event has shocked you."

She continued to stare at the man, but to Red she said, "And why didn't you defend me?"

"My dear, I was trying to give him an opportunity to clear his head and come to his senses." Red was speaking in a loud tone, his words clearly enunciated. "I didn't realize he was as drunk as he obviously is."

He used mindspeak.

'Let it go, Rita. Let the man up. We need to leave this room now.'

The mindspeak brought Margareatha's gaze around to Red's. Her face was blank, emotionless.

"Yes, yes, you are right. Please walk me to my room." Her voice was the meekest Red had ever heard it.

He guided her out of the parlor and past the man scrambling to his feet. The man was looking at them with puzzlement on his face. He put out his arm to block Red's progress.

"Take your arm away, or I'll knock you down again and this time you won't rise so rapidly."

The man stepped back mumbling, "Beggin' your pardon, suh."

They walked the length of the hall and Margareatha produced her key. Neither had spoken a word. Once they were inside, Red inclined his head towards the far side of the room and they walked over to the closed porthole before speaking in low tones.

"You know what you did, don't you?"

"But how, how was I able to do that? I even made him crawl with my mind. Are you able to do things like that? And I heard you in my mind speaking. Is that something I can do too?"

Red shrugged. "I never really tried to control a person that long, but I have made people step back or out of my way. As for you being able to mindspeak, we need to find out. Let me try something."

He used mindspeak. 'You have gained the ability to do what our father was able to do.'

Rita swallowed. "But how, Red?"

"No, think it. Don't say it aloud."

This time Rita licked at her lips and tried to direct her thoughts to him. 'But how, Red? I didn't do anything to learn to do those things.'

A huge smile snaked across Red's face. "You don't need to learn them, Rita. It seems this comes with a certain maturity. There's a man on board that I've been talking with about this."

"What?"

"He's on a wheat buying expedition, and for other things. It seems he would prefer a new agent. He wasn't going to speak at first, but I realized how agitated he was when he saw me. The conversations with him have been most enlightening. There's a whole new enterprise opening up for us. Do you think you can do books?"

"Books, you mean read?"

"No, I mean accounting, ciphering, putting figures down on paper and keeping track of things."

"Isn't that what bankers and clerks do? I've never done anything like that, but I can cipher with no problem."

"Good, I'm meeting this man in the morning. Did you want to be there?"

"How early in the morning?"

"Oh, no later than six-thirty or seven. We'll have a corner off to ourselves and may need to go outside. I think he'd like to avoid us, but he can't. There is no way off this boat until we dock."

"But why would he avoid you if you are making some sort of a business deal with him?"

"Because, my dear, he gets headaches when we are together. I've gleaned enough that the possibilities are enormous, and someway, somehow, this man is not of this country, possibly not this world and neither was our father. I'd like you to pay close attention to his clothes, how he looks, how he speaks, but don't go into his mind."

Chapter 45

The Man From Nowhere

Margareatha appeared as the two men were being served and she swayed to the table, her long green taffeta gown swishing as she moved. She waited for Red to pull out a chair. She knew how beautiful she had become since filling out. Men stared at her full bosom and tiny waist and looked with awe at her height. She could see the hunger in their eyes and the slackness of their mouths. Few dared to say "Good morning," or any other word. Others hurriedly looked away or ducked their heads as though caught in some felonious act.

The man sitting with Red wore an expensive, brown, perfectly-tailored suit. At first Margareatha thought it was light wool, but on closer inspection she couldn't really identify the material. He looked to be as tall as Red, his build was slender, his eyes brown, and his hair a deep auburn. His pale complexion showed no sign of tanning. His hands looked as though they had never performed physical work and it was difficult to determine his age. Like the other men his eyes opened wider when he looked directly at her.

"Mr. Alana, my sister, Margareatha O'Neal. Margareatha, Mr. Alana."

Red smiled at Margareatha. "It seems Mr. Alana is acquainted with our father. He has assured me, the man has no intentions of ever returning here."

The waiter brought three coffees and her oatmeal. The men had ham, potatoes, red-eye gravy, and biscuits. Conversation ceased until the waiter withdrew.

"I can't promise that will remain a fact. He isn't cognizant of your existence, yours or your sister's."

"Then don't tell him," advised Red.

"That may not be a choice."

"Avoid him at all costs then, or barring that alert us when he is planning to return."

"Once again, that may not be possible."

Red shrugged and swallowed some of his coffee. "I'd rather talk about shipping the wheat and other products. Who do you use as a buyer and shipper now?"

"We're using an agent from one of the warehouses, and I feel the man is in collusion with the men or companies shipping in the grain and food products. The quality is often substandard. This is dangerous for, ah, the people at the end of my destination."

"I see. Who owns the shipping company or ships?"

"Our money paid for the ships, but they act like it is theirs."

"May I ask why one of your people does not take over the business arrangements?"

"That would entail living here."

"And I suppose you would give the same reason for not being the Captain onboard ship."

"Yes, of course. It is not possible."

Margareatha found herself staring at the man. His words were creating a larger puzzle. There didn't seem to be an accent, yet each word was enunciated slowly and carefully as though English was not a natural speech process.

"Where is the grain shipped from New Orleans?" Red leaned back slightly in his chair.

"To a port in South America which creates other risks, but portage takes it to our warehouse, which is well hidden."

"Suppose we accompany you when you purchase the grain? Perhaps Miss O'Neal could go over your portion of the account entries and devise certain questions. It is possible that we could come up with a solution."

Alana's face took on a set look. "Then, of course, you would expect your share. Our funds are not inexhaustible."

"You have mistaken my intent. I was hoping to save you some money and show you that I would work much better as a broker, and, later perhaps a shipping outlet for you. If we do save you a considerable amount, would you and your, uh, company consider that arrangement?"

"Pardon me for asking, but is money the only thing you want?"

"Not quite, Mr. Alana. We'd like to know more about our sire and where he is from."

"I would have to discuss that with my associates."

Red smiled. "Of course, we understand. Is it a deal?"

Mr. Alana let out a breath of air. "For now, yes."

"Fine, we'll shake on it and when we dock in Saint Louis tomorrow, we'll meet you at the gangplank."

Chapter 46

Changed Plans

"There it is, Rita. War has been declared between the Union and Secessionists." Red tossed the paper over the entries she had been making.

Margareatha stared at the words marching across the front page of the St. Louis Dispatch and looked up at Red. "How will that affect us?"

"For one thing, the armies are going to want the grain. They'll fight over it. The Union isn't about to let a kernel of it go south. We need to change our base of operations."

"But where will you find that amount of grain?"

"In California or up in Oregon. I'm relocating to Carson City, Nevada and spreading out from there. They've found gold and silver in Nevada. The Union will not let that go to the South either, but their control will be weak. Anywhere there is gold there is money to be made–lots of it."

"Somehow, I can't see you involved in extracting metal from the earth."

"I won't be. The money is elsewhere. In selling something or providing a haven for men to relax. I have to leave here anyway. Missouri can go either way. I've absolutely no intention of having people shoot at me over slaves, cotton, states rights, or for whatever reason they are fighting. Bullets don't give a damn about your political or moral stance."

"Of which you have none."

"Don't become moralistic with me. If you don't like Carson City, there's always San Francisco. We'll have to ship from there. New Orleans is the South and they'll confiscate anything if they suspect it belongs to the Yankees. Damn good thing I hadn't moved everything to Galveston. Once the war is over, we can go there."

He grinned at her. "Y'all'd like to go back to Texas, now wouldn't y'all?"

Margareatha had her shoulders hunched. "I don't like the idea of Carson City. It's too new. There wouldn't be any decent houses there. Why don't we just go back to Texas? Maybe I can find out what happened to Mama."

"Why? You know what happened to her, Rita. She's either dead or a bona fide Comanche by now. If you wanted family, you could have gone back to your grandfather's place at anytime. I wouldn't have stopped you."

"And how would I explain how I have been living or how my clothes can be so expensive? Grandma Johanna didn't want us there before and she wouldn't be any different now. I don't wish to live in a house where I am not wanted and be a drudge."

"Then it's settled. We'll go west. Alana will be here within the week. Once we've sent the last shipment, I'll head out with it, ostensibly for Texas. I'll tell people I'm going home to enlist with my relatives, but I'll be sailing to South America instead. I want to see what is going on down there. You can take the Butterfield Stage to San Francisco and start looking for places to set up a warehouse and maybe an office for you."

"If you go to South America, you'll be gone for a year or more. What will Alana do for wheat, corn, flour, sugar, or whatever else you've been shipping?" She suspected that something about the poundage and the amount of money was wrong. Whenever she pressed Red for information, he ignored the question and brought out the book that Alana had given them.

She had read it in its entirety. To her, it was bizarre. Beings identified as Justine came from a planet named Justine and possessed two hearts, mind abilities, the same copper-colored eyes with a golden circle around the pupil, red hair, and lived for five thousand years. The physical description fit them and their father. There was also a planet called Thalia with huge warlike people. They had dark hair, dark eyes, lived about two to three hundred years, and possessed huge sexual appetites. Thalians would fight anyone, man or woman and perform the sex act with anyone, man or woman. There was another planet peopled by a more primitive group called Krepyons. Ayana had been a planet, but the Justines destroyed it and drove them away. The Ayanas were red-haired and brown-eyed and they possessed slaves. All slaves were blonde with blue eyes. Rita wondered what happened if babies were born with the wrong color of hair, but the book was silent on that and so was Alana.

"Damn, that's right, Rita. Right now I can't afford to be gone that long. There is too much to do. Alana may have to do without part of his cargo next time."

"Which part, Red? What else have you been shipping? The tonnage isn't adding up for the volume and the amount of gold. The gold is accounted for in two sections. The lowest tonnage brings the highest return."

"It's something they need to survive. Forget it, Rita. You haven't dirtied your hands on anything."

"And why would they be dirty?"

"The Justines chased the Ayanas out of their part of the universe. They're hiding here. They tried living on Earth, but the native populace wasn't suitable as slaves, plus the natives had the audacity to kill some of the Ayanian people. They fled elsewhere and began to import everything they needed in the way of, uh raw materials."

"How did you find that out?"

"I went into his mind when he wouldn't answer aloud. That's why it took an extra day last time to finalize everything."

"And you didn't tell me."

"What difference does that make? You never asked."

"And what constitutes 'everything?' "

Red gave a tight smile. "Nothing that you need to be concerned about as the, uh, shipments don't show on your books."

Margareatha stood and crossed her arms. "I shouldn't be concerned? I never believed that book like you did. The book said there could not be any cross (as they called it) species children. If that book is true, how can we exist?"

"Obviously, we do. I don't bother with niceties like that."

"Or any others, right, Red? Most of the 'native people' aren't blonde and blue-eyed, are they? We've been shipping human beings as slaves. They're people, like us!"

"Not like you and me, Rita. We're unique. I've just been shipping a few over-the-hill whores and some completely soused boozers that fit their needs. Those kind of people aren't even missed."

"No one would miss us, Red. I have to think about this."

"While you're thinking, you'd better start packing for San Francisco. You'll only be allowed one trunk on the Butterfield stage."

Chapter 47

A New Beginning

"It's the finest available!" The man's voice was filled with enthusiasm.

Margareatha eyed the dirty walls, the dirt floor, and the iron stove. The stove was an iron monster with a huge oven and a double rack. She could bake four pies at a time or two pies with one or two pans of yeast rolls.

"I'll take it if one of the other rooms is suitable for a bedroom and one for storage. Is the outhouse decent?"

"Yes, it is. You won't regret this, Miss Lawrence. You'll be making a profit within the week! Tucson needs a fine bakery." Mr. Alton Beasley was all salesman.

Mama had taught her to bake. The convent put her to work in the kitchen. The nuns might have considered her a heretic, but her rolls and pies they regarded as heavenly. Red had rented a house during the months they weren't on the steamboats gambling and she continued her baking. It was a source of relaxation for her. Sewing she hated. That was hired out.

She had been on her way to San Francisco when the Butterfield Stage pulled into Tucson for a noon meal and change of horses. The man sitting beside her on the stage had been extolling Tucson as the gateway to Mexico and all points north, east, or west. "We've got one of the two operating Post Offices in this part of the Territory." That mail delivery was spotty he ignored for he had lots and buildings to sell or rent. The man had kept up a running commentary to convince one and all to make Tucson their last stop.

No one had planned to take him up on it, but before they could reboard the stage, the driver announced, "Sorry folks, but we ain't going anywhere until tomorrow. The Apache have to be chased out of the area or move on of their own accord. They've been raiding anything that moves. The driver from Fort Yuma didn't make it. Right now we need another driver in his place and two extra men to ride shotgun. Lodgings can be found in some of the hotels or you all can spend the night here in the chairs. Won't be as comfortable, but it's free."

"Why ain't the soldiers put 'em to rout?"

"There's one problem with that solution, sir. There aren't any soldiers here. The Territory is still Union since we lost the Battle of Pacacho Pass. Right now we're relying on Arizona Rangers, but they've been busy trying to fight the Union instead of Apaches. The South says they own this territory, but they don't have any troops for here. That's it folks, lessen you all want to go fight the Apaches. Me, I'm going to go have a drink." The passengers had been left staring at his back.

"People are still coming in here and they need something fresh to gnaw on." Beasley continued to encourage the sale. "Y'all can set up a fine bakery and be real successful."

"It's hard to believe a woman could succeed." Margareatha was torn. She was not happy with Red's schemes. The fact that he was selling people as slaves she found repulsive. It went against everything she had learned from her mother, uncle, and der Pastor. Red had no morals. The only people he seemed to care about were his mother, little sister, and her. She wasn't entirely sure how much he cared about her. She held the secret hope that Mama was still alive and they would be together again. Mama would be bitterly disappointed with her if she did not change. The money she had saved was strapped around her hips beneath the voluminous skirts. It should be more than sufficient.

"You could be successful, ma'am, because men who would be your competitors are fighting for the glorious South. If not the South, they are fighting for the damn Yankees, beggin' your pardon, ma'am—either way they ain't here.

"Fact is that's why I'm offering you this. You mentioned that baking fresh apple pies would be one of the things you'd miss in San Francisco. Well, maybe, they wouldn't be fresh, but I'm told dried apples work well. This was a bakery until the man took off and his sister married and quit. It's lots of work and I don't think she was up to it, but you, ma'am, beggin' your pardon, look just a tad stronger than somebody shorter than most women. You have all this time until tomorrow anyway. If you like it, you can spend the night here and we could finalize everything in less than a week. Tucson's a growing place, ma'am, even with this fight for our Rights going on."

That Beasley assumed she must be Southern puzzled Margareatha, but then she hadn't bothered to argue with any of them on the stagecoach. It would have been futile for men paid no heed to a woman's opinion and she felt them too dense to understand her reasoning.

Beasley had brought her to the east section of Tucson's main thoroughfare. The town was a strange aggregation of adobe and wooden buildings. The adobe buildings tended to be thick and coated with various colors of paint or whitewash. There were few of the familiar two or three story wood or brick buildings that she could see.

"Why is everything so flat?"

"Why, ma'am, take a look at them mountains." He waved his arm towards the distance. "In the morning and night they'll look like they've been colored rose or purple. It's an inspiring sight."

"I wasn't speaking of the terrain, I meant the buildings."

"It does become a tad warm during the summer months, ma'am. We've found the adobe buildings keep things cool. 'Course they do need fresh mud and paint to keep the rain from crumbling them, but it's a minor point. It can be hot as blazes outside and fine and dandy inside. Wooden buildings just let the heat in and not everyone can afford a slave or two to keep the fans moving

"All you need to do is look. You can see how Tucson is growing. This here's the new part of town, but with so many coming in, not everybody has had a chance to build something. That's why you see some tents, but they're sturdy. Don't need to worry about the wind blowing 'em into your place." There was more cheer in his voice than Margareatha thought the place warranted.

Like so many of the structures, these walls were thick. On closer examination, she realized the bricks were underneath a thin coat of what? The paint had gone over that.

"What precisely was used to build this place? Is it brick of some kind?"

"Yes, ma'am, it's brick, but that's adobe brick. It's made from the sand and clay of our great natural outdoors. Finest material around."

"I didn't see any kilns. Where do they fire them?"

"That ma'am is done by our glorious sunshine. It's the best and cheapest way in the world to build a city from the ground up." Beasley laughed at his own joke.

The tour of the house convinced Margareatha that it was feasible. One room had a small wooden closet and the house could be secured by the heavy pine doors. There were shelves in the third room. She knew she was through with the false night life and cheating other people at cards.

"Very well, Mr. Beasley, as soon as I check the prices on flour, fruit, sugar, and pans we may have a deal."

“Why not buy it right now, ma’am? Someone else might come along.” Beasley favored her with a broad smile.

“Then I’ll continue on to San Francisco. I am not paying you one thousand dollars for this place. It has dirt floors. While I’m looking at prices, I’ll also ask about the costs of lots and houses here.”

Beasley’s smile faded. He had not expected a woman to behave like a man. He had long ago learned that tall women really wanted to be treated like all other women. Why was this one different?

Chapter 48

Lorenz

"What do you think you are doing?" Margareatha took four quick steps across the floor of her bakery and grabbed the youth's arm.

She had stepped into the storage room to retrieve another sack of flour from the chest when a sensation of someone near passed over her. She used her mind and realized someone had entered the bakery without calling out some sort of customary greeting.

The youth swung around, his fist clenched and Margareatha grabbed his arm. The stench coming off of him was beyond belief, his cloths were nothing but rags and his shoes were tied to his feet. His hair was a mass of dark, matted curls stretching down to his shoulders. She realized grey eyes were looking at her out of a face that could have belonged to her mother.

The grey eyes widened as he realized she was taller than he and had a head of thick, red curls. His mouth opened slightly, but no words came as he stared at her face and hair. A sick, puzzled look grew on his face and in his eyes.

Margareatha grabbed his left arm and tightened her grip. "Who are you? Where do you come from? Where have you been?" She realized her tone was too sharp, too harsh, but dear God which one was this? Daniel? Lorenz? It couldn't be Daniel.

He would be sixteen and close to full-grown. This one still had smooth, childish skin under the tan.

The grey eyes were blinking at her and still no sound came from his mouth.

She couldn't help herself. She shook him. "Answer me, what is your name?"

The eyes and mouth grew sullen.

"What difference theat make?" The entire sentence was drawn out and slurred.

"Lorenz Adolf, you stop acting like that."

His eyes widened in surprise and his mouth dropped open. His tongue flicked at his lips and he whispered, "Rity?"

Margareatha swept him into her arms, dirt, sweat, stink, and all. "Oh, Lorenzy, Lorenzy, where have you been? Where's Mama? Daniel? Auggie" She held him at arms length, touching his face in wonderment.

He shook his head. "I dunno. Ain't they hearh? Why didn't yu'all come back fer me?"

"I couldn't. O'Neal locked me up and sent me to a convent in Houston. Didn't the Comanche take you?"

He shook his head no.

"Then how did you live? Where have you been?"

Hardness settled over his face and eyes. "Comancheros."

Margareatha stared at him. Why would a band of renegades, degenerates from all races, let a child of four live? And horror gripped at her insides. Maybe it was best just to get him cleaned up and fed. Then they could talk.

"Oh, Lorenzy, you need some clothes, a bath. Are you hungry?"

The latter was a silly question and she knew it. He was bone-skinny, his belly sunken.

"Take that loaf you were reaching for and I'll pour you some milk. I was just mixing up the things for tomorrow morning.

Then we can get you cleaned up and go buy some clothes. I have to be up early to start baking."

"Where's Mama?" Lorenz's eyes and mouth hadn't softened.

"O'Neal said the Comanche took everyone." She noticed he hadn't asked about their father. Could he remember that that cold-hearted man had hated them?

"Then they're dead." The voice was harsh, flat, and still with that horrible border slur.

"No, no, I don't believe it. Somehow Mama's alive. You have to believe it. I know it."

For a moment the boy almost swayed in her arms and his eyes closed and then opened. He looked at her in wonderment. "Ah reckon," he whispered. "How yu'all know theat?"

She couldn't say God told me. All she could do was shrug. "It's something I know. Just like when O'Neal lied to me and then to everybody else, but we can find them. It'll take notifying the army forts, but until this war is over, we'll have to wait. While we are, you can fill out and get some schooling."

"Why I need schoolin'?"

"Because no one pays any attention to you if you talk like low-down trash. Now you sit at the table and eat that loaf of bread. I'll bring you a bowl of beans from the pot on the stove and I can spare a little milk. You eat that while I mix up the starter. Then we'll get you cleaned up and go buy some clothes."

"Milk's fer babies." Lorenz objected, but allowed her to push him into the chair. He hadn't eaten for the three days that he had been traveling alone and his diet had been sparse all month. If Rity wanted to get him clothes that was all right too. It looked like white men wore clothes no matter where they were. He was smart enough to have figured out that white men were regarded as a cut above everybody else. He wasn't sure why for from what he had seen, one color was just as bad as the other.

He tore chunks out of the bread and stuffed them in his mouth. Margareatha came back from the stove with a bowl of beans.

"What are you doing?"

"Mmphing," came from the overfull mouth.

"You can't eat like that."

She reached over and picked up her knife. Lorenz pushed back on the chair and stood with fists cocked when he realized she was simply slicing the bread. She wasn't coming after him.

"There, that's how you eat it; one slice at a time with some butter and jam or honey on it." She looked at him standing there.

This time Lorenz sat down in the chair. If she wanted him in a chair and eating bread one slice at a time as she called it, he could do that. He sat down and picked up the bowl of beans and began to pour them into his mouth.

"Lorenz, not like that. You are supposed to use a spoon. You've forgotten everything." Her voice was almost a wail and she sank against the table, her legs suddenly weak. How was she to handle this? She would have sat in a chair if she possessed another chair, but she had been thrifty, hoarding her money for an emergency. She knew Mama would want them together, but would Lorenz mind her now? He was at least five foot three or four, almost as tall as most men, and he had always been strong minded as Mama called it.

Lorenz looked at her and something seemed to fill his face and eyes and he swallowed. "We useta sit a table jest like this." He closed his eyes for a minute. "Yeah, ah had a spoon and would wop the table with it." His eyes and face transformed as he smiled at her. "See, ah ain't fergot everythang."

Chapter 49

Mamacita

Lorenz was on his way back to Rity's bakery after a day of shoveling shit. Margareatha had managed to find clothes, get him into a tub, cut his hair, and somehow found a job for him at the livery stable on the west side of town. Not many folks came in that way, but enough to keep the stalls packed with horse apples. Hay had to be shifted and fed to the animals. Tack always needed worked on too. The pay was miserly and his employer more interested in gabbing or playing cards with his cronies. One morning, the owner's wife had come by the stable to ask Mr. Pickens, the owner, for some money. Lorenz wasn't paying much attention to anything the woman said. Mr. Pickens refused her, but he was polite about it. The next day Pickens bragged to somebody about how he'd punished his wife for embarrassing him in public. Lorenz decided these men weren't any different from the men in the Comanchero camp. They just acted nice to women when there was a whole mess of people around. Rity wasn't the kind that would put up with that. He reckoned that was why she wasn't married—that and 'cause she was too tall.

Living in town had been a revelation. People always seemed to be going somewheres or busy at some kind of task. Most of them wore clothes that covered them from neck to feet; not only the top wear, but all sorts of underwear that itched or scratched in the most unreachable places. If you scratched in the wrong place in front of people, they scolded you. He'd argued with Rity about all the clothes, but she ignored him. She even threatened to hold him down and put each article on him.

"I did it when you were a baby and I can do it now."

Lorenz would have left, but he liked eating regular like and there was the promise of finding Mama once the fighting was over. 'Course Mama might not want him, but he had to know. Rity said she knew the way to Wooden and then to the farm they used to own. He wondered why they couldn't just go now as he sure hadn't see any soldiers fighting here. It seemed like all the fighting was someplace in the East. There didn't seem to be any young men in town. 'Course not all men were gone. From what he had picked up from the conversations at the stable, most men around here didn't care who won as long as somebody sent soldiers to fight the Apache, Comanche, or even the Kiowa if they dared to defy the Comanche long enough to raid in this part of New Mexico Territory.

Rity's threat to teach him letters and ciphering hadn't come to pass. She was too damn busy in that bakery of hers. He didn't mind. If everything didn't sell, the leftovers might be part of the evening meal. She sure could make a darn good fruit pie when there was dried fruit, and her rolls and bread were better than anything he'd ever eaten in the Comanchero camp. She kept insisting he drink milk and would pour it on his oatmeal or mush in the morning, if she bothered to make it. Half the time she just sliced up bread and slapped butter or lard on the slices. The lard was all right 'cause when she used that she'd sprinkle some sugar or spread some molasses on it.

His thoughts were interrupted by a figure darting out from between two buildings. It was a woman in a ragged skirt and blouse. Her hair was pulled back, but there was dried blood smeared on her face and into her hair. Both her eyes were black, and it looked like her nose was broken. Of teeth, she had none left in her mouth.

"Niño, help me, hide me. He's coming after me to kill me." Her speech was border Spanish which would someday be called Tex-Mex.

"Mamacita, how'd yu all git here?"

"I ran and walked. I could see the home fires in the distance. Hide me, Niño, hide me." She had grabbed his right arm and was taking turns looking at the road out of town and back at him. Her lips were cracked from a beating and the lack of water.

"Yu all mean Zale?"

"Si, Niño, si, por favor, find some place."

"Come on, Rity'll know what to do."

He grabbed her hand and pulled her along the streets. Rity had left the door open to cool off the place, but once at the door Mamacita stopped, her eyes wide with terror.

"No, Niño, no, they will lock me away."

"Mamacita, this is my sister's place. She'll help us." He pushed her inside.

"Rity, we need yore help."

Margareatha heard the desperation in his voice and looked up from her day's receipts and cash. She stared in wonderment.

"This is Mamacita. She kept me alive when they found me. I'da been dead without her. We gotta help her, Rity. She don't know how to live here."

"But where, where would she sleep? There isn't any room."

"She can sleep out back, Rity. She can work, carry things. He'll kill her."

Margareatha looked at Lorenz. "Who is going to kill her? Is anyone out there?"

"I meant Zale. He's the leader of the Comancheros I wuz with."

"Say 'was' not wuz."

Lorenz ignored her rebuke. "He's always beatin' on her."

Margareatha took a deep breath and looked at the woman. "Did you see him following you?"

Lorenz translated.

The woman shook her head no, although it was hard to tell as much as she was shaking. "I saw no one, Señorita."

Margareatha nodded while Lorenz translated. She had understood the word nada. She did need extra help. She wouldn't have to pay this woman at first as food, clothes, and a place to sleep would suffice until the woman learned to be useful. She refused to think how close to slavery such a bargain was.

"Lorenz, show her where she can wash up. I'll see about something for her to sleep on. Then you both can carry in wood and water for tonight and tomorrow."

Mamacita broke into sobs when Lorenz translated.

Chapter 50

Comancheros

"Lorenz, take Mamacita with you to the vendors stalls. The man you saw leaving said they brought in potatoes from Mexico. He saw the wagon pulling in. Here's a dollar. They're probably all gone if it's true, but if they aren't, purchase as many as you can."

Lorenz snagged the dollar and told Mamacita to follow him. He'd just returned from the shift at the stable. If he was lucky, he could parley the dollar into more than just potatoes. Mamacita followed Lorenz as she thought this was proper. Nothing he said convinced her to do otherwise. At the stands, she stood back, waiting to see if she was needed. She looked down the road leading into town and saw three riders coming. The big roan was easy to identify.

"Niño, we must go!"

Lorenz looked up and ran back to her. He grabbed her hand and they started running.

Behind him he heard shouts and hooves. He stretched his legs out farther, figuring Zale would kill him, too, for running and killing that man afore he left.

Why ain't they shooting, his mind wondered. Probably 'cause they're in a white man's town and somebody might shoot back. Nobody would care about killing some Mexican woman and a stray kid though. They were almost at the door of the bakery when they were surrounded by three horses.

Zale jumped off his horse, his face red from the sun and anger, the blue eyes filled with hate. He was a bone-thin six footer and about thirty-five. Lorenz curled his hands into fists and stepped out to meet him, and saw the knife coming toward him. It was too late to duck. All he could do was twist to the side. He felt the knife descend from his cheek and down the front of his body and to the side where the ribs deflected the knife. He found himself hurled to the ground

"Shoot him while I take care of her. No woman defies me." Mamacita had grabbed at Zale's arm, hoping to draw his attention from Lorenz. He turned on her and plunged the knife down into her time after time not noticing that Margareatha was in the doorway raising her shotgun.

Margareatha saw two guns being aimed at Lorenz and shot one barrel into the one on the right and another barrel at the one on the left. Both men bent over their horses' necks and their horses reared.

The noise brought Zale back to the world and he looked down at Margareatha's shotgun and realized that he had to stand straight to look at her eyes.

Strange they were; reddish-brown with a gold circle around the pupil. So strange he felt his legs grow weak and sudden fear made him turn and leap into the saddle. He rammed his spurs into the horse for townsmen were appearing with rifles.

Margareatha dropped on her knees beside Lorenz. Blood was puddling into the gravel from his face and side.

"Lorenzy, can you hear me?"

His eyes were closed and his teeth gritted as though letting out a sound or moan would disgrace him. He opened his eyes when he heard her, but they were becoming cloudy and he swallowed. "Doan call me theat..."

"Somebody get a doctor." Margareatha yelled at one of the bystanders. "Now! And somebody help me carry him inside."

"Tabling's gone for the doc, but I'd wait with taking him inside till you got some oilskin on your bed, ma'am."

Margareatha ignored the advice and looked up. "Someone grab him under the shoulders."

When no one moved, Margareatha picked him up and carried him through the bakery and into her bedroom to the only bed. She put him down as gently as she could.

"Oh, Lord, don't let him die now. How would I ever explain to Mama?" She took her apron and grabbed the sheet from the floor where Lorenz had been sleeping to staunch the blood flow. What did doctors do for something like this? How was she to keep him from discovering Lorenz's two hearts?

She was about to become frantic when there was a yell from the front.

"Anyone there? It's Doctor Shelly. Someone said there was a wounded man here."

"Back here, doctor, please come in. It's my little brother. He's not a man. He's still a boy."

The doctor appeared. He was about thirty-eight with curly brown hair. His mustache and goatee were luxurious. In his hand was the mark of a practitioner: the leather bag containing the tools of his trade.

"Keep that shirt away from the wound and get me some water and a rag. A spare sheet for bandages would be helpful."

Margareatha moved to the front room. She removed all the dishes from her dish washing pan and used a pot to scoop up water from the stove's reservoir. Rag, she thought, what kind of rag? She carried the water back into the bedroom. She ignored the people milling at the doorway.

The doctor was threading some strange looking needle.

"Where's the rag and the sheet for bandages?"

Margareatha gritted her teeth. "Use what's here." She had not had extra sheets made, but washed hers once a week. She needed this doctor. Lorenz would bleed to death, but how was she going to be able to let him work and keep him from discovering and then talking about Lorenz's two hearts.

The doctor shrugged. "If you have scissors, you can cut the sheet into strips. Do you have any whiskey or brandy to give him? If not, you'll have to hold him down when I'm sewing or go get someone to help you. There are plenty of folks standing around out there. Just make sure it's someone who won't faint."

"There is some brandy left from the special cakes I make."

"Get it. He'll need it. I can see you are right. This one has no whiskers. Do you know who he is?"

"I told you. He's my brother."

The doctor's hazel eyes examined her. "Is that your mother out there in the streets?"

"No, it's someone I hired that desperately needed a job. I don't even know her name. What has that to do with Lorenz?"

The doctor looked doubtful, but said, "I still need the brandy."

He took off his coat and pushed Lorenz's shirt out of the way. When Margareatha returned, he picked up his needle with the coarse thread. "Keep blotting with that towel and see if you can get any brandy down him." He ignored the blood on the side and concentrated on sewing from the bottom up.

It wasn't the best sewing Margareatha had ever seen, but then she had never seen a wound like that. What brandy she hadn't poured down Lorenz's throat the doctor swallowed when it was over. He set the empty bottle down on the floor and wiped his bloody hands on his canvas trousers.

"I need to check his heart. Then I'll write you a prescription for laudanum. It'll help him sleep. If you're lucky the pharmaceutical will have some left. It's hard to get now with the war on."

Margareatha looked at Lorenz. He had passed out from the pain and the loss of blood. She wasn't sure how she had been able to hold him down. She felt empty and drained, like she didn't even have the strength to walk outside.

"Will he live?"

The doctor pulled on his jacket. "Well, he might. He's young. It just depends on whether he gets a bad infection or not. Sometimes I can cauterize them."

"Cauterize? You mean burn?"

"Madame, that's all there is."

He fished his stethoscope from his bag and put the two ends in his ear before bending over Lorenz.

"Must you disturb him?"

He ignored her and held the round, metal over Lorenz's heart area.

Margareatha closed her eyes and directed her mind into the doctor's. 'One beat, one beat,' she kept mindspeaking into his.

Dr. Shelly straightened. "Hmm, it's slightly blurred. It could be the alcohol slowed his heart down. How old did you say he is?"

"I didn't, but he is twelve."

"Hmm, a tall one. Well, I'll be back in a couple of days to check on him. I need your table to write the prescription. He'll stay asleep for now."

She followed him to the front and realized the bread in the oven was ruined. She could smell the burnt aroma wafting in the air. She ground her teeth. How was she going to pay for all of this?

Dr. Shelly took out a pad and scribbled something on it. "Here take this into town. If they have it, you can give it to him twice a day. If they don't have laudanum, you can try for paregoric that's used for a baby's colic, but it will induce sleepiness. I suggest you keep a close eye on him for the first three days. Let me know if he develops a high fever. You do know how to nurse a sick person, correct?"

Margareatha nodded yes.

He handed her a small vial. "Here's enough laudanum for this evening. That'll be five dollars, Miss Lawrence, but that will include his care until I take out the stitches. It'll be another three dollars when I take out his stitches, but I'll be dropping by to check on him periodically." That she wouldn't pay him, he felt was a good possibility. Most people had a few coins and liked to trade or give him food like chickens.

"Isn't that a lot?" Margareatha looked up from the illegible scrawl on the paper. "I thought you only charged fifty cents or a dollar."

"Well, yes, ma'am, that's true for an office visit. This was a bit more. Tell you what, we'll make it three dollars now and you can send over one of your pies. Then it will be another dollar and a pie when I take out the stitches."

Margareatha swallowed. Her profits were down since Lorenz arrived for his appetite was double hers. At least he looked like he was filling out a bit, now this. How was she going to nurse him, go to the shop that sold drugs and herbs, and get up early to mix up the rolls and bread for tomorrow morning? How could she make pies while tending him? She needed to go shopping right now, but first she would need the laudanum to keep him asleep. Please God, don't let him get an infection, she prayed and realized there were still people milling around in the room. She ran back to look at Lorenz. His eyes remained closed, his mouth twisted by pain and pulled slightly upward from the stitching. Why wasn't there a real pharmaceutical here like in New Orleans? Maybe someone will watch him while I run to the herbalist ran through her mind and then came the realization that her cashbox was out front with all those people.

Most were the shopkeepers from the tents that had closed already. The Mexicans were outside of the door. Men and women had helped themselves to a roll while they were waiting.

"Those are a penny each, please." She tried to keep her voice even and not grit her teeth. She felt anger starting to build. They were robbing her. The crowd didn't look at it that way. They were there to offer their help.

"Why Miz Lawrence, I thought y'all might need a hand with carrying in the wood this evening."

Margareatha closed her eyes to blink back the tears. "I, I thank you, but there will be no baking tomorrow. Is there someone here that can watch him tomorrow while I go to the pharmaceutical?"

Chapter 51

Economic Reality

Margareatha hurried out of the telegraph office, praying that the telegram would reach Red in time. Lorenz had developed a fever one week ago. Her mind was in a complete turmoil. There had to be a solution for this situation.

The doctor kept going, "hmm," when draining pus from the wound. Surely those people that Red's shipments went to had something to help. She realized that should Red even get the telegram, it would take weeks before anything arrived via the stagecoach from San Francisco, and then only if Red could get it from Carson City to San Francisco. So far Lorenz's system was trying to fight off the infection and the fever. His appetite was huge, as though the food would rebuild the body tissue that was damaged. Her ability to keep the doctor from realizing that Lorenz had two hearts was severely tested each time. Dr Shelly examined Lorenz. He would look puzzled afterward as though he had forgotten something. To make matters worse, her income had fallen to nothing and her cash reserves were rapidly disappearing into Lorenz's stomach. There were three other things she was good at. One was playing poker, as her mind gave her an edge, accounting, and singing. She knew no one in this town would hire her for the first two and if they did, it would be long hours away from Lorenz.

She entered her home and found Josephina coming from the bedroom with an empty bowl.

"I think that's the last of the soup." Josephina spoke in Spanish and Margareatha responded in kind. Her accent was bad, but her mind had grasped the meanings.

"I'll make some more. Thank you, here's the dime I promised you. Were there any problems?"

"No, Senorita Lawrence, he really doesn't need anyone here except to keep him in bed and that is getting hard to do." She pocketed the money and left.

Margareatha walked into the bedroom and smiled at Lorenz. "Are you feeling better?"

"No, it still hurts like, uh, heck." He figured there was no use using hell. It would just throw Rity into a conniption fit and a tirade of words about Mama. What good did it do to talk about Mama? No way was he going to admit that he liked it or that secretly he believed she was alive. All it did was make the ache worse.

Margareatha laid her hand on his forehead. 'Damn,' she thought in her mind, aloud she said, "I'm afraid your fever is back. Did you want some of that paregoric to make you sleep?"

"Hel—uh, no. All that does is make me stop shitting."

"Lorenz, there are other ways of saying that." How many times had she told him?

"I'll sleep without it."

She walked over to the wall and opened her trunk, sorted through the finery she hadn't worn in six months, and pulled out a light green taffeta. It was low cut at the bodice and the shoulder had cap-like sleeves. The matching pair of gloves and the shoes were in the bottom. Then she pulled out a green dress of linen and a multitude of underskirts. She held up each item to eye them critically. Perhaps the dress would be better if brown, but Margareatha had nothing so subdued. The skirts and blouses for the bakery were too plain. There was one thing that she could do that wouldn't take her away from Lorenz for hours. If she had to use her mind to get the job, she would. It was barely four in the afternoon. She could bring in what wood they would need and clean her hands and nails before heading to the Orpheum. Her mouth was set in a straight line. They needed money; money for the doctor, for the drugs that were useless, for food, and if Lorenz became strong enough, money for the stagecoach. Respectability was a dream. *Mama, I'm sorry,* ran through her mind.

* * *

Branson McGuire looked up from his conversation with the bartender as the red-head with the fancy hat, green linen dress, and a matching parasol walked into his establishment. His blue eyes lit with interest. Where did she come from? The only tall red-headed woman he knew about ran the bakery and he hadn't heard of any new arrivals. This one was a high-toned saloon gal. She walked toward him as though she knew he was the owner or a man of importance.

"Mr. McGuire, my name is Miss Lawrence and I would like to speak with you." Her eyes were a strange copper color with gold circles around the pupils and she looked straight at him. To McGuire, the surprise was that she looked straight down at him for she stood about three inches taller.

Branson picked up his glass and twirled the whiskey around. "Well, now Miss Lawrence, it happens I'm a busy man, but if you like we can have a drink now and you can come back this evening to entertain the men. I've got a curtained room upstairs where a couple can retire." He winked at her.

"You are mistaken, Mr. McGuire. That is not my profession." Her voice was clear and well-modulated. The voice remained steady, no tremor, and no blush highlighted her cheeks. "I intend to return, but as a singer. The men here are hungry for that type of entertainment. There hasn't been an acting troupe through here since the conflict began."

Margareatha chose her words carefully. You never knew who was adamantly for the Union or for the South. Most of the people in Arizona Territory had quit caring. All they wanted was troops from either side to ride out against the Apache or whatever tribe stole their horses and cattle.

McGuire considered. What she said was true. The war had pulled men out of the West. Some were filtering back in, but they were beaten or broke. Those from California, Nevada, and New Mexico Territory might have funds, but they found little reason to linger in Tucson. In time, this woman should become more accommodating. A few drinks usually accomplished that. Women couldn't hold their liquor.

"What types of songs do you sing?"

"I sing everything from folksongs like Barbarie Allen to the latest Steven Foster songs like *None Shall Weep a Tear for Me*, and, of course, the popular songs from plays on the riverboats."

McGuire looked at her more closely. So that's where she came from, but no women had arrived recently. Then he realized that this was the bakery woman. She had transformed herself from a drudge into a fashionably dressed saloon gal.

Margareatha smiled. "Men will be happy to throw money my way and buy booze while I'm singing."

"Are you willing to sit with them afterward and let them buy you a drink?"

"No, I wouldn't, but perhaps during a break if they buy what I like to drink."

"And that would be what, Miss Lawrence?"

"That would be brandy."

A slow smile crept onto his face. That was a more expensive drink. "What time would you be here?"

"When is your establishment the most crowded?"

"It's usually more crowded about seven thirty to eight thirty. After that, it's the men who like to drink or gamble and they've been damn few lately."

"Perhaps by my second evening that will change, Mr. McGuire. I suggest you schedule me for two nights a week. Does that sound reasonable?"

"What about three?"

"Do the people here have that kind of money?"

"They will if they have a reason."

"What evenings do you suggest?"

"I'd say Thursdays, Fridays, and Saturdays are the best. Sunday evenings too many souls are praying for God to forgive them for their sins. It's the same on Wednesday evenings."

Margareatha put out her gloved hand in the lady-approved manner. "In that case, Mr. McGuire, you can expect me tomorrow evening at seven thirty. Is there a back entryway so that I can make my entrance a bit more dramatic?"

"Yes, there's even a place to wait while I have someone introduce you. I'll get the word out. If my sales go up, you can sing as long as you want."

Chapter 52

Saloon Singer

"Sing *Gentle Annie*," a man yelled.

"No, *Come Where My Love Lies Dreaming*," yelled another, "only this time make it real sad like."

Margareatha complied and slowed the tempo. She had been singing at McGuire's for about six weeks. The money was good and men stupidly threw coins, fractional currency (if they had it), gold lumps, or silver into the hat she had placed on a stool beside her. The men had gone wild over her. She didn't even need to use her mind to loosen the silver in their pockets. McGuire vacillated between hearty and leering, and becoming more ruffled with each failed encounter. She was seriously thinking of changing saloons or taking Lorenz and heading to Carson City without an answer from Red. The journey would be brutal on someone recovering from such a severe wound.

Lorenz had lost at least twenty pounds off his skinny frame and remained weak. He was finally able to get up and move a few steps. His food consumption was beyond belief. Somehow the food was repairing the internal damage, and he was growing. His system had fought off the infection. Dr. Shelly had been both pleased and baffled, but took full credit for the outcome. He too had made overtures since she began at the saloon.

Margareatha had nothing but contempt for them and for most men. Men looked at her and looked hurriedly away when with their wives. Without their wives they almost drooled, but still shied away from speaking in public. She was no longer respectable and she scorned them all; except when she was singing.

Her full, clear soprano would throb and ache with love or yearning depending on the lyrics. When someone requested songs like *Oh! Susanna* she smiled and made men laugh. If she took a break during the course of an evening, someone always bought her a brandy. A few would buy the entire bottle in the hopes of enticing her to their room or the alcove above. McGuire was delighted. The extra patrons coming to hear her and the purchase of brandy kept him at bay.

Margareatha finished for the evening and slung her long cape around the fancy off-shoulder gown. The cowl she would pull upward when outside. It fooled no one, but the ladies of worth could not accuse her of walking the streets in inappropriate clothing.

McGuire met her in the short hall leading to the back door.

"Stay awhile, Miss Lawrence. I've ordered a special bottle of brandy to celebrate all the business you've brought my way."

"Thank you, Mr. McGuire, but I must return home to check on my brother."

He grabbed her right arm under the cape. His huge hand clamped down in a bruising hold.

"Not this evening, Miss Lawrence, it's time we talked. It won't do any good to scream. My men will create a disturbance and they have orders to stop anyone foolish enough to investigate."

Anger, red and raw surged through her, and McGuire felt the pressure of a derringer against his belly.

"You will release me now. I've shot this before if you're stupid enough to think I haven't." With her mind she drove his hand from her arm and made him take a step backward. A puzzled look came over his face, but Margareatha side-stepped him and opened the door.

"Goodnight, Mr. McGuire. I shan't return." She banged the door closed. Men be damned. Answer or no answer, she was buying the tickets at the Butterfield Stagecoach office tomorrow. The stagecoach would take them to San Francisco. From there they would catch a local stage to Carson City.

Chapter 53

Margareatha Loses Her Temper

"Y'all going to let me have one of those women?" Lorenz's horse was beside Red O'Neal's after a morning of riding. They were on the way to the Sporting Palace, the fancy whorehouse Red owned. Red had given Lorenz a grey horse called Dandy when Lorenz had told about killing one of the Comanchero men that was trying to rape him. Lorenz couldn't figure out why, but the speculative look in Red's eyes alerted him. This man was expecting something, but what?

Lorenz figured it was because it meant he would grow up to be a gunman and rider like that Collins fellow working for Red. Red, however, was trying to determine if Lorenz's Justine mind abilities were maturing early.

Red looked at the boy. At thirteen, he was still incredibly slender and stood about five feet seven or eight. "We'll see how you do talking with the ladies today. Then maybe in a month or so I might permit it."

They tied their horses at the front.

"I need to meet with Madame Clarisse. You're allowed into the parlor, but no farther and no drinking. Remember these whores are fairly high-class. They don't want to hear a bunch of cussing or see you spitting or hawking anything."

Lorenz looked at Red. He seemed to be serious. "Ah thought all whores were nothing but tramps."

They stepped to the front door.

"No, these have a certain amount of education and expectations. That's why they are here instead of the other place."

"I thought it wuz 'cause they're prettier." Lorenz refused to speak like Rity wanted. She was always bossing him around.

Red grinned as he knocked at the door. "They are prettier, but that's because my customers want young and pretty."

A dark skinned maid opened the door.

"Why Massa Red, come in. Y'all want some coffee and cream?" She looked surprised at seeing Lorenz. He was tall enough to be a man, but anyone could see he was still a boy.

"Callie, you are going to have to quit calling me that. I pay you wages." Red smiled. "And instead of cream, put a shot of whiskey in the coffee. Where's Clarisse?"

"She's in what she calls her office, suh." Callie pointed towards the kitchen. "Do y'all want me to give this," she started to say child, but changed her mind, "young'un anything?"

Lorenz smiled. "How about the same as Red's?"

"No, give him a cup of coffee with cream. Anyone else up?"

"Some of the girls have wandered down, suh."

"Good, they can keep him company."

"Ah don't want any cream. That's fer babies."

"And don't break the cup when Callie brings it." Red guided him into the parlor furnished in gold, blue, and white upholstered chairs with small dark tables beside them, and a deep, white velvet sofa, a fancy table by the door, gold brocade drapes to keep gawkers away, and a maroon carpet. A maple stair wound up to the second floor. Lorenz was awed. Never had he been in a room so richly furnished. Rity was buying fancier things as she could afford them, but most were made by local tradesmen.

Two sleepy-eyed young women stood the moment they entered and curtsied.

"Mr. O'Neal, can we be of service?" the blonde cooed.

"Service, Daisy? What an odd way to put it." The other woman was a brunette, and she smiled at Red. "You name it, Mr. O'Neal, and I can match it." Her brown eyes sparkled at the thought.

"Why, thank you, ladies, but that will need to wait until evening. I've brought my young friend, Lorenz, and if you will, ahem, keep him entertained while I speak with Clarisse, I'll appreciate it. By entertained, I do not mean initiating him into the ways of manhood. Just sing songs or talk."

Red turned and walked to the back.

Lorenz was red-faced. He had never been around such pretty girls. Rity didn't count. She was his sister. He felt the swelling between his legs and hoped they didn't notice.

Both young women hooked one arm around one of his and led him to one of the over-sized upholstered chairs. "Haven't you been with a woman, honey?"

Red flared up Lorenz's cheeks. "Uh, no." He tried to think of something to say that wouldn't sound stupid.

Daisy, the blonde, half-pushed him into the chair and plopped down into his lap. She put her arms around him. "There, doesn't that feel nice?"

Lorenz's mouth opened and he pulled in a breath of air. "Yes, 'um."

Both giggled, and Daisy brought his hand up to her breast. As though following some deep rooted instinct, Lorenz began to squeeze. That felt good. He liked it.

The foyer door banged open and red-headed fury came barreling into the room.

"Get away from him you two bit floozies!"

Before either could move, Margareatha grabbed Daisy by the hair and pulled her off Lorenz. She used her parasol to thump the other in the chest. Both were screaming.

"Just what do you think you are doing? Mama would skin us both alive if she saw you here."

She grabbed Lorenz's arm and pulled him upright.

Clarisse came running into the room with Red following her. "You have no right to disturb my young ladies in this manner."

Margareatha took her parasol and drove it into the Madam's midsection.

"Wait a minute, Rita," Red began when Margareatha's parasol caught him in the midsection. He didn't join Clarisse on the floor, but he grabbed his stomach.

Margareatha gripped Lorenz's shoulder and propelled him out of the room, through the foyer, and out the front door. She was using the parasol to bash him whenever there was room enough or Lorenz tried to twist away.

"Not out here!" he yelled at her as they stepped onto the street.

Red appeared at the door. "Miss Lawrence, if..."

"You may take care of his horse. I'll see you later," she raged back and continued to pull Lorenz down the street toward her house using her parasol whenever she could get in a good whack.

Inside her house she fought him into his room and used his belt on him. She failed to notice that his eyes had turned to ice and no sound came from his lips.

Lorenz knew he had endured worse beatings. He'd sworn to kill the man who had administered them and any man that tried to do that to him again. But this wasn't a man. This was Rity, his sister. He couldn't kill her, but she'd never have the chance to do this again. He gritted his teeth. He knew he would leave here. In a couple of years he would be big enough and strong enough that nobody could stop him. First he would kill Zale and then go find Mama. All he had to do was survive and he was damn good at surviving.

When Margareatha judged it punishment enough, she tossed the belt on his bed. "I expect to see you've written out your name and alphabet when I return. Mama would never have forgiven either of us if I left you there." She banged the door on her way out, fearful that she might have gone too far.

Her mood was no better at her Poker Parlor. There were several tables downstairs, a small bar, and an upstairs with an office for doing all of Red's accounts. Placing numbers in a row soothed her agitation. When she looked up, she realized she worked through supper. She decided to ready herself for the evening and order something through her bartender.

Margareatha pinned the green plumes to her hair. The plumes swept down the left side of her head. Her dress was a dark green with a shoulder shawl. The bodice outlined every feature of her full upper figure. Doing the accounts had put her in a better mood. She left her office where she kept the accounts for Red's whorehouses, saloon, her own establishment, and Red's shipping business. She locked the door and placed the key into her beaded embroidered purse. That was slipped into a special pocket sewn on the side of her skirt. She could hear the scrape of chairs and men's laughter below. Parson was dealing already. No one knew if that was his name or whether it was the theology he spouted when too deep in his cups. It didn't matter as long as he stayed sober while dealing.

She lifted her head and saw Richards leaning against the left mahogany newel post. He straightened and smiled as she approached.

Margareatha nodded at him. She ignored him as she did most men. This one was tall, his build good but his shoulders slumped from long hours at the poker table. Bags were under his eyes from heavy drinking. His belly had a definite paunch.

He put his left arm out and grasped her waist to pull her into him.

"Miss Lawrence, you must have a drink with me, but first a kiss."

Margareatha drove her knee up into his groin. A look of surprise and pain filled his face. His grasp loosened. Margareatha stepped back and drove her right fist into his soft belly. As he bent over, she grabbed his hair and tried to heave him down the stairs. Richards managed to grab the railing by the third step down and hauled himself upright.

"You bitch!" He started to double his fists when Margareatha's left caught him on the nose. She followed through with her right square on his chin. He slumped downward desperately hanging onto the railing.

By this time men were gathered at the bottom gawking upward. They had never seen a woman use her fists so effectively on a man. Margareatha gathered her skirts and stepped around Richards.

"Somebody throw him out. He's barred from here." She descended with her head held high and took her seat at the head table.

"Morgan, you heard me. Throw him out and bring me a brandy." She smiled at the men looking at her.

"Anyone ready for a game?"

Inside she was seething against all men: Red, Lorenz, and the apes who wanted to paw her and beat her into the ground. That evening she showed no mercy. Other evenings she might lose a game to throw a sop to the men playing against her. She stalked home still belittling men in her mind. It was a relief to walk into her house to peace and quiet. She checked Lorenz's bedroom to make sure he was asleep and found herself looking at a slightly rumpled empty bed.

She sank against the doorjamb whispering, "Mama, forgive me. What have I done?" He was gone. She knew it. A quick survey of the kitchen confirmed her suspicions: bread, beans, two empty lard cans, and a knife and spoon were gone.

Margareatha ran to The Sporting Palace and barged in on Red's conference with Clarisse.

"He's run off." In mindspeak she shouted, 'We have to find him! Now!'

Red removed the cigarillo and looked up at her. "We can't do anything until morning. Did you check the livery stable?"

"No! I didn't need to. You have to go after him now!"

"Darling sister, I cannot see in the damn dark and neither can anyone else. Morning will be time enough, besides which way would he go?"

"He's gone to look for Mama." She was screeching, not caring who she disturbed.

"How do you know?"

"Because that's what he wanted to do once this war ends."

"There, you see. If I can't catch up to him, he might be at Wooden. I was planning on going to Texas anyway." He used mindspeak to explain. 'My mother has sent a letter with information I can't ignore.' He didn't bother to tell her it involved a shipment of Confederate gold.

"If he's in Wooden, I'll find him. Now if you'll excuse me, I have certain business concerns that must be resolved."

Chapter 54

The Wounded Soldier Returns

Kasper pulled the cart to a stop by the Blue Diamond Freight loading area. MacDonald's letter had stated he would be riding with the freight coming in from Missouri.

He had been wounded, and was returning home. Anna wasn't to worry as it was just a thigh wound, and the doctor had extracted the bullet. They had threatened amputation if the infection didn't heal. He had managed to keep some of the medication from the *Golden One* with him and then use it without the doctor's knowledge. He wasn't proud of it, but he had used his mind to make the doctor write him a discharge and a pass. Anna's letter about the hostility of the Texans had driven him homeward. He was stopping at Blue Diamond Freight as the logical place in Arles to lie low if he needed to rest.

People had stared at Kasper and Anna who was holding Mina when they drove through Arles. She had rarely visited Arles after her marriage. She had convinced Kasper to take her along. People wouldn't recognize her. Two barrels of cornmeal and one of flour had come through. It was better than nothing and he could not let Anna traipse around the countryside alone. Jackson and Jesse might be Rebs, but they wouldn't hurt Gerde or the Rolfe family. Herman Rolfe would watch over both ranches and the town.

MacDonald stepped out of the building as they approached the loading dock. He was using his cane in his right hand, cradling his Henry with his left arm, and carrying his satchel in his left. He favored his left leg as he walked. Kasper swung himself down from the large cart. Anna was fuming. She had to wait for him to come around and take Mina before she could climb down. MacDonald solved the problem by walking over to her side and taking Mina. The smile on his face and his eyes told her how much he valued them and she almost jumped the distance to be in his arms. Kasper came over to shake his hand when a shout interrupted their reunion.

"I told you all it was them damn Yanks. Git 'em."

MacDonald turned and faced them, handing his cane and Mina to Anna. He stepped forward and braced himself. Anna shoved Mina into Kasper's hands as MacDonald swung one massive fist into the first man's face. He pivoted and brought his left smashing into the other's face. The first man had dropped, but by this time the third was at his other side and he couldn't swing around as rapidly with his bad leg. This assailant landed a blow to his cheek.

The second man shook his head and moved in, fists cocked, his right arm coming back to swing a haymaker at MacDonald.

Anna swung the cane into the back of the man's knees, knocking him downward. She lifted the cane and swung it again, clipping the man on the side of the head. He keeled over in the dirt. The red rage was in her and Anna raised the cane again, oblivious to the screams of their daughter. She cracked the cane down on the man's ribcage and raised it again, this time aiming for his head when a force stopped the cane from moving.

"My love, if ye do that, ye may well kill the man."

MacDonald had knocked the other two out and was now holding the cane. He found himself looking into a pair of slate grey eyes that saw nothing but the enemy. Dear Gar, he thought, she tis ready to kill. He smiled.

"Mrs. MacDonald, I still have need of this cane. Twould be a shame if ye break it."

For a moment her eyes fixed on him, and then she released the cane and hugged him, not saying a word, just holding him as though assuring herself that he was alive and safe, and hating the clothing that kept her from touching him. For a brief moment he held her.

"Now we need to leave. I'll hold our lassie when it tis safe. Mayhap ye should be in the back of the cart and I twill hold my rifle."

Freighters had thrown the three barrels into the cart not caring whether they broke or not. Damn Andrew for making them load the damn Yankee's cart. It seemed the damned Yankee had paid months ago and he, Andrew, was honor bound to deliver it. They felt differently. Why should it go to Yankees when supplies were getting low at Stanley's General Store?

"I advise a steady pace." MacDonald sat beside Kasper balancing the Henry rifle on his right thigh, his finger on the trigger.

"Ja." Kasper flapped the reins. "Yo, team, up."

Neither man looked in the back, but Anna had pulled her shotgun up into her lap with Mina. She knew how to use it and would if they were attacked. If there had been more men in town, they might not have been able to ride out, but this was January 1863 and the South needed men.

Towns and farmlands had been depleted of young and middle-aged men. Even boys were enlisting. General Lee had inflicted heavy losses on the North, but the damn Yankees just kept coming. It was rumored that they would be using slaves to fight for their side. Weren't the Irish enough? And England still hadn't declared for the South. Instead England was talking about slavery like it was the issue. Everybody knew it was for States Rights and the glorious South to maintain her traditions.

"Should I quicken the pace a bit?" Kasper's knuckles were white, but his face was stoic with no change of color.

"Nay, ye should wait until we are a good five miles away and then stop to let me get into the back. Wait till the road curves a bit and I twill make the transfer. I shall watch to see if we are followed."

There was no way for Kasper to know when exactly five miles had been reached, but years of living here honed a man's senses. One-half hour later he cracked the reins against the team's back and they went into a trot. He knew they couldn't stay at that pace and within the hour, he slowed them for MacDonald to switch places with Anna.

"We twill nay camp at the usual spot, Kasper. I want ye to keep going. There tis a place further on that tis one of the false fording areas. The willows and cottonwoods grow thick there. Twill help hide the cart."

"Do you think they'll come after us?" Kasper let worry creep into his voice.

"Oh, aye, but it twill take time for them to get up their courage. How are they for man power?"

"Most of the able bodied men have joined the Confederate forces. Those that were captured and agreed not to fight for the Union have gone to Nevada to work in the mines. Some of the freighters might be under the same terms and "officially" based elsewhere. There are people like Marshall Franklin and Elias Clifford that are in their 50s or late 40s."

"They are still capable men, but I canna see Marshall Franklin going on a raid."

"They hate us." Anna's voice was hard and strong. "They chased the farmers off in parts of eastern Texas."

MacDonald turned slightly to look at her. "How do ye ken that?"

"The cobbler, Diest, came through and told us."

Anna felt she must confess. "I had him make both of us a pair of shoes. Mine were breaking down and he didn't know when he would come through again. If it isn't rebels, it's Comanche or Kiowa, and now there are white raiders too. The country isn't safe anymore."

MacDonald turned back to watch the trail. "Dinna feel bad about the shoes. Ye needed them and ye are correct. I may need them ere he returns.

"Kasper," he lowered his voice. "The people in Arles ken that it takes us about four and one-half days to make the trip. If we push on an hour longer and start an hour earlier, we can make it in less time. We twill stay at the ranch one evening and come into Schmidt's Corner the next day. Ye can tell Rolfe what has happened. If he is nay there, I twill try to find him without straying too far."

"We can't leave our ranch to the mercy of them." Anna was adamant.

"By ourselves, we could lose. I want ye and the wee one safe. If it twas just us two, aye, we twould make our stand there."

"Why not come straight into Schmidt's Corner then?"

Kasper's question caused a strained silence. He did not see his sister's cheeks redden.

"I have been gone for over a year. I have missed our wee one's first steps and first words." Such a thing twould nay have happened in Thalia, but he did not mention it. "I want one night in my own house, one meal with my wife and wee one, and one night in my own bed that tis built for someone my size."

Chapter 55

Home

It was a brutal pace for the horses, but they pulled into the Rearing Bear Ranch a day early. Kasper knew he had to discharge his passengers, water the horses, and head towards Schmidt's Corner. Daylight would slip away within three hours and he wanted to be home.

Mina had been fussy all day. It had done little good to pass her between MacDonald and Anna. When they pulled into the yard, Mina tugged at her mother's sleeve.

"Mein potty, Mama." Mina would mix English and German until she started school lessons with Uncle Kasper.

"Ach, she has not been for three days." Anna picked her up and ran for the outhouse.

MacDonald tossed his satchel and cane over the side. "Did ye wish the rifle or the shotgun for yere drive to town?"

Kasper shook his head. "No, I wouldn't be able to hit anything with either one. I do have a shotgun at home. Maybe if they attack there and I know Gerde is in danger, I would be able to shoot someone."

MacDonald grabbed Anna's shotgun and boosted himself over the edge of the cart. His leg was on fire and dropping to the ground added to the pain. He needed Anna to clean the wound and apply the salve that he knew was in one of the kitchen cabinets. That is, it would be there if Anna had not used it for some other purpose. He was also hungry and kenned that his lassie twould be too. It twould be better to eat and have Mina in bed before Anna tended to his leg.

He hobbled into the house carrying the shotgun and rifle. Kasper followed behind him with his bag. It was an annoyance to MacDonald that he could not carry everything at once, but he needed the support of the cane. It took another trip back-and-forth to bring in Anna's bag and the cooking utensils.

Anna still had not returned with Mina when Kasper drove off. MacDonald pumped water into the bucket for the evening's drinking water and began carrying in wood for the kitchen stove and fireplace. Then he saw that Anna had carried in the wood before leaving. He started the fire in the kitchen stove and the fireplace in the great room. He heard the kitchen door close.

"We wash our hands now," came Anna's firm voice.

She appeared in the doorway speaking German. "Bread and clabbered milk are in the springhouse. The bread will be dry, but there are still some jars of the applesauce I made from the last shipment of apples that Papa was able to send. Do you want some coffee?"

"Nay, save that for morning. How do ye still have coffee?"

"We don't," retorted Anna. "It is nothing but chicory and bark."

He grimaced at her retreating back. Mina was standing in the doorway watching. She decided this was a good time to toddle to this huge man who had held her so much of the way home so she wouldn't feel the bumps and jolts of the wagon.

MacDonald caught her with a flourish and held her over his head while she went into gleeful giggles.

"Now wait patiently whilst yere fither finishes starting this fire to warm the home. Then I twill get a blanket to warm our bones till it tis warmer in here." He was well aware that this was an inefficient way to heat a room, but that was all they had.

Another small iron stove was in the bedroom, and he planned to start that after dinner.

Anna returned to the kitchen and then left again. He picked up Mina and the cane and started to follow her outside when he realized she had taken the extra bucket. She planned on washing the dishes this evening. The woman didn't stop. MacDonald considered. He couldn't carry Mina and the bucket right now. He decided to set the table in the kitchen. The iron stove would put out heat faster than the fireplace. He set Mina down.

"Be patient whilst yere fither helps yere mither."

Mina was too young to realize that men in this world didn't set out bowls and utensils when there was a woman around. MacDonald was opening the applesauce when Anna returned. She frowned at him, but dumped the water into a metal dishpan sitting on the back of the stove.

"I did nay object as ye twill need hot water to clean my leg once Mina has gone to bed."

Anna nodded and slipped off her coat. ""Why did you set the kitchen table, Zeb?" She was puzzled. Breakfast was the only meal eaten here.

"Tis warmer in here for me and the wee one." He picked up Mina and sat in one of the chairs.

"Yere fither shall have the pleasure of holding ye and feeding ye..." His voice trailed off as Anna carried in the highchair and lifted the tray section upward.

"She feeds herself, Zeb. She isn't an infant."

He shook his head. "The wee ones grow so fast here, but on the trail we twere feeding her."

"That made sense and less dishes." She tied a bib on Mina and sat. She folded her hands and launched into a prayer thanking God for the food and for bringing them safely home.

After dinner MacDonald started the fire in the bedroom stove while Anna dressed Mina for bed. Mina's crib was in their bedroom against the west wall and several feet from the stove. Mina would sleep in their bedroom until she was older. Then her bedroom would be in the room across the hall until she was old enough to be upstairs. This room would become the formal living room and the other bedroom theirs.

MacDonald had the pleasure of holding his wee one, telling her some nonsense story, and putting her into the crib after she fell asleep. He checked the fire, put in another log, and returned to the front before collapsing into the rocking chair.

Anna appeared with a washbasin of warm water, a roll of bandages, and a towel.

"I twill need the salve in the blue can if ye have nay used it."

"Ja, it is in my apron pocket. You need to drop your britches." She smiled as she used his word.

MacDonald stood and undid the canvas flap and let the britches fall down around his ankles. Anna noticed the bloodied bandage. The bleeding must have stopped once they were out of Arles for it had not come through on his trouser leg.

"Zeb, you have been bleeding. Is it safe to use this salve?"

"Aye, tis the other one that heals the scars. This one twill pull out any infection and help it to heal whole." He looked at the small container. "I hope there tis enough; else I twill need to return to the *Golden One*. I did nay wish to do that till the danger tis over."

"Stay where you are and I'll get my scissors. I need to cut that bandage away. If you sit down I won't be able to clean it properly." When she had her scissors, she cut away the bandage and set her lips in a straight line before she began cleaning and bandaging the wound.

Anna looked up at him as she tied a knot in the bandage. "There, that should hold it. I'll clean up and you rest. Mina should be sound asleep by then."

She rose and picked up the dirty bandage and towel. She turned more slowly than normal to keep from spilling the water and went into the kitchen and then outside to toss the water.

MacDonald shook his head. She had to be as tired as he was from that trip, possibly more so and now that the salve was soothing the wound a more pressing need arose. He picked up the scissors, returned them to the sewing machine drawer, and grabbed his coat before stepping outside. Ye gods, Anna had carried the water clear out to the garden. She was running back.

"What are you doing outside?" Moonlight streamed around them.

"I'm going to the outhouse before bed."

"Ach, you could have used the pot."

"I prefer this, and ye need to put on a shawl or coat ere ye come out here." He rushed off toward the small building set below the garden.

* * *

He entered the bedroom while Anna was putting the dishes away. After he disrobed, he considered putting on what Anna called a nightshirt, but rejected the idea. He would just need to remove it in a few moments. He put another log into the fire and looked down at his sleeping wee one. How he longed to show her to his elder Lamar.

Anna entered and began removing her clothes. The moon provided sufficient lighting and she was undoing the button on her last long slip when she realized a very nude MacDonald was looking down at their child.

"Zeb, what if she sees you?" The horrified words hissed out.

He turned, a wide smile creasing his face. "She tis too young to remember." He walked over to her.

"Let me help ye with that."

"Zeb, we might start the bleeding again."

"Ye twill have to be gentle with me my love. I have been too long away from ye."

Chapter 56

Raid

MacDonald stirred the fire in the iron cook stove. Rolfe had not been at Schmidt's Corner. He'd left Anna and Mina there after warning everyone of an impending raid and went in search of Rolfe. This was the third day. Time was running out and Rolfe was nowhere to be found. He didn't think anyone could afford to hire a wolf hunter now. Had the man gone off to the Comanche tribe he visited? If so, there was nay telling when Rolfe twould return. He needed to be in Schmidt's Corner with his counselor and lassie. He felt the raiders would burn his place, but they would be too many for him to defeat by himself. He threw a handful of chicory into the coffeepot and headed for the outhouse.

On his return he saw the outlines of men and horses on the road to the south. He veered to the north to be positioned behind the washhouse. If they rode this way, he would have just enough time to get inside and grab his Henry. He had braced it against the kitchen table. Why had a Thalian Warrior left his weapon? He could hear Rolfe saying, "Dummkopf!" The words Rolfe had used when he had erred in the early days.

The seven men out on the road saw the smoke coming out of the chimney. They had missed seeing MacDonald stepping behind the washhouse.

"Burn it," two of the men muttered.

"He's there."

"He can't stop us."

"He can kill enough of us or slow us down. If we burn this now, it will alert the people in Schmidt's Corner. It would be better to hit there first and then get this ranch on our way back. Besides, he might have some liquor stashed away somewhere if that fence sitter Owens doesn't have any."

The group continued towards Schmidt's Corner. They did slow their mounts and look down towards the first place Rolfe had created for his ranch before bringing out his wife. It was a simple hovel dug into the side of a bluff that once fronted a much larger, swifter moving river. A timbered roof extended outward to keep off the sun. A small campfire in front of the roofline had a coffee pot swinging over the fire.

"Well, he's somewhere. Let's keep going. We'll pick up the pace when we're closer to the damn Yankees. We don't want to roust him. He's probably out in the bushes somewhere."

They walked the horses for two miles and then broke into a fast trot. They were a quarter of a mile out of Schmidt's Corner when the leader pulled a white, homemade mask over his head and neck and raised his quirt. The other six emulated him and a harsh yell broke from their lips as they spurred forward.

No shots from the Rolfe home greeted them and three men dismounted long enough to set fire to rags and place them alongside the house. The rest started firing while riding through town. Ben Jackson slung his hammer at them and they shot him. Then they began to shoot up his house. Slugs tore into Owens's Tavern and the Phillips's home. Jesse was standing at the backside of the tavern and started to yell, "I'm a Southerner," when he saw three men setting fire to the Phillips's place. He ran into his tavern, ducked down behind the bar and came up with his shotgun. If they wanted a fight, by God, he was a Southerner and knew how to shoot.

Anna was in the garden weeding and wishing she was home weeding in her own garden. Mina was playing on a rug placed a few feet away. At the first shot, Anna stood, bent over, picked up Mina, and ran bent low to protect Mina. She could hear yells and galloping horses as she ran for the house. Gerde and Kasper were standing wide-eyed in the kitchen, both incapable of moving. Anna shoved Mina into Gerde's arms.

"Here, put her behind the big chair.

"Kasper, where is your shotgun?"

He pointed towards the hall. It was impossible to tell if he meant the office or the front of the store. Anna whirled and took her shotgun down from over the kitchen door. She went nowhere without it. She would not be defenseless if Comanche struck again.

"Get it!" Anna was yelling. She clawed at the box with the shells and stuck two of them into the breech.

Her yells woke Kasper and he ran towards his office.

Anna heard someone come into the store and she stepped through the kitchen door into the hall and fired both barrels directly at the man in the store.

Kasper appeared in the office doorway.

"Mein Gott, Anna, you've killed a man."

Someone grabbed the downed man by his boots and pulled him out. More bullets sprayed glass from the windows and Kasper ducked down.

"Get back!" This time he was yelling at anyone who might be near.

The smell of smoke began to fill the air. The Phillips's place was burning rapidly. The raiders had ridden out of range, but they turned and came roaring back into town.

Olga was pulling Young James by the hand and running for cover to the barn. Flames were licking up the front of their house and she feared for their lives.

No one heard the hooves of two more horses as MacDonald and Rolfe barreled into town. They had met up in front of Rolfe's dirt home and pushed their horses the six miles into town. Both had their Henry rifles out and were guiding their horses with their knees.

Rolfe was screeching a war scream and no one understood MacDonald's bellow of "Thalia!" One slug took out the raiders' front rider and another raider felt the smashing pain in his leg that began spurting blood. The Henry slug kept going and the rider's horse went down. They had set the town on fire and knew it was doomed. Three of their men were down; one badly wounded and the other two dead. Bullets were firing from six different locations. They turned, rode behind the Phillips's house, and then headed back towards Arles. They were not young fighting men. They were men in their late forties and fifties that preferred town life over ranching or farming and offered quick access to a saloon.

MacDonald and Rolfe fought the urge to charge after them for Rolfe's home and children needed saving. The fire was rapidly spreading upward.

"Mama's organ. It's in there. You can't let it burn. It's Mama's!" Olga's screams angered Rolfe

"Shut up. Ve're trying to save der house!"

"We can't, Friend Rolfe."

By this time everyone had grabbed buckets for carrying water from the river to keep the fires from spreading. MacDonald threw his hat on the ground, dumped the bucket of water from Anna over his head, pulled his kerchief up over his nose, and ran into the house through the kitchen door. Smoke filled the place and seeing was difficult in the haze. He knew where the organ was. It sat against the back wall of the room a few feet in front of him. His long legs carried him to the doorway. Sunlight filtered through the small front window creating a greyish yellow smoke blanket that hovered in the room. He pulled the organ towards him and the door. It had not broken into flames, but the wood was heating up. Once he had the rosewood organ into the kitchen, he pushed it toward the door.

At the kitchen door he stopped. It was narrower than the front door and he needed to enlarge the opening. MacDonald kicked at the doorframe several times, the blows landing solidly, and chunks of wood began flying outward. It left a jagged line of lath and plaster, but now he could barely breathe and he felt the heat increasing at his back. He pushed the organ outside, hefted it to his shoulder and staggered across the porch. He grabbed the post by the steps leading to the ground and felt fresh air enter his lungs. From somewhere came the sound of cheering and Rolfe's voice.

"Mac, get the hell out of there. Vhat's der matter mitt du?"

He looked out at the men and women cheering, took another deep breath, and straightened his back before walking down the steps while trying to ignore the pain in his left leg.

The buckets of water were futile. The Rolfe home and the rest of the contents burned to the ground. One charred stud remained a defiant finger sticking upward.

"Keep the Jackson's place from burning. The fire twill spread if we dinna." MacDonald bellowed after placing the organ nearer to the barn.

"An ember has hit Smitty's stable." Jesse reported on a trip back from the river with a sloshing bucket. Everyone ran to refill their buckets. If the stable hay caught, there would be no Schmidt's Corner by nightfall.

Every man and woman was sweat-soaked and smelled of smoke by dusk, but the fires were out. The back portion of the stable had been spared. The front portion was blackened and they tore the charred timbers away from the rest of the structure. The store and the rest of Schmidt's Corner remained.

Rolfe and MacDonald nodded at each other and both went for their rifles and horses.

Chapter 57

Taking Stock

"Tante Anna, where are they going?" Olga pushed a lock of hair behind her ear, smearing smoke-stained sweat across the side of her face.

"They are going to track the men who did this and check on our ranches." Anna let herself look to the south. She took a deep breath when she saw no smoke.

Olga swallowed. Her home was gone along with their clothes and linens. She had saved her mother's china, but that was all. There was no food. She started to walk forward and then stopped. Where should she go? To the barn? The thought of sleeping there made her skin itch. It was dirt floors with hay in the middle portion and manure covered the stable area.

Anna's arms were around her. "It's all right, Olga." She looked at Gerde.

Gerde was no exception to the rest. Her clothes and exposed skin were grey and black. Strands of hair had escaped from her tight bun of rolled dark hair.

"Get everybody together and maybe a little cleaned up. We'll all eat at our place and decide what to do." She nodded at Kasper standing by the men.

"Why are they pointing to the cemetery?"

Tears were running down Olga's face. "I saw Mr. Jackson on the ground when we ran out of the house. He—he's dead, and Tom's fighting for the South, and we don't even know how to write to him." She hiccupped.

Anna's mind was too tired and numb to realize that Olga, almost eighteen, had a crush on the only young man in town.

"Then they are probably talking about burying him." She turned to her sister-in-law.

"Gerde, you are right. We need to clean up and start dinner.

"Mein Gott, Mina." She ran for the house.

"Mina, Mina, Mama's here. Where are you?"

Anna burst into the kitchen and saw nothing. She ran to the hall and hesitated. Should she look in the store or in the living room? She had told Gerde to put Mina behind the big chair when she ran into the house, but had she? If so, had Mina stayed there? Rage had swept through Anna when the attackers shot at the store and bullets came through the open door. It was the same red rage that had plagued her all her life. When it started, Anna would strike out against the opponent. It didn't matter if she used words or a weapon. All she could think of was to destroy the enemy. Today she had feared for Mina's life, but the fires started and they had to be put out. Fire was the enemy once the shooters from Arles had left.

Mina was lying beside the chair, eyelids closed over a tear-streaked face and a wooden block in one hand. She must have gone into the kitchen where the play blocks were stored in a box under the sink, and returned here. She had pulled a doily down from the little table and the Bible that had rested on it lay on the floor.

Anna scooped her up and held her tightly. Mina looked at her mother and tears started rolling down her face.

"My heart, my love, I thank God you are all right. Will you ever forgive your Mama?" It was a question that would plague her for years. Dear God, forgive me my horrible temper.

"Is she all right?" It was Gerde on her way to retrieve another towel.

"Ja, she is fine. A little frightened. I will need to hold her for awhile."

Gerde nodded. "The fire in the cook stove went out and it will take a while to finish cooking the beans. They aren't enough to feed everyone. I've maybe enough bread and pickles. We can share the clabbered milk, but our sugar supply is getting low. The Rolfe's store of honey is gone."

"What about the crab apple jelly Johanna sent?"

"There's some. We've tried to conserve everything. If Mr. Rolfe could get us another shipment down through Indian Territory, we'd be all right. How are your stores at the ranch?"

Anna closed her eyes before answering. "We have enough to share, but Mr. MacDonald won't think to bring any back with him when he comes—if there is anything left."

Kasper had walked back over and was bringing Olga with him. As he stepped through the door, he spoke to them both. "We need our spade. We'll bury Mr. Jackson tonight and hold the ceremony tomorrow."

He turned to Olga. "You and your family will stay here until your Papa decides what he will do."

"Thank you, Uncle Kasper." Olga's eyes sought Gerde's for a confirmation. The invitation meant her, Martin, and Young James. James was now the same age as Hans was when Hans died. Would Gerde accept him in her house?

Gerde gave a quick nod of yes to Olga and looked around. "Where is James? He can carry the bucket of water from the river for washing. We need more than what is in the basin now."

"We'll go downstream and rinse off after we bury Mister Jackson. Tomorrow we'll see what is left of the Phillips place. I don't think there is anything more than the fencing and the back shed."

"Why did they burn the Phillips's place and shoot Mr. Jackson?" Olga's crying was turning into wails. "They were on the same side."

"A bunch of drunken fools don't care about that. They just wanted to destroy us. They are worse than the Comanche." Anna began to feel her rage returning. She set her teeth. There was no one to fight.

"Olga, why don't you find Young James? He can carry the water, bring in more wood, and if necessary watch Mina."

Gerde was busy stirring the fire in the cook stove to life. "Some more water is needed for the beans too. They soaked up all the broth."

"I'll get the first bucket while Olga finds James." Anything to keep Olga busy. She had lost her mother and now the house and everything in it but the organ. Anna didn't realize that Olga had managed to rescue her mother's white china. At least the Rolfe's have chickens.

Anna tried to put Mina down, but she clung to her mother's neck.

"Mama, Papa?" Mina was crying again.

"He's chasing the bad men away to keep us safe. Now you stay here with Tante Gerde like a good girl."

Mina tightened her grip.

Gerde looked up. "You'd better keep her with you. She's different from your others."

The words struck a cold chord within Anna. Had Gerde realized how different two of her children were? Had Gerde been around the children that much? Rather than argue, Anna nodded, perched Mina on her left hip, went out the door, and picked up the bucket she had used to throw water on the flames.

Chapter 58

News from the Front

Anna looked up from her washtub to see a lone man staggering into the yard. His Confederate uniform was tattered, a crutch under his right arm helped him walk, and the left wooden leg kept poking holes into the ground. The man wore a hat that was as tattered as his clothes and she could see the bandana underneath. The shoulders were broad, but the man was a mere shadow of a healthy adult. His worldly goods were on his back, held by leather bands running across his chest. He leaned against the fence and tipped the bill of his hat upward.

"Would it be possible to rest here on your porch, Mrs. MacDonald? I'm not sure I can make it into Schmidt's Corner today. It's been a long walk from Arles."

"No von gave du a ride?"

Why, thought Anna, would the Rebs of Arles let a returning soldier walk?

"No, ma'am, not when they heard where I was going. It seems nobody recognizes Tom Jackson without his leg." The man's voice was bitter and pain-filled.

"Mein Gott, Tom, I didn't recognize du. Du haf lost so much veight. Come in, come in. Some cold vater du must be vanting, and something to eat, ja?"

Tom looked ready to break down. "Thank y'all, Mrs. MacDonald. Yes, to both of your offers. I don't think I could have walked any farther."

He opened the gate and clumped into the yard. "Do y'all mind if we go through the back door? Then I won't have to walk up the step to the front porch."

"Ach, ja, come in, Tom." Anna was busy drying her hands on her apron and walking towards the kitchen door. Mina was playing in the shade of the crab apple tree that had reached ten feet and the branches had started to come over the fence. Her toys were blocks of wood from Uncle Kasper. He had cut and sanded them from the lumber left over from the Phillips's place.

"Mina, come mitt Mama."

Mina looked at Tom with widened eyes.

"This is Mr. Jackson, Mina. Come now. He ist hungry and thirsty from his long walk."

"That your daughter, Mrs. MacDonald? I can't wait to see Pa. I haven't heard from him the last two years. 'Course that doesn't mean anything. No mail really comes to a hospital or a prison camp."

Anna knew that she had the task of telling Tom about his father and the raid on Schmidt's Corner. That was why the people of Arles had let him walk.

"Ja, this is our daughter Wilhelmina. Ach, Tom, so much has happened." She stood back and let him precede her. It was the first week of May and already too warm to keep the door closed. She would need to shoo out the flies before fixing something for Tom.

Tom made it as far as the kitchen chair and sat. "Just some water will be fine, Mrs. MacDonald." He wasn't sure how deep the resentment ran. These were damn Yankees. He had hoped his leg and his youth would be enough to get him back to town. No one in the South could afford anything and no damn Yankee was going to hire a cripple, and how the hell could he help Pa as a blacksmith with one leg and a shrunken body?

Anna handed him the filled water ladle and grabbed the kitchen towel and began flapping it vigorously to drive the flies from the table and counter out the windows and door.

"Now some nice bread and butter mitt coffee, ja? Und some clabbered milk mit—no, that's with some apple butter? The beans are not yet done. Then du rest and Mr. MacDonald vill take du into town tonight or tomorrow. He's over at Mr. Rolfe's. They some branding are doing." She almost tripped on Mina who was trying to stay well behind her skirt.

"Mina," she reproved her, but picked her up. "I must the butter and clabber go get from the springhouse."

She disappeared out the door. It was cowardly she knew, but she was trying to figure out how to say the words. If only she could say them in German. The news would be just as bad, but she would be able to say them with clarity, and she felt, with much more compassion than she could say them in English.

Mina was delighted to be up in her mother's arms. Papa always picked her up, but not Mama. Mama was always so busy.

Anna pushed the heavy springhouse door op and set Mina down. Then she picked up the covered butter dish and bowl of clabbered milk. It was cool in here and she stood for a moment before walking back outside. She handed Mina the butter and pulled the door shut.

"Come, Mina, back inside ve go. Du carry the butter for Mama."

Once inside the kitchen, Anna saw that Tom had his head down on the table.

"Are du asleep, Tom? Ach, I forget, du a man now are. I am sorry, Mr. Jackson."

He had removed his hat and his dark eyes regarded her and a slow smile came on his face. "Mrs. MacDonald, Mr. Jackson is my father."

He saw Anna blink and swallow.

"Is something wrong with my Pa, Mrs. MacDonald? Is that why I haven't heard from him in two years?"

Anna set both bowls on the table and wet her lips.

"Mr. Jackson, I vish my English vas better, but, ja, something has happened. They killed your papa vhen they tried to kill us, and I—I am so sorry, but he thought he vould be safe mitt dem."

Tom halfway rose from the chair and sank back down, a stunned blank look on his face.

"Who killed him?" His voice rasped out of his throat. How would he live? How could a crippled man track down killers or Injuns?

The drunken, rebel fools from Arles. They tried to burn Schmidt's Corner and run us out. They vere shooting all over der place. Even Mr. Owens, the bullet grazed, and they burned the Rolfe's and Phillips's places. Embers vere flying and set fires in other places. Vone took part of Mr. Schmidt's stable and the side wall of your cabin. Thank God, Mr. MacDonald and Mr. Rolfe got there vhen they did. They chased them off, but ve fought fires all afternoon and kept vatching for them to break out again."

Tom closed his eyes and hid his face. It was too much for a man to bear. His Pa, his home, all gone. Where would he sleep tonight? The nerves from his missing leg and the stump where the peg leg fit hurt like hell and he knew he needed to rest before going on or it was another night on the ground. Worse, it wasn't even damn Yankees that did it. It was his own countrymen.

Anna looked at the shattered man and patted his shoulder. "There vas lots of vood left from the Phillips's vainwright spare stock. The people in Schmidt's Corner used it to repair the side of your cabin, Jesse's shed, and Kasper used some for his garden fence. Mr. Rolfe took the rest to his other camp and made a place for them to live.

"I don't know how your place looks inside." Anna's voice became apologetic. "Ve tried not to disturb anything more. Ve buried your Papa in the town graveyard. Mr. Schmidt made a vooden marker for him and ve held a town service for him. Mr. Schmidt led us."

Tom lowered his hands. "I have a house to go to? Y'all mean Yankees did that? Why? I was killing your men—before this happened." He nodded at his leg, his voice full of bitterness again.

Anna smiled. "Your Papa vas our friend. He vas an old man. Vhat else could ve do? Ve are Christians. Ya, it vas bad, but soon, soon, this var must over be."

Tom's face grew tight. "Ma'am, it is. General Lee signed the surrender paper April ninth. That's why they let me out of prison. I caught part of a ride into Arles with the Union Cavalry that's setting up camp there."

It was Anna's turn to stare opened mouth. Then she closed her eyes, folded her hands, and prayed in German. "Thank you, dear Father in Heaven. It's over. Amen." She opened her eyes and looked at Tom.

"It's easier to pray in Deutsche. It's vhat I'm accustomed to doing.

"Miss Rolfe vill be so glad to see du alive are. She vas upset und crying vhen ve had no vay of vriting und telling du about your Papa."

She turned and began setting out the bowl, knife, and spoon. "Miss Rolfe vas the first vone to see your Papa on the ground; she and Young James vhen they ran out of their house. It vas burning."

Olga's crying hurt Tom to the core. Olga had just started to grow out of childhood when he left to join the Cause. He wondered if her lips were still that strange raspberry color, and why the hell think about that? What woman wants half a man? Not that he couldn't be a man, it was just most women wanted somebody whole that could support them.

Anna placed everything in front of Tom and he could not stop himself. He practically shoveled the clabbered milk into his mouth. He tore great chunks out of the bread and gulped the chicory brew she set beside him. After chewing the mouthful of bread, he took a deep breath.

"Y'all must excuse my manners, Mrs. MacDonald. I cannot begin to tell y'all how hungry I've been." He bowed his head.

"Thanks for the food, Lord."

"Mr. Jackson, I understand. The Comanche did not let me eat. Du enjoy and du vill for supper stay tonight."

Chapter 59

The Dream

It was one of the few nights that MacDonald and Anna did not exercise their marriage rights. He had not returned from taking Tom into Schmidt's Corner until nearly midnight. Anna had mended after they left. Material for making new clothes had not been shipped in for over two years and it was either mend or go unclothed. Anna then set the food in one of the warming ovens for her husband before retiring.

MacDonald carried the rifle into the bedroom, set it against the wall on his side of the bed, and shook Anna awake and hugged her.

"Anna, my love, I will need to ride into Arles again. Captain Richards is commanding the Union troops there and they need beef. Nay twill sell to them so they have been confiscating cattle and causing more ill feelings. Tom says they twill be happy to buy beef from us. I twill leave tomorrow afternoon. Herman twill make sure we have horses and cattle ready to go. There tis even better news. The Blue Diamond freighters told Tom they will be receiving a shipment. Kasper twill be getting part of his last order."

She looked at him startled. "So soon? How did that happen?"

"I dinna, but I suspect it tis because there are Union troops in Arles." A smile lit his face.

"Anna, if we sell the beeves, I twill buy ye a present."

She shook her head at him, but contentment filled her and she let her mind drift before falling asleep, and Anna found herself in that strange land of not awake, yet not asleep. This time the vision was sharp, clear, and in full color. It was her children and they were here, in this house! They were gathered around a small Christmas tree in the great room. Lorenz looked to be in his teens. He was skinny and broad shouldered, his hands bony, and he was smiling. For some reason his mouth seemed to be pulled up and to the right, giving him a sardonic look. His dark hair was combed up into a wave at the forehead, but stubborn curls seem to run down the side into his sideburns.

Margareatha was a beautiful, full-grown woman with her red hair pulled up and away from her oval face. Her clothing was a surprise; rich, satiny green fabric that gave off its own glow in the lamplight. Daniel was seated in one of the dining chairs, but the height of his broad shoulders over the top of the chair told Anna that he was tall. He looked young, but there was a full mustache. His hair was straighter, waved back, but the same type of curls swirled around his sideburns. Zeb was standing there holding Mina. Auggie was not there. A ghostly presence seemed to hover between MacDonald and Daniel, but it was small. She could not tell whether Auggie lived or died for it could have been Auggie or Llewellyn Gerhardt.

Anna started to toss and moan, her sounds growing louder. She held out her arms as if to embrace the reality of the dream and then Zeb was holding her.

"Shh, tis a bad dream, my love. Ye are here, safe in my arms."

Her eyes flew open and she was gazing into the darkness of the room and Zeb's strong arms were around her. His closeness filled her nose with his scent.

"No, no, it was a good dream. My babies were here. They will be here." And her voice broke. She looked up at him, seeing his strong face in the shadows of night.

"But it won't be right away. It will be at Christmastime. Lorenz is only fifteen, but he will be almost a man when they are here. Mina didn't look any older. You were there and holding her. It was so strange. But you are Papa.

"Oh, Zeb, why can't it be now? I want to hold them. My Auggie, he wasn't there. There was just a whitish image of a baby. I don't know if that was him or, or the one I lost." She hid her face in his chest.

He held her close, stroking her hair. "Anna, how right are these kenning visions of yeres?" He did not remind her that a fifteen-year-old boy would be considered a man or almost a man in this land.

Her muffled voice was low, but emphatic. "Always."

"How do they ken to come here? How could they be together when they were separated during the raid?"

"I don't know, but Margareatha was with Lorenz that day. She was twelve-years-old. She would remember what Kasper looked like. Daniel and Lorenz looked like him." She left out the part about Lorenz's strange smile.

"Then that Christmas we twill celebrate. Now we need to rest." If ye can, he thought.

She drew away and took a deep breath. "First I need to thank God that they are alive." She folded her hands and said a low prayer before putting her head on the pillow.

MacDonald took a deep intake of air before closing his eyes. He hoped the vision gave her comfort and then his eyes flew open when the realization of the potential this opened for him. Anna had said that Margareatha and Lorenz had two hearts. That meant they would probably have some of the Justine mind abilities and long lives compared to Earth beings. If he could win them over, they could go with him when he returned to Thalia. He was about to close his eyes when he remembered that Anna had said O'Neal's son was Toma's son and looked like Toma. Did that mean there was another being with Justine abilities?

He would need to search for the man when Texas became safer. He kenned full well that certain Earth beings could close their minds to a Justine. They too could be fighters if convinced to take such an adventure. He would learn the math and the way to chart a starpath. Perhaps Mina would have children with his Thalian or Justine abilities. If he could gather all of Toma's children as helpers and a fighting force of Earth beings, it would be possible to defeat the Justines. A smile of triumph flitted across his face before sleep claimed him.

About the Author

Mari Collier was born on a farm in Iowa, and has lived in Arizona, Washington, and Southern California. She and her husband, Lanny, met in high school and were married for forty-five years. She is Co-Coordinator of the Desert Writers Guild of Twentynine Palms and serves on the Board of Directors for the Twentynine Palms Historical Society. She has worked as a collector, bookkeeper, receptionist, and Advanced Super Agent for Nintendo of America. Several of her short stories have appeared in print and electronically, plus three anthologies. Twisted Tales From The Desert, Twisted Tales From The Northwest, and Twisted Tales From The Universe. Earthbound is the first of the Chronicles of the Maca series.

Lightning Source UK Ltd.
Milton Keynes UK
UKHW021856020121
376048UK00019B/435/J